AF256034

The B.G.

HIGH SCHOOL WANDERINGS

Larry Kaniut

Paper Talk
Anchorage, Alaska

© 2020 Larry Kaniut interior manuscript

© 2023 Larry Kaniut cover design via AI Midjourney.

All rights reserved. No part of this book may be reproduced or transmitted in any form or by any means, electronic or mechanical, including photocopying, recording, or by any information storage and retrieval system without written permission from the author.

ISBN 978-1955728041 print
978-1955728058 epub

DISCLAIMER

The obscene language presented herein is not meant to offend. I've tried to minimize it by substituting entire words with the first letter of same. I apologize for offensive references that I selected in order to maintain the realism of the paperwork research.

ACKNOWLEDGMENTS

I was privileged to have up to 10,000 students during my five-plus decades of teaching-coaching. To them I am grateful and acknowledge them—they taught me more than I taught them.   (3/25/19)

In my attempt for clarity, I used two different fonts to designated different voices:
- *narration is written in Calibri*
- conversation is written in Times New Roman

In some cases these fonts may overlap in a paragraph.

Original writings retain misspelled words intentionally as these were quoted from the sources.

A special thanks to Sarah Larson for her diligence in editing and updating the manuscript.

Jody Winquist at Northern Printing in Anchorage deserves a huge round of applause for her creativity and formatting ... and unceasing effort.

Sharon Aubrey of Relevant Publishers LLC created the cover design and helped with interior formatting revisions.

Several former students have expressed interest or made suggestions for the "work in progress" ... as have some family members and friends.

DEDICATION

The B.G. is a tribute to students—one and all—who enlightened me for over half a century...they're important, we need to love and to protect them. They were my delight. It was my privilege and honor to work with them. I dedicate this book to them.

In the process of seeking approval for use of actual names of students, I posted a query on Facebook to CAF. Tim Melican responded to me:

"My real name can be used as one of the many of us Dimond Graduates who are disappointed 30 years later that we never were in your class."

I thought posting this here would get Tim into the game and validate so many of the comments about BDK in this book.

INTRODUCTION

What you're about to read is <u>from the hearts and minds</u> of high school students...a culmination of my teaching-coaching-participating in public schools. Although fictionalized in part, most accounts are verbatim from student, staff or parent communications, with different names. My files reveal numerous student notes, poems, compositions, journals and, of course, the suggestion box on my desk.

In 1983 I considered writing a book about a year in the life of a high school. The book you're holding is that book. Written in three parts—*The B.G* (kids are important), *Dawn* (show them that you love them) and *Save the Dogs* (protect those kids)—the book chronicles students' heartbreaking cries for love.

How do we tell kids that they matter, that we love them, that we will protect them?

Anchorage Times, (Oct. 5, 1991) "Choice is clear" letter to the editor:

"When will someone have the courage to say what is plain—if men and women want to have and rear emotionally healthy children, they had better consider the infant's needs and meet them.

"Some things simply cannot be safely delegated to others. A child should take precedence over a career, at least for a while, or we are all in real trouble.

"There is nothing demeaning about the very rewarding work of rearing a happy, sane generation. Best of all, everyone benefits."

Patricia B. Jasper, Anchorage

One of the most significant writings I ever read was *I Taught Them All*. It helped me focus on what was important about school and working with kids. I hope *The B.G.* captures the fact that kids are important and need our love and protection.

I Taught Them All
I have taught in high school for ten years. During that time I have given assignments, among others, to a murderer, a pugilist, a thief and an imbecile. The murderer was a quiet little boy who sat on the front

seat and regarded me with pale blue eyes; the pugilist lounged by the window and let loose at intervals in a raucous laugh that startled even the geraniums; the thief was a gay-hearted Lothario with a song on his lips; and the imbecile, a shifty-eyed little animal seeking shadows.

The murderer awaits death in the state-penitentiary; the pugilist lost an eye in a brawl; the thief, by standing on tiptoe can see the window of my room from the county jail; and the once gentle eyed little moron beats his head against a padded wall in the state asylum. All these pupils once sat in my room, sat and looked at me gravely across worn brown desks. I must have been a great help to those pupils...I taught them the rhyming scheme of the Elizabethan sonnet and how to diagram a complex sentence.

Naomi White, November 1943

Part 1
The B.G.

September-October

Tragically the head on collision resulted in two fatalities. It wasn't pretty. It never is when the Grim Reaper makes his play on the highway. Hospital-bound for Liberty Heights, the lone survivor charged away amidst blue and red flashing lights and a screaming siren.

BDK always said a composition or speech should have a beginning, middle and ending. In this case I chose to begin at the end. You will discover the details of the beginning and middle as you read. And, of course, you'll discover more about BDK and the B.G.

We're the Liberty High Angels. Some fantasize about being America's team but we're not. We're like any high school—the good, the bad, the aborted. Change the era, change the locale, change the culture. We pretty much share the template of high schools everywhere,

whether we're talkin' racin' the bay, the chariot, the Porsche...

whether the cliques include stoners, Geeks, Dagos, preppies, parking lot crowd...

whether you name those good and those lousy staff members...

whether our parents are together or not and love us or not.

We share the teenage affliction called high school.

Yellow-orange school buses single-filed behind each other, students dressed in multi-colored outfits spilled from the buses' steps, one after another to an overwhelming distant rumbling that grew louder. Students spread across the sun splashed parking lot and the adjoining sidewalks, moving toward the high school. In the midst of the conglomeration of young learners, almost on cue, a canary yellow 1956 Chevy Tudor hove into view. With pistons pounding and straight tail pipes popping, the vehicle rumbled into the lot… and shook the ground in its casual, wolf-like search for a victim.

With driver's window down and a cheerful but confident facial expression, Tuffy scanned the area for Clancy's red '32 Ford Deuce.

Parked at the center of the second row, the candy apple red beast reposed sublimely, Clancy at the wheel and talking to a couple of classmates.

Tuffy rolled up in his yellow chariot. "Hey, Clanc, how's about meeting at The Beeg Friday night to run the rods?"

"Tuffy, you're not telling me again that you think that yellow streak you call *Terminator* is really a challenge to my *DAD* do you?"

"We'll see Friday night if that red slug makes it till then."

"Okay, Tuffy. But don't bet on winning."

Tuffy departed his rod in a tattered and sleeveless T-shirt, trying to catch one his girls and wondering if he should have worn a shirt for the first day of school. Clancy caught him and jabbed him from behind. "So, what's up big man? How was Alaska?"

"Man, do I have stories for you."

"I'm looking forward to them."

"I told you when I left in June my uncle had me a job. But it was way more than a job. It was an adventure. I worked for this guy named Sprinkle. He owned Fuzzy's Trucking. But more than that, he was an historic racing figure in the state."

"What kinds of stuff did you do?"

"I worked in the shop and office. Did a ton of work around his trucks. Fuzzy journeyed to Alaska from Priest River, Idaho, where he grew up. His father was a bus driver—ran twice daily between Priest River and Spokane—and taught Fuzz to drive. In time he came to visit but returned four years later. He loved it and put down roots. Even though he'd never seen one, he was asked to race snow machines. But he became so good he also raced stock cars. Actually went to Eagle River, Wisconsin, and took second place on a Skidaddler snow machine. I loved listening to his stories.

"He had to borrow money to join the Teamster's Union. Since 18-wheelers have fascinated me forever, it was a perfect job. Even though I expected KW's or Petes, I was surprised when he told me his first rig was an International. Because it was available. He ended up running eighty-three trucks—some his; some others'. But he left Alaska for warmer climes where he drove school bus."

"Sounds pretty boring compared with trucking."

"Hey, Clanc, what would be boring with a bus load of rowdy teenagers?"

"Well…"

"He even taught his kids to drive trucks, even Da Lonna, the girl. She's pushing rigs as we speak. In Alaska of course. All of his kids names start with "D"; and his wife's name is Delight. How cool is that?"

"Sounds like you had a really neat boss."

"Yeh. He drove school bus in the winters because trucking shut down."

Faculty Lounge

The faculty lounge buzzed with the normal "can't wait till the weekend," "did you hear about…" and much ado about nothing. One discussion of note involved take-no-prisoner counselor Muley and one of the least liked teachers Mr. Nozall, "When you wrote last year's evaluation, along with the other teachers of his, did you really intend to say Clancy Fitzsimmons was 'absolutely worthless'?"

"Without a doubt. He's the worst student I've had in ten years of teaching."

"You couldn't find one thing useful about him?"

"Zero."

"Is it possible something should be said about your teaching…maybe it lacked something to inspire him."

"I stand by my comments. The kid was a zero. He'll never amount to anything."

Knowing Clancy would be in his class, BDK had reviewed his student folder in the school counseling office before school started. Big Daddy read his previous year's evaluation. Clancy had a history of failure. Pretty much failed every class before this year. Absolutely zero positive comments from any of his teachers the precious two years. Appeared Fitz didn't really have any academic motivation. It was all over in his file. How could Big Dad best help Fitz? BDK didn't know the reason but suspected turmoil at home. Looked like most of Clancy's previous year's grades were "D's" or worse. BDK took roll in his English 10 class then invited Clancy Fitzsimmons into the hallway.

"Clancy, I know you're taking English over because of your grade last year. I've reviewed your student folder in the office and know a tiny bit about your school grades. What your grades were and the reason you're re-taking English this year are none of my business. But I want you to know a few things. First, I'm not interested in your past bad grades. Second, I won't hold them against you. And third, I'm interested in you. I can't read your mind but hope you'll let me know if I can do anything to help you have a good year in my class. "

"Ahhhh. Okay. Thank you, Mr. K."

"Okay, Clancy, let's go back inside."

Shock, almost beyond belief, flooded my mind when BDK addressed my class that first day. *Am I hearing what I think I'm hearing?* I'd heard about this guy…wonderful things:

"Big Daddy K is the best teacher in the school."

"If you have a chance, sign up for Big Daddy's class."

But what did he just say? What have I gotten myself into?

"Okay, ladies and gentlemen. Sometime I may refer to you as kiddos but I usually call you Miss or Mister and by your last name. Welcome to tenth grade English. The two most important things you need to know today are one, are you in the right room with the lamest teacher in the school and two, do you know your bus number so you can find it after school? And one other thing, I'm here to learn you the goodest English I can."

I don't remember anything else he said because the rest of the period I considered transferring out as soon as possible. Time would change that but I didn't know it then. After all I'm only an idealistic young lady. The rest of the day went by in a blur—till the last period bell rang (at 2:00 o'clock) and I found my way to my locker and walked to my bus.

Riding home and into the evening I considered the English class slash misadventure. Wow. *Can I learn anything in that class? How could all those kids be wrong about Big Daddy?*

BDK offered his traditional speech about English, "Some of this stuff won't be fun. In order to identify subjects and verbs, you'll need to learn at least five groups of words: helping verbs, prepositions, personal pronouns, subordinating conjunctions and relative pronouns. It's okay if you speak or write incorrectly. The main thing is to communicate. But if you want to sound ed-ju-ma-ca-ted, you don't answer the phone "This is me." You say, 'This is I…or It is I.' The reason is simple. The subject here is either *This* or *It* and the personal pronouns *me* and *I* are objective and nominative case respectively. Since the predicate nominative needs to agree with the subject or antecedent, it necessarily should be the nominative *I*, <u>not</u> the objective *me* pronoun. So, you see, it's important to know the five groups of words in order to better determine subjects and verbs as well as nominative and objective cases. It does matter."

To illustrate the point he said, "It's every girl's desire to go from rags to riches and ride off into the glorious sunset in the lap of a good looking knight in shining armor like me." Then he asked what was wrong with that sentence.

Mr. K's senior aide, Lu Lu, piped up, "The girls were thinking of yours truly…as in me, myself and I. Ha, ha."

"Actually," spoke up Brenda, "Mr. Kandel, 'in shining armor like I' would be the correct way to say it."

"Bingo, Miss Brennan. You get an 'A' for the day."

And, Lu Lu, had a comeback, "That's a Magoo." You could almost always depend upon Lu Lu to say that or "have a duck soup day."

BDK then explained the nominative and objective cases, using the personal pronoun chart. Of course, that was after we'd studied direct and indirect objects…which take objective personal pronouns. "You may not have heard it here first, but you did hear it here."

The first week of school, with a girl on his arm, Tuffy swaggered up to Coach K between classes in the hallway. Proudly, if not arrogantly, Tuffy proclaimed, "I'm going to be a state champ this year."

Coach took that into consideration, recalled the past two years coaching Tuffy and said, "Tuffy, come into my room for a minute. Think about what a state champ is."

When they were inside, Coach K asked, "What's your definition of a state champ?"

Tuffy stated, "Taking first place in your weight class."

"That's right, Tuffy. But there's more than that. A state champ is an athlete who is committed to himself, his team and his school. He is one who is a role model and a hard worker. He is one who can be trusted. He can be counted on. A state champ is more than a first place in a weight class.

"Remember the last two years when I was assistant coach and you rarely did what I asked…you bypassed me to the head coach?"

"Well, yeh, but…

"Tuffy, remember last year when you took a bathroom break from practice?"

"Well, yeh, but…

"It came to my attention after the season that you were in the parking lot with two of your buds drinking beer. Does that ring a bell?"

"Well, yeh, but…

"Tuffy, I don't plan to have you anywhere near the team this year… unless you're in the stands rooting for the Angels. One rotten apple tends to spoil the whole barrel. I don't even want, nor expect, you to turn out for the team. Where do you see yourself in this picture?"

"I'm a senior, coach. I really want to wrestle."

"Time will tell. We work on the principle that nothing in life worth having is free…or easy. And we stress conditioning and execution as factors to achievement. But you've got a lot of growing up before practice begins."

Wall Talk

Liberty hallways have numerous painted 2x4 hall benches attached to the walls. Many a story has been told along these hall benches. ..as well as the locker users.

Spinning tales excels in the hallways and locker rooms...as in lying and rumor spreading. Oh, the ghastly words that are spun. Stories about the big, bad jock who has a chart of the chicks he's been with...but never really had a date. Kinda like the Bigfoot who stole a computer and wrote a book about coming from an alien space ship and running for President of the United States. Or is it? Hmmmm.

The ultimate student anarchy. Those lockers run the gamut. Whereas guys' lockers are decorated with big or little chested chicks, monster trucks, motorcycles or cars, girls' lockers are much more ornate and organized, like they took a lot of time decorating them. Most girls' lockers have pictures of cute guys, horses, maybe some home decorating scene or natural-pastoral scenes. Then, again, you have a disparity among the classes. Take for instance the maturity, did I say maturity ?, of senior lockers spiraling downward to freshmen lockers. Ghastly.

The locker room is another subject of despair. At Liberty we're talking—take your preference, nasty or Ga-nasty—gray battered lockers in rows along the walls with a center part for baskets parked above cold, concrete floors. Oh, did I mention the olfactory differences? Yeh, the girls' locker room baskets have deodorant, cologne, bras, mini or maxi-pads; but the boys' have sweaty gym socks and evidence of male enhancers as well as a jock strap or two. Like I said, Ga-nasty!

A couple of seniors sat in the hallway between the student center and "C" hall, awaiting a bevy of beauties, hoping to view the fairer sex as the girls passed by…and grading them from 0 to 10, 10 being the ultimate chick.

When Suzanne K wiggled by, the seniors hooted with joy.

"Now there's a 10 if ever I seen one."

Bumpy Stillwag added, "Yeh, we won't see no higher score today. Maybe some near 10's but ain't likely."

"Wow," whispered Conner, "here comes one destined for the Purina dog chow award. She could beautify America if she had some underalls."

After she'd passed, Roy silently woofed *bow-wow*.

And yet another barker passed and Bumpy said, "She has the personality of a turnip."

Conner added, "Don't overrate her now, Bump."

"Some of those girls should be taken out, even if it's with an old blunderbuss."

"Oh, here comes Myrna. I'd like to blunder onto her busts."

Yes, those hallways and lockers have their own stories to tell. We have class or clique hallways, meaning freshman through senior and jocks, preps, stoners and so on. In some ways the hallways ID the student, maybe label him. Sad.

Oh, and lest I forget, the bathrooms have their wall "literature" also. Some of the "writing" is horrendous. You either need a strong constitution or ignore the vulgarity. Even though some students claim the walls provide more education than the boring books, or teachers.

A disgusted student wrote, "Some of that bathroom graffiti pales by comparison to that on student desks, messaging each other. I don't feel it is necessary or appropriate to write such obscene language on school property. So in the future please refrain from this behavior. It hurts my young eyes. I bet you are a couple of druggies who are failing this class. It would be more beneficial if you paid attention in class instead of continuing an argument that has no basis in reality. Do you even know each other?"

Smoking Public's Voice

While awaiting the arrival of his newly ordered vehicle, BDK parked his aging car in front of the school office instead of parking it in his customary spot in the teachers' parking lot. Didn't know he was going to get flack from the smokers across the street who left notes under his wiper blades.

As has been the tradition for who knows how long, an annual smoker's group made its presence known across the street on the south side of the school grounds. They had no shame and wasted no time in denigrating the jalopy that inhabited a parking spot since the first day of school. But Mr. K fought back.

September, Week 1

#1 To the owner of this heap. Move it or it will be towed. It's an absolute eye soar. The Smoking Public

#2 We warned you recently to move this crate from the front of the school. We may be smokers but we still attend this public

Wall Talk

"You can have the kid or me."

"What does that mean?"

"You can abort the kid or you can forget about having me, the father."

"You can't mean that."

"I do mean that."

"If you love me, you'd want the baby. It's yours."

"If you love me, you'll forget the kid."

"Jason, I can't do that. It's our child—yours and mine."

"Okay, Alana, we're through."

"It's a choice. Life's a choice. What do I choose to do? If I abort, that's a choice. The unborn has no choice. Do I steal that opportunity from our child-to-be?" Alana talked with friends for their opinions.

How could things have gone so wrong between these two teen lovers?

It was Friday night at The Beeg, The Battleground. When we address The Beeg, it's with reverence—not because we worship it, but it's kind of our testing ground. That's one place where we make it or don't. Liberty and The Beeg have a lot in common. We gain approval there. You might say to some degree we compromise and conform in order to be accepted. And because of our respect for The Beeg, we capitalize the "T" and the "B." And call it The Beeg.

On occasion Marshall and Mazzie drove to The Beeg...and took a limited number of sandwiches and apple cider for anyone interested.

Cars have arrived along with the "partiers," some drive, some drink, some do drugs, some try to score. As the night develops, rumbling engines, gasoline fumes, blue smoke and noisy voices prevail.

Dressed for the occasion some wore jeans or shorts, tank tops or T-shirts, flip-flops or casuals or running shoes. Some of the girls were proud to display their bodies in see through thin fabric or low necked blouses, and, of course, short ragged jeans with buns hanging out.

Seventy degrees felt nicely comfortable. Dark threatened then descended, the only light coming from the metallic monsters as they rumbled into position, a constant drumbeat of engines awaiting their turns. Booze flowed, some couples found their way inside cars or the tall grass to celebrate their freedom.

The Terminator jockeyed into position, rumbling as a hungry lion, next to Clancy's DAD...Death and Destruction. Highlighted in red, white and black, red-orange flames all but crackled from the radiator across the front fenders and hood, reaching a foot beyond the firewall on the doors.

Both drivers looked at each other, motioned the thumbs up and focused on the starter. Lu Lu faced the drivers with both arms straight out at shoulder level, both palms facing the drivers with the fingers on each hand spread. Simultaneously Lulu closed one finger at a time, beginning with the thumbs...going from 5 to1. Then zero!

When the little fingers disappeared, spinning-squealing tires grabbed the pavement and rent the night. Blue-black smoke rose from screeching tires and exhausts until the gear boxes registered the shifts into second gear. Again tires screamed. On the third shift, which was identical for both drivers, there was little screeching of the tires. Racing side by side in a perilous ride toward the finish line. However on his last shift, Tuffy missed third gear with engine wound tightly.

Roaring engines drowned out the yelling boys' and girls' voices, cheering the red or the yellow.   The Deuce seized the advantage as it jumped ahead and finished before the Chevy.

Clancy smiled as he glanced over at his pal. "Bad luck, Tuff. Maybe next go around."

"Yeh, Clanc. I missed my last shift, wound out. You got me fair and square but I'll get you yet."

Other cars lined up to continue the evening, Lu Lu kept his position and counted down from 5 to 0 time after time. Many duels, many challenges, many happy or disgruntled drivers. Even a couple of young ladies competed. One drove a Camaro and the other a Mustang Cobra. Neither car was as sleek or as hot as the young maidens.

A mysterious, phantom-like scribe secretly places comments in the staff mailboxes... venting concerns and hoping for action. Will we ever learn the identity of this person who named himself Corner of the shadow?

Corner of the Shadow

The educational institution to which we cling is our mainstay. I seem to hear from the administration ONLY when there's a problem. Are there

Mr. Wade sits in the faculty lounge commiserating with Mr. Blankenship. "I'm thinking about the Corner of the Shadow notes we've been getting. Any idea who it might be?"

"Not really. I s'pose it could be any number of people."

"You think Doofeld might be the Shadow?"

"Bill? Nah. He's arrogant and nasty enough. He's not smart enough. Just smart enough to be a jerk. If he were smarter, he'd have avoided a number of shenanigans that have gotten him into trouble. Maybe you've never heard about the beating he took as a bouncer? He threw a guy out of the bar but the guy came back with reinforcements. Bill spent the rest of the summer in a leg cast. Maybe you didn't hear the one where the administrator transferred Bill after he pulled a titty twister on the ad man's daughter. Did you know he blackmailed our principal to guard the school from his motor home in the parking lot, before moving into his classroom and sleeping on the couch? I guess that's the reason we have tenure—to protect the guilty. And we can thank the local order of the National Erasers…er Education Association."

BDK's Suggestion Box

Mr. Kandel told his classes he was thinking about a suggestion box for his desk so that kids could put any suggestions in it. Within a short period of time three of his tenth graders provided him a three-fourth-inch thick box about 5 by 8 inches with hinges, a hole in the top and a hasp for a padlock. Hmmm. He set it on his desk and invited all comers. He didn't have long to wait.

Mr. K, I've heard if you can't get a real job, you can always teach. Don't you have to know something before you can teach a subject?

TNP (Take No Prisioners)

Wanna go a coupla rounds with me?   Italian Stallion (Rocky)

Old Movie Guy

The night is dark and I am far from home.

Literary Jeanie

Who said, "There's more than one blessed way to remove the ectoderm from a feline"?

Miss Quote

Do we really have a choice in our gender?

A to Z

Was the U.S. justified in bombing Nagasaki and Hiroshima?

I B American

Why does Mr. Wiggles' camper antenna wiggle most days during lunch?

Mr. Query-us

Mr. **?**-us

Why are boys so attracted to boobs?

Myrna Garfield

Mr. K, are you up for a roll in the hay? (Hey, K and hay rhyme and have assonance!)

Secret Admirers

Student Writing *some thoughts on abortion*

Mr. Kandel,
You have no right to make fun of someone who gets pregnant in high school! You've never been in that position so how (excuse the French) the Hell would you know. But I do and it's really s---. Ron and I were suppose to love one another, or at least I thought. Anyway, I got pregnant and had an abortion. Believe me it's not that I wouldn't love the baby but GOD I was only 14. He would have made a great father. I'm just sorry I killed the only part of him I'll ever have. Now tell me you've gone through this Hell and torment! I was scared and why shouldn't I have been? I know I'm going to hell, but I pray and PRAY that my baby and it's father will go to heaven. The father doesn't know, and he never will! I love him. I just feel so isolated and like no one is there.
No one.

Me

Mr. K,

Personally I think that if you did "make fun of" someone who got preganate or got someone preganate. I think they have a right to be made fun of! Granted it may be tough to go through but...If you have to sleep around like some jackrabbit then you pay the price and all the consequences that go along with it.!!!

Anonimus

Mr. Kandel,

She liked him alot. She got drunk and screwed around last May. She got PG and had an abortion at the end of July. He never helped her cope with the deal. She still likes him alot and doesn't enjoy the fact she could have had been so stupid.

Sam Harvey

Mr. Kandel asked students early in the year to list topics they'd like to discuss in class, time permitting. He compiled their answers putting the most suggested topic first and so on.

Students listed teachers, parents, dating, drugs, world affairs, child abuse. Current events and life made the list as write ins.

And one standup comic —probably Lu Lu—suggested the topic of child abuse. He wrote "there are some children in this class who need to be abused!"

Mr. K always referred to class discussions as B.S., brainstorming. We get it. Our first discussion of the year was...what else? Dating.

Class Discussion Dating

On the subject of dating our class kicked around numerous aspects of the activity. We started with gals and ended with guys:

What gals look for in guys:

Well built, tan, blue eyes.

Size of the lump in his pants.

A normal, not arrogant, narcissistic guy.

Personality.

What guys look for in gals:

Fun to be with. Nice eyes, chest, sweet. Old-fashioned values. Nice buns too.

Looks, personality.
She must be slightly insane and a little scary.
A caring person.
Sense of humor.
Does not go to fake and bake. Not snubby!!
I would not date a girl who would lift me by my testacles.

It was a pretty lively discussion. Probably some of the more gullible or straight kids may have missed some of the information, but it flowed without interruption.

Smoking Public

September, week 2

>*#3   Please find some gum and put it underneath the wiper. Because if we come out here and set our books on it again, it might fall apart. Thnx. The Smoking Public*

>*#4   What, no gum? Your lucky this time we had gum on us. I had set my camera bag on the car and it really shook a lot!!! Please leave some bailing wire next time I don't think gum will work. Your friends, The Smoking Public*

>*P.S. Tell us who owns this car sos we can have it towed and repaired when we knock it down.*

>*Response: The classy vehicle of which you jest is owned by Mr. Congeniality.*

>*#5   Dear Mr. Congeniality,*
>*We think yer smoking something. We think the beater bug has more class than a petrified ant. See if you can figure out this joke: MR snakes; MR not; OSAR; CMBDI's?; MR snakes.*
>   *Sincerely, The Smoking Public*

>*Response: I'm wondering if those beady snake eyes belong to the Smoking Public?*

Coach K inherited a group of eager young men who seemed to want to run. Only problem was he didn't know how to coach them. Contrary to "win a few, lose a few," he felt "you win a few and you lose a lot more." He'd coached a bit in Oregon but was limited. He didn't even know the distance of the cross-country course and told the athletic director who asked him if he'd want to coach, "All I know about cross-country is that they run into the woods and out of the woods, and I don't know what they're doing in the woods."

So, there they were at their first meet with the number one team in the state—the Wildcats. The young men warmed up for the race and when the starting pistol sounded, they disappeared beyond view...

One of the runners who also endured both Coach K's rookie seasons as cross-country and wrestling coach said later, "Coach K was serious when he said, 'Manhood does not hinge on the language you use so much as the language you choose not to use. If you don't develop and practice good habits, bad habits will dominate your life.' I know because I ran extra laps when I transgressed the no swearing rule."

Student Writing

Composition for BDK, "A Plea for Help"

CARS! Cars and more Cars. The theme of my youngster years. Whereas most young men had pictures of girly pin-ups on their walls, my walls were plastered with cars—wall to wall. I could hardly wait until I reached sixteen so I could get my license.

The question is, when, or if, will it happen?

I'm a sophomore seeking adulthood but with totally overprotective parents who have given me a 5 PM curfew. I have very few freedoms. I can't go to malls. Can't go to a movie alone. When I'm out, I must call home to catalog every new venue. It's easier to stay at home.

My folks want me to get a job. Dad chooses to spend money on his habits instead of me. Funny. How can I get a job without a means of transport to get me to work? I need a job to get a car and a car to get me to a job I don't have.

My mom thinks I'm gay because I appear nervous when she brings up the subject of girls. Not true. It's just that if I had a date, I'd have to take her on the bus, call home every five minutes and be home by 5 PM. Not a swank image!

My mom always uses the number of things I do wrong as an excuse to keep me from doing anything...instead of giving me a chance to drive and accept responsibility. She keeps telling me how many wrecks I'm going to have. My dad says we have no parking space and doesn't want me on his stinking insurance policy.

I'm a car obsessed wheel freak who can't ever drive. Isn't that kinda like taking away Piccaso's paints or cutting off Liberace's hands?

I would trade everything I own—stereo, TV, both dogs, MY SOUL— for just one little plastic card that says James. R. Welvin is capable of doing something by himself.

Smoking Public

#6   You forgot to lock the door in the Blue Beast and the key is in the ignition. Why is the key inside and what's it for? Your favorite people of The Smoking Public

Response: Believe/not, the key is broken off in the ignition. You could start the car with anything you stuck into the ignition and turned it because the key is there to stay. BTW did I mention my other car has three wheels?

#7   We assume yer a classless student since you drive this heap. No one on the staff would have such a dinosaur, eh? That beater would take all comers in the paper's heap of the month contest—for all time!   The Smoking Public

P.S. What's with the 3-wheel stuff?

Response: There you're wrong, S.P. Anyone with class would love to own this VW bug. And, I doubt any staff member here could afford a Rolls Royce which would be more showy.
Hunk

P.S. "3-wheel stuff." How about I give you a clue: Cessna, Piper, Aeronca, Citabria.

Inter-office Memo

From: Terry Star, Athaletic Directar and Head Football Coach
To: Coach Kandal
Subject: WRESTLING MAT
The new wrestling mat in the Liberty fan room needs to be put away.
Cc: Mr. Wild, Mr. Usels

During the homecoming assembly—as with most assemblies—the teachers stood along the south wall of the gymnasium. A very small number of them made their way into the stands to sit with the students. Seems like they were comfortable there, needed to sit, didn't want the attention of students staring at them or whatever. BDK always sat with the students.

Sky blue banners proclaiming dozens of conference and state championships for just about every sport over the years hung from the ceiling, ivory lettering telling the story. Most prominent were cross-country, volleyball and wrestling.

The assembly brought together the student body and staff. One of the highlights was the ROTC drill team and their synchronized performance. It seemed almost like drill master Jamal Lashawn Green had prepared for this his entire life. He was a seriously dedicated and rigid young man, thoroughly qualified for his job. He whipped his team into excellence. The team's performance at the assembly was as good, if not better, than any performance by any group of any time.

With commander Green in full voice and charge they marched in syncopated fashion without a flaw from the gymnasium sidelines onto the court in four rows of four. White gloved hands held bayoneted rifles as the young men marched in coordination, thumping rifle butts on the floor, lifting and pointing them to the ceiling, spinning rifles into the air and catching them, tossing them to each other and crossing them with other drill team members... a completely choreographed routine. Their white hats, gloves, belts and rifles contrasted sharply with their navy dress blues.

Part of the homecoming activities always included the powder puff football game. The young women played each other, the frosh vs. the sophomores and the juniors playing the seniors. On the second day the winners met in the final. Surprisingly the freshman girls—with a ton of talent— won their game and faced the seniors for the championship.

It was a tight game for the first half, actually tied. But half way through quarter number three the seniors blew it wide open. Mr. Kandel's daughter passed and ran for two touchdowns and the senior girls won by a convincing score of 28 to 7.

After the seniors won the powder puff final, Lu Lu proclaimed of their victory, "That's a Magoo!"

Somewhat confused, Peter Bandal asked, "What are you talking about, Louie…a Magoo?"

"Magoo is a good thing. A positive effect. You know how helpful and supportive of the students our custodian Magoo has always been? He's one of us so I decided to give him some credit. Whenever I hear or see something that is positive, I'm going to call it a Magoo. So, the lingo, Ringo, is Magoo."

The next big event was the torching of the bonfires. Traditionally each class gathered flammable items and stockpiled them near the field for the homecoming bonfire. This year was no different. Students, staff and some parents gathered around the celebratory event before heading off to the game.

On the way to the stadium a couple of ballers talked about former teachers.

"What's with La Shandra Williams? I had her in junior high for two classes. How'd I luck out? She wasn't qualified to teach either one. My mother's an accountant and called the school to volunteer to teach Williams about math because the teacher couldn't balance a check book but taught personal finance. What's with that? How did she receive a degree in teaching? And it was in physical education, not math."

"Yeh, she's a lotta mama. Last year my friend said she had a drawer fulla Playboy mags. She's a nice enough lady but has no teaching skills. When she was sick earlier this year, one of my friends said she musta gotten some bad plankton."

"Quincy Cochran said she blew out a heel on her shoes."

"Cookie said that? He's pretty astute."

"Yeh, Cookie's the man. But Williams ain't alone. Do you know anyone who's had Mrs. Meene? There's a real model teacher. She lives up to her name. Probably the most hated teacher ever. She had those little seventh graders scared out of their minds. She ruled her classes with an iron fist, threatened them, constantly creating an atmosphere of fear. But my friend Lenny gave her nightmares. He got his tax dollars worth of education…and never got caught. I can't remember everything he did but he plugged her car's tailpipe with mud, removed a spark plug wire from her car engine in the parking lot, filled her mailbox this horse manure, stole staples leaving her stapler empty and left nasty notes from her in teachers' mailboxes."

"What about the Professor?"

"You mean Mr. Snooze, the history teacher no one understands?"

"Yeh, he musta thought we was brainy-aks cuz last year the only thing I understood about his class was that he spoke English. Everything else was way over my head. I made my way outta his class the first chancet I got."

"That's right. He was well qualified to teach college."

The homecoming court consists of seven young ladies and seven young men. As might be expected, most all of them have high grade point averages and are involved in sports, music, theater, debate and/or student government. We will profile bios about them in our next issue.

The princesses (in alphabetical order): Mary Betts, Amy Chandler, Betty Dotson, Margie Faldorf, Meredith Mc Guire, Sophie Phelps and Gretchen Tibbit. They are feted for the homecoming parade, football game, week's events and prom where one will be crowned Queen.

Those young men chosen to be princes are none other than Brett Cavanaugh, Warren De Lotus, Bakers Morris, James Peabody, Rick Plantis, Barry Romans and Conner Stark.

(Also watch for our expansive presentation of homecoming week along with the court.)

Before the homecoming game the prom court arrived in their fancy dress and chosen vehicles which included a dazzling Corvette, 1957 Ford T-Bird, Rolls Royce, 1931 Model A convertible coupe, Camaro, Trans-am and modified Hummer. If I forgot to say they were all dazzling, they were all dazzling. Spiffed out to the max.

The court would walk onto the field at halftime and the queen and king announced to the audience. It was always amusing and, probably frustrating to some, as usually a football player was among the prom court—he arrived to lead his princess onto the field…but was he embarrassed or was she, that he wore a football uniform instead of a suit or tuxedo?

Once the game began, it was reminiscent of the Four Horsemen of Notre Dame that Grantland Rice wrote about in his 1924 piece. I love that piece where he wrote, "Outlined against a blue-gray October sky, the Four Horsemen rode again…they are Famine, Pestilence, Destruction and Death." Then he named them.

Of course, we didn't have gray skies. It was a perfect, blue sky day in September. Even though our Liberty Angels didn't have Stuhldreher, Miller, Crowley and Layden, we were just as dominant with Ayers, Frentress, Mastuka and Bivins.

At the end of the first half we were knotted 7 to 7 in a tightly defensive ball game. However Ayers hit Bilbo Bivins out of the backfield for a 30-yard TD bomb and Mickey McGowan drove the PAT through the uprights for a 14 to 7 Angel victory.

During the season our quarterback, Joe Ayers, took some heat because he was a southpaw but that didn't stop him or the team. We had dual monster linebackers—Mark Frentress and Marty M, AKA Bad Mas—who stopped all comers with 56 solo tackles each and both were selected to all state at the end of the season and stalwart Sid anchored the line. By season's end the Angels were on cloud nine, so to speak.

And we lived up to our war chant led by the cheerleaders:

> Liberty, Liberty, do or die
> Let this be our battle cry.
> Are we in it? No we're not…
> We're not in it, we're on top.

Corner of the Shadow

Recent rumblings indicate the head shed sent us a prince pal to punish us. Numerous faculty members want to save our family-oriented, professional dignity and students. What say you?

Please fill out the poll in your mailbox: Is it the head shed's plan to bring this school down?

Attached: letter to staff from Prince Pal Meredith

Dear Staff,

I apologize for the rift that exists at Liberty. Change is inevitable with new administration. I'm hopeful we can work together as a unit in order to be the school we all want…rather than a split faculty or harsh environment. I have noted your concerns and I wish to work in tandem with you for positive change. Liberty has an excellent reputation and I hope to maintain that with you.

Sincerely,
Principal Meredith

Dear Suggestion Box,

Why does Myrna have such big melons?

Temptation is pretty easy to nibble on if it comes in the right gown.

The 8th and 9th wonders of the world are Dolly Pardon's breasts.

You don't have to make a down payment on the merchandise to know what it's worth.

Did you know there's only one verse in the Bible that addresses baseball? It's Genesis 1:1…In the Big Inning!

Dragon Slayer

Letter to parents

Dear Parent(s),

Although each school year brings excitement, it is especially exciting to see students whose parents are Liberty grads. It is my privilege to be working with your young adult and I will do my best to assist your teenager to acquire the fundamentals for 10-1 English.

I will be sending home a "progress report" with your student approximately every two weeks so that you can keep appraised of your young person's progress.

I would appreciate your looking at the attached course description and indicating that you have seen it by signing your name below and returning only this letter portion to me with your young person. The course outline is for student use (to be kept in notebook).

Sincerely,
Mr. Kandel
English Department
345-4673   (HOPE)

As usual BDK told his students "I'm here to help you any way I can…legally. I'm not going to the parking lot to puff weed, toke a doobie or whatever with you but I hope I'm more than an English teacher."

He felt that was a good way to let them know he cared about them and wanted to support them. Sometimes he knew, like the time he asked a 9th grade girl who had never read a book. He gave her a book and said, "Here is one of my favorite stories. I'd like you to consider reading it and to tell me what you think about it. Why not take it home and think about it over the week end?"

"Okay, Mr. K. It's pretty thin and has pictures. I'll think about it."

On Monday after class Lisa approached Mr. K and said, "I want to return *Charlotte's Web*. I read it and looked at the pictures. It was a delightful book. I loved the pictures and felt kind of a part of the story. I've had some experiences like Charlotte's."

After several minutes of obvious joy and answering Mr. K's questions about the book,

Lisa admitted it wasn't too hard to read.

Mr. K said, "I'm glad you liked it, Lisa. You've just done your first book report. You did great."

Faculty Lounge

"I had a student re-take algebra from me. She received a 'D' on her report card last year. Since she didn't want a grade lower than a 'B,' she re-took the class. She confided in me that I explained things better and she understood more than her previous teacher. She got her 'B.'

Smoking Public

#8   Dear "Hunk"?

I question this name, or as they would say in the Old West, moniker. Hunk you ain't. My offer for your broken down "car" is $15.00. Your favorite member of The Smoking Public

Response: $15.00 is not only an insult to me, but also an insult to Volkswagon.   TG

Good afternoon Ms. Mc Kenzie. I'm Marshall Allen Perry at your behest. I brought you a bucket of flowers…not to be confused with a bow-kay. I haven't seen you in a while and wanted to pop by your house before our final year in prison begins. I know we've been together most of the summer, when we weren't working, but I figured it would be kind of cool to start off the year with some flowers for my lovely. "

"Oh, Marsh, you shouldn't have."

"No problem. You remember my neighbor Mrs. Gunderheit? She always tells me I can have all the flowers I want. What better use than to give them to the girl I'm going to marry? She totally agrees with me that you are the crème d'la crème.

"Okay, Ro-May-O. I can't say no to those kind words nor the flowers."

Lu Lu is none other than Louie Ellis. He is kind of the class clown. Very funny. Very smart. We think he knows what he's doing all the time. His AKA is Lu Lu. Don't know who hung that sobriquet on him but it stuck. Sometimes, because of his goofiness, he's called Looney Louie. But most refer to him as Lu Lu. He is funny, clever, sometimes a pain in the behind… but there is something about him that you have to like. One of his favorite lines is "I have breakfast every morning with Mr. Kellogg."

Circular File, AKA Waste Basket

About the big-chested Ms. Dolly...
When we guys see her we think golly,
Do those big jugs of hers make her proud?
She knows she should not be allowed
To show them near completely bare
Simply making all young men stare...
Hoping to share all of her joys?
All boys who don't... ain't really boys!

Student Comments

Barry: "Did you hear Principal Wild reprimanded the German teacher for wearing slacks to class instead of a dress or skirt? What's this school coming to?"

Clint: "Yes, I did. Do you ever wonder about principal classroom visits or evaluations of teachers. Sometimes I think principals are jealous or just plain stupid"…

Barry: "Or…maybe they're products of the Peter Principle?"

Clint: "Yeh, climbing the stupid ladder. I heard one of 'em thought the science fair was an absurd idea…and he also tried to get Jaylin Stanford banned from the shop class. Said it was for boys. She wanted to build a hope chest for a friend."

Blake: "Back to your question about what this school is coming to."

Smoking Public

September, week 3
#9   Hunk,
Have you heard from The Smoking Public lately? Leave a note tomarra.

Response: No, I have not. I approached the car and found a nicely folded note under the windshield wiper. Those two burned cigarette holes in the note were creative, artsy and classy.
Hunk

#10   Dear "Hunk?"
I think I finally found who really owns this car. If I am correct.

Good. We appreciate your concern for our health but as for this car outliving us. This is highly impossible. I still say that gum would be the best choice and bailing wire would be our second choice.

Yes, we have seen pictures of black lungs and I have seen video tapes of same.

The Smoking Public

Response: Would you rather have a pink lung or a gray-black one? TG

#11   TG, we are trying to figger out the initials TG...We are sorry you were insulted by our newest member, about your "car." We hope you will forgive us. It's really not a bad car. I think Apples are better than I.B.M.'s too. What kind of printer do you have?

With humble apologies,   The Smoking Public

P.S. Your car may be trash but I don't even have one. I'm envious.

Response: Dear S.P. or should I say T.S.P.—Congratulations! Not only are you thinkers but you're also quite observant. I am not only a hunk but I am also a tough guy, thus T.G. It's getting colder and may snow soon so you better consider wearing some warmer coats. Winter is on its way.

One weekend Clancy arranged to drive to Tuffy's to help with the ranch work, have some time away from family and chill. It was a gorgeous, sunny, fall day. Marshall Perry had also volunteered to help out Saturday but couldn't commit for Sunday.

The last cutting of had been raked into windrows earlier in the week and baled into square bales. Tuffy welcomed Clanc that Saturday morning, made sure he had remembered his leather gloves, gave him a general explanation of their plans for the day and headed out to the field in the pickup, tandem axel trailer behind.

At any rate, the wrestling teammates took turns driving or loading. Marshall drove, Tuffy took one side; Clancy took the other. Once they'd gotten two rows of bales stacked onto the trailer, Marshall traded with Tuffy and hauled the bales onto the next layer. When the bales reached the fifth level, the guys headed for the barn and the conveyor belt.

Tuffy's mother was in charge of the belt and Tuffy off loaded the

23

bales that chugged their way up and into the barn loft where Clancy, Marshall and Tuffy's dad stacked the bales.

They hauled several loads to the barn before lunch and while the guys made their way to the field for the last load of the day, Mrs. Bidar headed for the house and her masterful menu for the evening meal. She didn't have long to wait after the table was arranged when the guys showed up and ate until they couldn't move. It took a while for them to let the food settle before they attacked her fresh made apple pie topped with vanilla ice cream. They all agreed they wouldn't be able to eat like this when wrestling season started.

As much as he hated to, Marshall said good bye and left for town.

After a good night's sleep, Tuffy and Clancy had a sumptuous breakfast and saddled a couple of horses for a ride around the surrounding area.

Tuffy told Clancy about Alaska's rugged beauty and the great times he had landing off runway, explaining that many Alaskan pilots fly their planes into the Bush, or what is known in Australia as Outback, and recreate. Tuff told Clancy that he got to fly in a Super Cub "where these bush pilots can land on a dime." He related fly-in contests of flour bag bombing and short field takeoffs and landings...how pilots competed by reducing weight and flying with a gallon or two of gas. He didn't tell him about the numerous planes that were never found but he did mention catching salmon till his arms hurt.

They enjoyed themselves and touched on a number of topics including school, racing, future plans and wrestling. They laughed when discussing a principal's suggestion that they smile more when wrestling. If that wasn't funny enough, they recalled the athletic director's admonition to Coach K that wrestlers should not lose weight. And they got a good laugh when they remembered the football coach's threat to Coach K that if either of them were injured and couldn't play football, he was holding Coach K responsible. Tuffy asked Clancy, "Do you actually think Coach K was afraid of our football coach." And Clancy answered, "That's a laugh."

Lu Lu was always up to something. One of his practical jokes was by gluing things down on teachers' desks. One time he put a thumb tack on Mr. Kandel's chair. Somehow Mr. K missed the tack, or has a cast iron butt. Lu Lu asked him how he felt. Bad mistake. The next day Mr. K placed two tacks on either side of Lu Lu's chair, one for each buttock. As class was about to come to order, Mr. K told the class to have a seat so that he could take roll. About then there was a gigantic yell from Lu Lu.

Mr. K looked up nonchalantly, "What's up, Louie?"

"Oh, nothing." Then a second yell arose as Lu Lu found the second tack. *Hmmmm.*

Because of marginal grades and thinking it might be good therapy, BDK suggested Clancy Fitzsimmons write a composition for extra credit. "Maybe we could then discuss your paper. Never know. Something good could come from it."

"Okay, Mr. K. Will you grade me down on grammatical errors?"

"How about, for every error I find, you give me a dollar? No, Clancy, I'm not grading on errors. I'd like to hear your story."

"Okay, I'll do it for you. Is there any hope?"

"There's always hope, Clancy."

"Okay."

Clancy wrote his autobiography:

I was more than a stinker. More than a brat. Even more than a a-hole. Maybe a criminal is the correct word.

My trouble started in the second grade when my teacher made me hold out my hands for the class to see. I chewed my fingernails. By third grade I'd suffered enough inner termoil that I struck back. Had a chip on my shoulder and chose nasty means of getting ravenge. It kind of started when I stuffed crayon boxes with frozen dog pooh.

It did not help that my mom was the class mother, always there.

Everyone knew I lied because I did it to cover my bases.

I had a friend who was my sidekick and I was his right hand. We stole lumber for a tree house from a construction sight and dropped dirt clods into the exhast pipe of a Catapillar tractor. When the workers returned, they tried starting the machene. It puffed, coffed, belched black smoke and blew up.

Neighbors told the crew about the two kids steeling lumber. One became a watchmen. We returned. Caught. Punished with grunt work—digging holes, removing scrap lumber and cleaning up home sights—until school started.

We sneaked behind school to smoke cigaretes. In fifth grade friends and me oogled the girls at the skating rink on Friday and Saturday nights. We rolled the wheels and the dice, hopping to score.

My friends parents told their sons to "stay away from the Fitzsimmons kid" because I was bad news and bad medacine to everyone.

In sixth grade I got even with Mr. Crumb who said he hated me. I covered his car engine, exhast pipes and heater with limbergur cheese. Uuuhhwwee, did that smell! But he failed me. My parents complaned to the school board, had me take an entry exam for 7ᵗʰ graders and I passed. Bye-bye, Mr. Crumb.

I mellowed to a degree in seventh grade but the next year I was admited to the hospital for an overdoes of asparin and booze, a suacide attempt that went south.

From the ninth through the bulk of tenth grade, my rap sheet read:

9ᵗʰ: ran away twice, started drinking in bars and getting thrown out, sent to juvenile detenshun for bar room drinking, forgery, drunk driving, disorderly conduct and prostatution.

10ᵗʰ: theft of shopping cart full of groceries, prostatution and painting a cop car red.

From the 7ᵗʰ thru the 10ᵗʰ grade I received one "D," the rest were "F" grades.

P.S. Mr. K, it is very hard for me to change from bad to good. I still drink a lot. The good news is that I'm not causing trouble anymore. And I'm not going to. But I could use your suggestions as to how I can stop drinking.

Teacher Concerns

We need a united tardy policy

Too many students come to class unprepared—no pencil, paper, notebook

Eliminate bicycles in the halls

Cut out intercom announcements. Boring, Trite, Useless.

Communication is terrible. Administrators need to be more receptive to staff.

Corner of the Shadow

Staff comments Regarding Principal Meredith: she refuses to be responsible for her actions. Daily she blames inexperienced assistant administrators. She has hamstrung teachers when it comes to student assistance. Teachers want to be part of the picture but their input is repulsed. Security guards are given little credit for anything.

You are being ignored.

Mr. Ferris told his class one day, "Some of you use the eenie, meanie, miney, moe shuffle…going down the page of multiple choice answers and shuffling."

Smoking Public

September, week 4
#12   Tough Guy,
We did get caught up in homecoming. ..the powder puff football game, the hall decorating and the tug-o-war.
Your Friends, The Smoking Public

P.S. "three wheel" from the past. Would that be—those terms, Cessna, etc.—a plane?

#13   Dear Mr. Kandel, So your going to start moving your car now, huh? Well we'll find your car no matter where you park it. We know who you are now, I herd you bribed one of your students with early dissmisal to deliver your note. So what have you been up to today?
Your Friends, The Smoking Public

Response: Dear S.P.,
What I keep wondering is the reason you continue calling me L.K. and Mr. Kandel. I thought I made it quite clear that I am Hunk, Mr. Congeniality, T.G., Kerm. Also, I thought you were perceptive. Who seems to think I am trying to hide my heap? I drew you a map showing you where it will be parked.

P.S. "3 wheel"...BINGO. LOL.

Mr. Kandel had students sign and date the following agreement...
The most important items in the class room are
The student
The instructor
The learning environment
In order to assist the student in learning, rules have been established.
I agree to obey these rules:
I will not be tardy (I will not be truant).
I will not talk out of turn.
I will use no offensive language.
I will bring no contraband to class—food, drink or "electronic" devices.
Because the learning environment is a key to healthy learning, it is essential to protect it—to combat distractions/disturbances.

If I am guilty of any of these disturbances,
*   I will lose 1 point for each and*
*   I am subject to a conference (with teacher, parent, counselor).*
Repeated offenses could result in loss of class or credit.
I understand this information and I take full responsibility for the
consequences.

"Zie, Kitty sent me a thumbnail of her month at the drug rehab center. She suggested I share it with you since I know you've asked about her."

"I'm honored, Cassandra. I'd like that."

"Here it is."

My parents kidnapped me in the dead of night. I had no idea what was going on. Next stop, airport. When I landed in another state, I didn't even know where I was. A man and a woman introduced themselves and said my parents had given permission for them to keep me 6 weeks in a drug rehab center with them and their staff. It was all clandestine.

We drove until we reached the center. I filled out f------ forms like a half asleep zombie before I was taken to my cabin. Disallowed everything, including toothpaste and any alcohol related items which kids put on cigarettes and smoke.

Everyone here is chemically dependent. We're all part of alcohol or drug anonymous. The kids try to get away with sneaky stuff. But we have drug tests. I know I need to change.

I have a cool roommate. We get along real well.

Many are suicidal. Emotions are all over the place—high and low. Nearly everyone tries to be accepted, like at Liberty; some choose appearance; some choose personality; but all need help. A common theme is, "It's hard because I'd like to quit drugs, but don't have the will power. When someone offers me drugs, I accept."

I miss Tom terribly. Hope he still loves me.

After probation I got to call home a few times. As always, Mom's okay; dad's a dick

Our daily schedule is kinda like school. Includes classes, discussions, chores, meals, recreation. I'm guessing part of rehab is doing the chores—doing dishes, cleaning room and buildings, vacuuming. Maybe to teach responsibility. Our recreation is swimming, bowling, ice skating, skiing, hiking forest and roller skating.

We have AA movies and discussions. Former users talk. We saw the Outsiders the other night. Some confessions and discussions are helpful. Some kids bull s--- their way through the program. Someone's almost dogging on you all the time, in spite of the good you're doing.

Students go from here to a halfway house. Some don't make it and go home.

One 38-year-old male counselor is very helpful.

We got a ugly new female tight a-- counselor. She escaped from the zoo. We all hate her. She's a real b----.

Went to airport to pick up new students—3 girls and 2 guys

I've endured-survived-outlasted a month. Think I can make it. Then back to Tom, you and Liberty.

"Zie, Kitty's actually thinking about writing a book about high school life. She said she might see if Mr. K will help her."

"Do you think she'd have enough stuff for an entire book?"

"Oh, yeh. She's kept a journal forever. For instance earlier in the year she let me read it. She wants to tell parents what school is like. But mainly she wants to say that kids are important. I think lots of teenagers could write that book. If you want, I'll see if she'll let you read it. She might even…wait. I'll see if she'll write you about it so that when she returns, maybe she will let you read it."

"That would be awesome, Cassandra. I'll look forward to hearing from her. I would like to encourage her as much as possible. After all, couldn't her plight have been any of ours?"

"I think so."

Suggestion Box

"Water, taken in moderation, cannot hurt anybody."

Literary Jeanie 

I'd ask but it's obvious the school was desperate when they hired you to teach.

TNP 

Can you direct me to a phone booth?   *Clark Kent, Superman*

Old Movie Guy 

BDK, were you a virgin when you married?

Secret Admirers

Is it normal to have pain from breast implants?
Myrna Garfield

Who really killed President Kennedy? And his brother Robert?

I B American

What are the advantages of automation?

A to Z

Who said, "A stitch in time is a penny earned"?
Miss Quote

Why do we get detention or suspension for petty stuff while Mr. Wiggles stuffs his petty?   *Mr. Query-us   Mr. ?-us*

Angels' Halo

Heap of the month—could be a moth-balled, rust-coated junker… or a gen-u-wine glitzy mobile. We'll be featuring a vehicle every issue so stay tuned.

Ask Buckwheat (another Halo column)

Nearly everyone has had an embarrassing moment. If you haven't, just wait. Your time will come. I've listed some from our Angels.

I was a freshman laying out at the beach when a strange man walked by and told me, "Your bosom is hanging out of your swimsuit."
Myrna Garfield

I went to a concert, felt embarrassed to leave in the middle of a song, barely made it to the men's room and discovered a long row of stalls. Whoops! Fortunately no woman was present.   Lee Avalone

I went to pick up my date, a truly beautiful girl. When she came to the door, a strikingly ugly girl appeared, I nearly fainted…until she told me my date lived next door.   *Tuffy Bidar*

Body surfing in Hawaii when my swimsuit fell off.   Max Malone

Class Discussion

We continued our dating discussion with some questions about intimacy:

How do you come on to a guy without him thinking your a nympho?

How do you know if you're moving too fast?

Why do some guy's only go for the body and not brains? We need to do something about it.

How do you tell your date he has something green in his nose without being embarrassed?

What should a guy do if a girl who looked good last year isn't so pretty this year?

What do you do if she has bad breath?

Locker Room

"You want to hear something absolutely stupid?"

"Not if it's one of your corny jokes."

"It's not. It's about Mr. Jones. You know, the algebra teacher."

"Yeh. I know enough about Jones to keep way away from him."

"Well, get this. He couldn't decide what to name his son. So, guess what it was?"

"You mean Wilt?"

"Yeh. Wilt. But that's only part of his name."

"How so?"

"Jones liked three names. Couldn't decide on one so combined them. Wilt. Dinger. Platypus."

"Platypus is a name? I thought it referred to an egg laying mammal, a marsupial…duck-billed platypus to be exact. Never been to Australier, mate?"

"Yes, it does, goofy. And, no, I've never been to Australia. But who's goofier, you or Mr. Jones?"

"So, Jones hung that platypus name on his kid?"

"Yeh, WiltorDingorPlatypus."

"Wiltordingorplatypus Jones? That's too much. No wonder he's called Wilt."

"Yeh, but sometimes he goes by W.D.P."

"His old man wanted to see if his kid had what it took or was a chip off the old block…hoped he'd see his son in the principal's office so offered $100.00 for anyone who might egg his kid into a fight."

"How dumb is that?"
"Yes, a real boxcar brain, as in hollow skull."
"I feel ya. Cuckoo, Cuckoo."

Somewhere in the sacred halls of Liberty High there lurks a mysterious body nicknamed Cocoa Bunny. This person, probably a goofy guy, leaves his calling card on the bathroom walls and it strikes of digested food. At first the phantom pooper Cocoa Bunny left his card in "C" hall. He's left his mark in at least three bathrooms. Seems like he's making it his goal to have a "message" in each building. Will Cocoa be caught and how soon?

Wall Talk

Lu Lu: "Here comes Mr. Wiggles."
Shane: " Why do you call him that?"
Lu Lu: " Watch the parking lot some day during lunch, his camper's antenna wiggles a lot. He's always in there with a chick creating a wave of excitement."

November-December

Prom night was a big night for the gomers. Some had planned a year in advance.

Whom Shall I ask? Will someone invite me? Does the occasion call for a new dress? Should I rent a tux? What will we do after the prom?

Some would double date and/or meet other couples at the hotel for the night.

Some would not attend the prom. For some gomers it was not a big deal - they couldn't care less.

Girl Talk

"Rosalind, have you heard about the game played on road trips by the basketball team?'

"No, Beth, I haven't. What's the score?"

"You're joking, right? That's the name of the game. They have a point system to see who scores the most points during the season."

"Okay. I'll bite. What's it like?"

"It has nothing to do with basketball and everything to do with machoism and disrespect. They prove they're macho while denigrating girls.

It's a 'game' where they try to score. They tally their conquests and have an end of the year party to acknowledge the winners.

"The game goes like this. On the way to or from, even before or after the bus' departure, the players get points for four activities: 1 point for kissing a cheerleader; 2 points for touching her inside her bra; 3 points for touching inside her panties; 4 points for the ultimate, if the ball drops into the hoop. How disgusting is that?"

"They've got little respect for nothing but themselves…and very little of that."

"True."

"Ros, you're not making this up? Does the coach know about this? What about Mr. Usels, does he know. After all, he's in charge of activities."

"I'm guessing the men are clueless."

"Shouldn't we do something? Maybe drop an anonymous note?"

"Let's do."

Faculty Lounge

Mr. Clifford, science teacher known for his humor, told fellow teacher Horace Ferris, "She wanted me to sign the cast on her arm. So I wrote, 'This class is boring.'"

"Did you hear the one about Mr. Crimmons. One of his students promised him herself for the night if he passed her?"

"I heard he considered the bars of prison and had no problem giving her an 'F.'"

Class Discussion

On a third shot at dating we covered stuff from where to go on a date to sexual favors.

At what age should you date? Why?

Where should you take a girl on a date?

What if you're on a double date and you're attracted to the other guy?

How soon after the first date should sex become a factor?

Circular File

My boyfriend was doing me on the coffee table when my ma come in the room. I told her to get lost.

Early in November a female tenth grader asked Mr. Kandel after class if she could talk with him in private. "Of course. Hopefully I can be of some assistance. Could you meet me in the library today at lunch?"

After he met with Reilly half dozen of her friends confided in him with numerous problems. He was always truthful. He always reminded them they should not submit control of their lives to someone else and that they could greet life every day with gusto and gratitude.

He admitted he was learning along with the students and that even though he was the only adult in the room, he reminded them, "I don't want to be an adult because I know too many of them." Kids believed in him because he never gave up on a kid. Little did he know that he would receive a harried phone call one Friday night from Reilly.

"Mr. Kandel, can you help me kidnap Amber Purcell? She took a bottle of aspirin and her parents won't let her out of her house or take her to the hospital."

"Reilly, I can't do that. I'd be arrested or shot. Call the police. Is there someone who can talk with her parents?"

The next week the stories ran rampant.

"Did you hear Amber attempted suicide over the weekend?

"No."

"It's all over the school. Reilly called BDK and asked him to kidnap her friend Amber. Seems Amber had downed a bottle of aspirin."

"You're kidding? Amber?"

"No, I'm not."

After BDK told Reilly he couldn't kidnap a person and that she needed to call the police, he called Youth Services. It was Friday night and he didn't expect positive results. Seems as though Amber's parents realized the danger and got her to the hospital.

Although he pursued a solution via police and youth services, it blew over and Amber returned to school. Amber wrote Reilly: "Nothing was more comforting than knowing somebody liked me and cared whether I lived or died—that somebody didn't want me to be perfect—just myself."

Locker Room

"We had a guy here last year in swing choir who bragged about his conquests. Seemed he was lying, bragging or something. Always showed us his wallet full of condoms. His boast was something like this, "I be ready. Like the Boy Scout motto. My mama din' raise no fool. My wallet's got a full display of condoms. I never know when I be needin' one. I be prepared."

"Kinda sounded like a dumb jock."

"A dumb jock?"

"Oh, excuse me, are there any dumb jocks?"

Lu Lu invited Marshall to a party but Mazzie had a volleyball match which Marshall planned to attend.

"I appreciate your offer, Lu Lu, but I promised Zie I'd be there to cheer her on tonight. After the girls' game the boys play. I want to see that freshman Kandel kid, Kelly's little bro. I hear he's pretty hot stuff, has awesome court skills, spiking ability and vertical leap. Kind of like his big sister the setter. You might remember their sister Gigi…she graduated a couple of years before from Central. Maybe a rain check is in order?"

"Sure, Marsh. We can aim for another night. Have fun and tell Zie I said hello…and to win one for the Angels."

And volleyball proved to be everything expected. Ribbons in bows and innertwined in girls' hair, balloons, posters and individual player placards punctuated the arena—Marshall never saw so many attractive young women as the faces on the placards and the court.

Some of the other schools on their schedule included Cannondale, Lincoln, Ruby Lake, Preston Prairie and Loganville.

Student Concerns

Better counselors needed

More discipline is needed

Don't have rules you don't enforce. Don't enforce rules you don't have.

Expel troublemakers after given a fair chance

Sometimes going to that guy's class is as confusing and, at the same time, as amusing as going to the circus and seeing the bearded lady, sword swallowing man, fire eating guy and three-headed lady—all at once. Kinda scary but always an adventure.

Circular File

I like what Mr. Timmons said about writing a book for us kids: This hitching post is dedicated to all the fair, young maidens in the land who seek a knight in shining armor and who wish to ride off into the sunset in his arms astride his great, white stallion. They deserve a shot at the lad and the lad deserves a shot at the young maiden. Sometimes she finds the guy with the white horse but he can't find his saddle.

Marshall took Mazzie on a picnic. When they arrived at Wild Goose Lake, overlooking Wilderness Peak, they were quite surprised to discover that their potato salad, ham and homemade biscuits were ready for them but the honey was quite lethargic in its container. You had to be there in the 30 degree atmosphere.
Don't you know.

As was his custom in keepings parents apprised of student progress, Mr. Kandel periodically provided progress reports to parents. His early October report for Crystal Feller indicated she had a 3.3 grade point average, "B" to "B+." Even though it was a reasonably nice grade, she indicated to him on his student evaluation a short time later that she was having "trouble distinguishing between phrases and clauses." He had provided a form allowing students to indicate areas they'd like to improve and/or in which they needed help: writing, grammar, usage, organizational, punctuation, mechanics and reading. Under "optional" he had listed areas of hindrance which included work, time organization, study habits, misunderstanding materials, relationships (parents, boy or girlfriend, other classes and teachers).

Crystal checked all boxes under relationships and indicated she had too many absences and her "guitar teacher misunderstands me." And she wrote, "I would just like it if not only could you be my teacher, but be my friend."

Shortly after Thanksgiving break Mr. K received a nicely handwritten note from Crystal, on December 1.

Mr. Kandel,

Hi, I am feeling pretty down because of my many absences and make-up work. I was hoping you could write down all the assignments and tests I've missed and when I can make them up? I'm sure my grade has dropped in this class and this is my favorite e class. I am going to do my best in making up all my work and I am sorry to have to hassle you about it. You are an excellent teacher and a great writer. I am glad that I switched from Mr. Baolotin's class to yours at the beginning of the year. As soon as I get all my make-up work and tests done, I will start writing for you and for myself. I already have a lot of poems and I could show them to you sometime.

Thanks.

Crystal Feller

On December 1, Crystal Feller received a progress report from Mr. K indicating her second quarter grade point average was 1.7. Combined with her first quarter grade of 3.3, her average was 2.5 or "C."

It was exactly four days before Crystal took her life, leaving a ton of unanswered questions for her family, friends, teachers and others.

Inter-office Memo

Principal Wild informed the staff and students

From: Principal Wild

Subject: Crystal Feller Update

There is an invitation tonight at 8 PM at the D.R.N. Funeral home. Continue referring any students who have requested to see a counselor. If you feel a student needs to be referred to the nurse or the counseling office, arrangements will be made to escort the student to the counseling office.

It is important that all staff attend the faculty meeting Wednesday at 2:10 PM.

For those students who had Crystal in class this year, please meet today at lunch with Ms. Thomson, Counseling Dept. Head

Thank you.

Principal Wild

Principal: suicide counselors were in attendance for students and staff the next few days at Liberty High.

Crystal's obituary in the local newspaper stated she enjoyed music, her pet cat, fine arts camps, skiing and bicycling. She lived with her mother and was separated from her father by several hundred miles. The article also stated the venue and time of her memorial service.

Crystal's funeral service was at St. John's Episcopal. As expected the two hundred mourners were somber. Her grandmother read a poem. A priest in white robe with gold collar, read Psalm 46, "Lift up your Eyes unto the Hills." After a series of prayers and meditations Crystal's mother read her obituary. After that mourners held hands and sang Amazing Grace.

Angels' Halo

On December 5 my best friend Crystal Feller took her life. Because she was my best friend, I'd like to know why she didn't share her hurt with me so that I could have helped. I was hurting and decided to walk to her house and tell her my situation. When I arrived, I was stunned. It can't be true. She can't be gone. But police cars and an ambulance were there. She took an entire bottle of pills.

I blame myself. I knew her best. She felt her choice was her last option. She was so blinded by her inner pain she couldn't see those who cared for her. She only saw what caused her pain.

No matter how much you hurt, suicide is not the answer. The hurt will eventually go away and you'll surmount the agony.

Every night when I turn out the light, I cry for her, for me, for all the friends she left behind, for her memory.

Keeping her promise, Cassandra looked up Mazzie and gave her a letter from Kitty in which she expounds upon her desire to write:

"Let the Truth be Known" by Kitty You Know Who...or do you?

I've wanted to tell what's boxed up inside me ever since I was young. At a typewriter now I pour out my feelings onto this paper and tell everyone. It's my chance to open up to someone. Hopefully some day I can find the right person and share this.

Running free in an open meadow with no one there to judge me for how I look or what I'm wearing has always been my fantasy. I don't want to worry about homework or what people say about me. If they judge me, let it be for what is inside and not outside. And for what's in my brain.

I want to be free...to be loved and listened to. I want to play the way I choose and not worry about someone else's rules.

I want all people to live in peace with each other. I want all selfish killing of humans and animals to stop. I don't see any point in destroying life.

The last and most important thing that I want is for the world to start over again. I want to clean the slate. Just erase the deaths of John Fitzgerald Kennedy, Bobby Kennedy, Martin Luther King Jr., Abraham Lincoln, Albert Einstein, Tito, Winston Churchill, Jesus Christ and Ghandi. Someone wanted change and these people died.

I am fifteen years old and I have yet to live life to it's fullest. I have yet to love, to have my heart broken, to be married, to have children, to watch them grow, to see them love, to see them marry, to see them have children, to have grandchildren to spoil and to one day pass away, leaving a memory of me that no one can forget. I want the opportunity for my words to change the world.

Stereotyping and hate should stop. That is the main reason I've dedicated my life to our oceans. One day I will change the world with my views. I dream that I can open secrets of the F.B.I., C.I.A. and government. The public has a right to know. I guess I'm going to have to be the one to stop it. Let the truth be known.

Each Friday we students were to turn in our research on an American who made a difference. Mr. K gave us the option of substituting those on the list for another person. Some on the list include: George Washington Carver, Glenn Cunningham, Amelia Earhart, Patrick Henry, John Paul Jones, Jesse Owens, Jackie Robinson, Will Rogers, Wilma Rudolph, Jim Thorpe and Harriet Tubman. I'm guessing Big Dad assigned those biographies in order to give each student experience researching, writing and getting an easy grade...to up their grade point average.

Marshall talked with Louie about his choices.

"Louie, you know you're one of my best friends. I'm concerned about you."

"What about me, Marshall Magoo? What could trouble your little ol' head about me?"

"We've been pals since grade school. You're a great guy. Smart. Funny. But I'm concerned about your drinking."

"My drinking? You know I can handle it. You know I don't drink to be cool. I'm already cool. Everybody knows that. I drink because I like it. Maybe some day I'll outgrow booze but for the time being it's not a problem. I'm not addicted."

"Okay, Louie. You win this time. Just know I love you like a brother and want you to be happy in your skin."

"Trust me, Marsh, I'm happy. And I can't be in anyone else's skin, now, can I? So there."

"Okay, buddy. Just know I'm praying for you."

There were times when Mr. Kandel stepped in it. But when he recognized such, he always apologized. I remember once he alluded to the word *Nigger* in discussing a class novel, thinking the lone Black girl was sufficiently strong emotionally to handle it. There were repercussions for which he apologized and explained his theory about the girl's strength of character. He felt badly for disappointing the girl and her parents. He would not make that mistake again.

Another time was when Mr. K lost it with his lethargic sixth hour class and told them they didn't "give a s---." The period bell rang and he realized he'd shocked himself. He could hardly wait for sixth hour the next day when he said, "Yesterday I was upset and used a term I shouldn't have. I'm not in the habit of swearing so I'm apologizing to you for my breech of etiquette and behavior."

Wall Talk

"Hey, Jas, ever wondered about the initials for B.G.? We know it stands for battleground or the shortened version, The Beeg. But what else could those initials stand for?"

"Louie, I don't have a clue how long The Beeg has been here nor how long it will stay. Can't think of many words those initials stand for. Could guess, though."

"Okay. Guess. Think about it. What other words could be represented with "B" or "G"?

"Louie, I'm thinkin' about our very own Myrna Garfield and her melons. I'm a guessin' yer thinkin' Boobie Girl?"

"Hey, Jas, not bad. What about Bad Girl, Bad Grass…or Breeding Ground? Anything else?"

"Hmmmm. Let me think. What about Big Gal…or Boys-Girls?"

"How about Big Guy? Marshall Perry's always mentioning he knows the Big Guy in the sky. He even refers to Him sometimes as Big God."

"Yeh, that's right, he does."

Suggestion Box

Is doing the best you can really doing the best you can?
                    A to Z

What's the dope on 666? Will the Mark of the Beast be a micro-chip…or sumpen else?
                    I B American

You're living proof that abortion could have saved us.

TNP

"A penny saved is a waste."

Miss Quote

Shouldn't Mr. Wiggles be in the Gray Bar Hotel?

Mr. Query-us   Mr. ?-us

What's logical about letting trans-genders compete with women in sports?

Myrna Garfield

Big Dad, Have you considered having a sexual explosion with a student?

Secret Admirers

If I had been in the garden with Adam and Eve, I would have slain the dragon.

Dragon Slayer

Teachers come and teachers go. The cycle continues. However good, caring teachers are hard to come by. So, when Mr. Timmons retired, it must have been a God-thing because Mr. Kandel started teaching about that time. Mr. K cared for kids like Mr. T.

Not only did Mr. T teach and inspire kids, he also wrote some exciting books. He considered writing one about his teaching experiences. Then Alana Marie Holland confided in him and loaned him her journal via a friend. A heartbreaking journal about her father's incestuous relationship with her. Later she had a weight gaining problem from her boyfriend and Mr. Timmons wrote her a note and tried to counsel her through her friend but then lost track of her:

Dear Young Lady,

I wanted to thank you for your willingness to share your dilemma, to encourage you to "hang in there" and to apologize for my fellow males (as a whole) for our lack of compassion and understanding.

As you know, I would like to see our world brightened and peoples' lives uplifted—not degraded.

Your recovery and future happiness are most important. I wish you happiness. That you bear your burden with confidence and that the hurdles are not insurmountable. If I can be of any help, please let me know.

We are a sum of all our parts and we are a part of what we've been.

Our lives are affected by what we've experienced, but we can rise above the base.

I'm sending a quote which I hope will encourage you. Jeremiah 29:11 states that God is here to help. I've replaced the "you" with your name. "For I know the plans I have for Alana," declares the LORD, "plans to prosper Alana and not to harm Alana, plans to give Alana hope and a future."

I wish you the very best and hope your days are filled with sunshine.

Mr. Timmons

Inter-office Memo

To: Mr. Wild
From: Coach Kandel
RE: improper postal procedure
Mr. Wild,

I would like to know who and why the package in the mail room addressed to me was opened. Thank you.

Coach Kandel

Janitor Concerns

Vandalism
Rudeness
Pop machine mess
Eliminate study halls—they merely allow more students in the halls

Geno McKay picked up a new challenge and a nickname. Seems some of his pals dared him to "squeeze Myrna's melons." Geno needed no inspiration, the challenge and the twenty dollars from his pals was enough. One lunch in the student center Myrna sat on the wall benches when Geno approached her, confidently...maybe even with a smile on his face. His buddies witnessed the scene. He gave her a double handed quick squeeze and shouted, "They're real!"

Whether she expected the situation or not, Myrna went straight to the office, reported it and called her mother.

The next day Geno was called into the office and told he'd be called from his class as soon as Mrs. Garfield arrived on campus.

Sure enough, midway through third hour Geno got the message to report to the office. He admitted his action, told it was on a dare and Mrs. Garfield told the administrator that her daughter wore her clothes and was "larger than I am." Obviously Myrna had some trouble keeping herself all in at times.

Bottom line: mom confronted Geno; Myrna still wore tight sweaters and blouses; Geno got a three-day suspension. But he had the last laugh...got twenty dollars and probably more satisfaction.

Oh, and Geno got a new nickname: MelMan.

Just after the event with mom and his return from suspension Tuffy's friend and hockey player Geno, the squeezer, got word that Myrna's boyfriend and buddies were going to visit from Central High to get some revenge. Word got out and Geno the MelMan had several volunteers to defend him in the parking lot, including Tuffy. Seems word returned to Central and the "fight" was off. So much for defending a woman's honor.

Smoking Public

December

#14   Dear Hunk,

It's been a long time since we last wrote. We haven't seen your bug lately. But now you have one of us in one of your classes and who, when should keep you guessing. To write back leave a note in your box.   Smoking Public

Clancy never felt comfortable in school since his kindergarten year but something about BDK affected him in a big way. Clancy actually looked forward to attending Mr. K's class. BDK was fun and funny. He seemed to make English enjoyable, if that's possible.

Maybe Mr. K had the ability to make his student's believe in themselves.

BDK shared with Clancy that he had had zero plans to teach. His college supervisor evaluated him student teaching and told him he was one of the best teachers he'd ever observed. So here he was at Liberty.

Mr. K suggested that Clancy check with Mr. Rose who was auditioning students for a play. "I'm not much into plays, Mr. K, but I'll follow your suggestion." Lo and behold, Mr. Rose turned Clancy into an actor and theatrical person at which he excelled that year.

Clanc had a lead role in Twelve Angry Men and did a lot of the production work. He was a natural.

Inter-office Memo

From: Coach Kandel
To: Terry Star, Athletic Director and Head Football Coach
Subject: printed wrestling programs
Coach Star,
Is it possible to order some programs for our fans in the stands? I've checked with local printers who have given Liberty a good price. In addition to you, I've sent samples to Mr. Wild and Mr. Usels for consideration.

From: Terry Star, Athaletic Directar and Head Football Coach
To: Coach Kandal
Subject: wrestling programs
okay on Wrestling programs as long as cost is held under $75.
(signed:) Terry Star
ps: I need elgability list today
Cc: Mr. Wild, Mr. Usels
To: L. Kandel
From: Mr. Wild, Principal Liberty High
Subject: HEALTH EXAMINATION FORMS
In the future, please do not hold these forms. The boy in question did wrestle without the form tuned in to Mr. Star. This could jeopardize the entire meet when you allow members to participate without proper eligibility forms completed.
Cc: Mr. Star

From: Coach K
To: Mr. Wild
Subject: eligibility forms
I told that boy he could not wrestle until he was cleared. He did NOT wrestle. He informed me that he had already talked with Mr. Star about it. Someone drop the ball?

One of the hazards of hiking the hallways of Liberty is the wheelchair avoidance. We're the only high school in the district with one floor, facilitating those wheelchair bound. We have a number of students confined to their wheelchairs, including mostly special needs kids with some sort of physical or mental issue. Running down the hall, late to class, Clancy bumped into a chair and nearly knocked Marybelle Edwards from it. He apologized and sped on. After that every time he saw Marybelle, he blushed and said "hi."

Corner of the Shadow

Here we go again. Another (attached) letter from our esteemed Prince Pal. (second letter from Principal Meredith:

Dear Faculty and Staff,

Our goal is for our students to learn and to grow. There is no place for dissension. Because learning takes place in a comfortable, supportive environment—my desire for Liberty students and controversy has arisen and resolution will take away from our major objective, I feel it is best that I move so that harmony can be restored and students become a top priority.

I wish you the best.
Sincerely,
Principal Meredith

Inter-office Memo

To: Mr. Wild
From: Mr. Rose
RE: Parking lot activities
Mr. Wild,
Please note the blue and white van owned and driven by the Clarkson sisters (Donna and Cheryl) is used each morning as a pot smoking wagon. This AM I noticed at least six kids in it.
Thank you.
Mr. Rose

Clancy Fitzsimmons had a chip on his shoulder and didn't care. Before BDK talked with him. Before he wrote about his childhood hooliganism. That was before. One day after class Clancy stayed. He wanted to tell Mr. K that his father beat him until the year before. "He never explained the reason. Sometimes he beat me until I was breathless. The two most joyful days of my life were when I discovered I could outrun him and when he died last year. Maybe acting out was my way of rebelling.

"I'm not doing great in your class, but I'm attempting to develop better study habits and turn around my life."

"That's wonderful, Clancy. Let me share a story that may encourage you. It's true. Seems there was a back to school night and the teacher with two elementary boys named Ted was eager to meet the mother of the good one, thinking the other mother would not show.

"The teacher told the mother that her Ted was her favorite student, did everything she asked and got tons of 'A' grades. The mother was impressed and thankful. Departing, she thanked the teacher.

"When mom arrived at home, she told her son how much his teacher admired and praised him. Wrong Ted. This kid was the one who did everything wrong . . . if he did anything. But guess what?"

"The bad Ted became the good Ted."

"You're right, Clancy. He became a model student and later valedictorian of his class. So, the teacher goofed but her goof was a blessing. It shows the importance of a pat on the back. You have decided to change, to make the most of school. I'm pretty impressed and really believe in you."

"Did you notice, I don't chew my nails anymore?"

One of Liberty's teachers was kind of a renegade. Seems Kathleen Wisdom Wharton was disturbed by senior students' inability to perform well in English so she got her elementary degree and taught all grades from K through 12. She settled on teaching seniors.

School Nurse

The nurse's office became a hangout for lots of kids...a veritable first aid station if not rescue post. There's no doubt some were sick. But many went there to lean on a listening, compassionate ear. They knew she was a doll and cared about them.

Some cried on the shoulders of this security lady. She was a favorite who gave them some sympathy, if not empathy.

Inter-office Memo

To: All Liberty High Staff
From: Student Assistance
RE: Drinking and drugged driving week, week before Christmas

Dear Staff,
The Holidays are approaching rapidly as is the high risk for all drivers, including, perhaps, pedestrians and other innocent folks. Please review the pre-holiday awareness with your students in order to reduce our students of driving or riding with impaired drivers.

1. Each morning we plan to have students read several appropriate statistics
2. On Tuesday all physical ed classes will view *Drinking and*

Driving the Toll of the Tears in the gym.
3. Since not all students will be exposed to the movie, we have several video tapes that explain the drinking-drug problem. (*Under the Influence; Drinking and Driving, a Deadly Combo; Driving and Drugs; No Accident; Saying No to Drinking Drivers*)
4. We will avail copies for those students wishing to commit NOT to drink, drug and drive or ride with an impaired driver.
5. We hope that you will apprise your classes that more than 40% of all 15-19 year old deaths result from motor vehicle crashes. And half of those fatalities are related to alcohol.

Speaking of alcohol...the party scene tends to prevail at Liberty High, at least for some. There are those who engage in order to be accepted. Others enjoy the liquid diet. Some don't seem to mind worshiping at the Porcelain Goddess or Ralphing in excess.

Summer parties differ from winter ones. Summer offers open spaces and opportunities like camping, parks, lakes whereas winter ones are pretty much held indoors due to the weather. Summer activities include swimming, football, Frisbee.

Kids used to come to school to learn. Granted, they didn't all rush starry eyed into class and hang on every word of every teacher. But they did show some semblance of regard, if not respect, for their teachers and/or the subject. Students today, however, seem to go to school for a party map, a nickel bag and a condom.

Different locales furnished party map "headquarters" on the weekends...maybe McDonald's beckoned...or A & W Root Beer a long block from school. Get the info. Get the map. Get to the party. Who will be there? Are the parents out of town? Will we get busted?

Class Discussion

Dating prevailed again and we covered sexual aspects, including rape.

Some girls give up their virginity to be accepted.

Some girls give up their virginity to keep the guy.

What about girls who are date raped? They get pregnant and life becomes a living hell.

January-February

Marshall tells Louie religion isn't a bad thing. "You party most weekends. Have a good time. But you complain about the headaches and hangovers, not to mention the waste of time. There's also the danger of accident or death. I know you feel religion is not worth your time. But it saved my life. When I met the Master, I became a more positive and productive person. I'm learning that happiness is in your heart, inside you. You don't find happiness on a tire rack, inside a Mercedes, in a woman's panties or a guy's big boy undies. Not that you're interested in some guy's undies."

"You got that right, Marsh."

You didn't have to be a Ben Carson brain surgeon to realize BDK's efforts to help kids feel good about themselves were legion. For instance he has a different student each day take roll—it familiarizes them with classmates, helps bring them closer together, gives roll taker more public exposure and helps with confidence and self image. That activity gives each kid a little extra Kudo. Think about it. If roll takers amount to twenty kids a month, each kid takes roll 2 times every 3 months or 6 times a year in a year long course.

Mr. K also gives assignments that involve parents, neighbors, siblings, family, others. He might have students ask those others what kind of education they had growing up, encouraging discourse between student and adult. Or he might have the students compile a list of things those adults like, dislike or remember...all while trying to improve the kid's self-esteem via interviewing, taking notes, reporting back to the class. Sometimes his assignment queried the student's family military service or volunteer activities or other activity they enjoyed.

He regularly has kids go to board to write class comments. An example would be the class discussion regarding specific words like spontaneous. What is the definition? What other words are derived or attached to it...spontaneity, spontaneously, spontaneousness? What are some synonyms? Antonyms? And the board student(s) writes down this information. He has students come up with other words that incorporate uce, words like reduce, induce, seduce, spruce, adduce, abduce, almuce, produce, introduce, super-induce, photo-reduce, out-produce, coproduce, sauce, transduce. Then they discuss the meanings of those words. Amazing stuff.

Two high school baseball buds Doug and Brian reminisced about their Christmas vacation.

Doug: "Remember the time we were in Hawaii and sent a post card addressed 'Dear Mr. K?'"

Brian: "Yeh, that was the one with the two nudes pictured with sand on their backsides, kind of where their tan lines were supposed to be."

Doug: "And the next year we sent him a card from Florida addressed 'Mr. Conoot.'"

Brian: "We used some creative writing skills to tell him we were trying to figure out what these half nude or nude creatures were."

Security Guards

The first ever security guard was hired here some years back. He was a dazzler. Girls loved him. He was about 26 or so, wore a suit and tie, totally outshone the teachers in looks and dress. The girls went gaga when he walked the halls. Some teachers even had the hots for him.

But he left here after one year and returned to LA. Later he became a councilman and dusted the mayor and another councilman. His name was Dan White. The first—maybe only—defense ever used for him became known as the "Twinkie Defense"—because he was sugar coated from Twinkies and Coke, his attorney said his mind wasn't right. You can Google this information, just input Danny White, Mayor Moscone, Harvey Milk. There's quite a history to be learned.

Marshall drove over to Mazzie's to help her with her homework. Mr. Mc Kenzie met him at the door. "Hey, Marshall, how's it going?"

"Very well, sir, how about you?"

"Fine. Fine. Zie said you were coming over."

"Yes, sir. She said she needed help with trigonometry. Since she's smarter than I, I was baffled by her request for my assistance."

"Marshall, I can assure you, she won't get much help from me. I'm still trying to figure out the 'X' from algebra."

"It can't be that bad."

"Maybe she misses you and used trig as an excuse."

"I s'pose that's possible, Mr. Mc Kenzie."

Suggestion Box

What are the advantages of automation?
I B American

BDK, how often do you and your wife get it on?

Secret Admirers

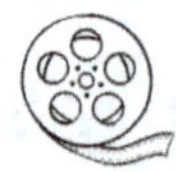

If you're born with one of those or one of those, you're either one of those or one of those.

A to Z

Did I miss you at Pearl Harbor?   *Tora Tora*
Old Movie Guy

Did the chicken climb the mountain because it was there?

Miss Quote

Mr. K, Your glasses and clothes aren't the only thing about you that are ugly!

TNP

It was the best of times, it was the worst of times.

Literary Jeanie

What's the definition of statutory rape?

Mr Query-us   Mr. **?**-us

Are big breasted girls more appealing than flat chested ones?

Myrna Garfield

BDK offered students help...sometimes a contract to "give anyone in this class a 'C' if you agree to turn in every assignment. You may fail some and get 'A's on some, but the average will be a 'C' at the minimum." I don't think anyone ever took him up on his offer.

In his efforts to help on one occasion Mr. K provided student feedback via a questionnaire—they could check any of twelve options and/or respond to "other." One student Kegan Hubert checked the boxes "I'm lazy" and "I have other homework." Under "other" he responded "To keep up the grades I have in all of my classes (mainly math) I don't worry as much about English and I forget about my English homework because I don't think as much about it. The way you are teaching is fine. I think I just have to try harder."

No doubt Looney Louie would call Kegan a "chaw dodger." Then he'd explain that anyone who avoided spittle from tobacco chew was a chaw dodger—they avoided it. As a chaw dodger shied away spittle, so a lazy person shied away from work just like one from the spittle. It was Lu Lu's term for LAZY.

I remember Mr. Kandel offered extra credit for 5 misspelled words on test. I found all five and asked if we got extra credit if we found 6. Whoops! He then told the class to look for six.

Mr. K assigned students to read one chapter each overnight from *The Scarlet Letter* and write a one sentence summary. The next day he took their chapter summaries, had a discussion of Nathaniel Hawthorne, compiled all thirty papers—one sentence per chapter—and handed them out the next day so that the class could "read" the entire book in one day. Then the class discussed the book. Obviously it wasn't the same as reading it page by page, but he accomplished in less than a week what would have taken much longer and bored half the kids to death.

Pierre wrote that it was a stroke of genius: "The idea of reading a chapter is brillant. Continue the good teaching."

Cathy agreed: "Mr. K, Although confusing to a degree, it was much better having the class read the book in part because it was so boring most of the kids wouldn't have even looked at it. We all learned the book's theme. You're full of good ideas. Merry Christmas."

No name: "I didn't like it. It would have been better to not read the book at all. Ha, ha."

Smoking Public

#15   Dear Hunk,
Here we are, another great Friday. Have a great weekend and good luck this weekend. hope you do well. Write back by lunch, Sincerely, Your Friends The Smoking Public

#16   Dear Mr. K,
We're sorry there was no letter yesterday. I hope your having a smurfy day. Wondering why this letter's on red paper, well it's close to valentine's Day. Your Friends The Smoking Public

Dear S.P.,
You have a Hap...py Valentine's Day.
It's been real and it's been fun but it's not been real fun. Get it? You've entertained me and left the bug in one piece but I'm in my new ride if you can find it in the parking lot. Have a great year,

eh?

Secretary Concerns

Be responsible to all students, not just yours. If they know we are interested in them, communication will be great and we will again have good discipline.

A kid finally took Mr. Jones up on his offer to start a fight with Wilt. It happened at lunch. WDP was standing outside watching some kids in the parking lot when Glenn R called him a name. Wilt didn't take kindly to it and met him on the sidewalk. Glenn sucker punched him and Wilt dropped like a sack of spuds. He lay on the ground without moving. Kids gathered around. Here comes security. They radioed the office for emergency help.

Inter-office Memo

To: All Staff
From: Administrators
Over the weekend, one of our students, Jody Milder, lost his life in an auto accident. Two other sophomores in the car, Bently Silver and Sam Carl, are hospitalized at Liberty Hospital in intensive care. As of this morning, their conditions have been upgraded to satisfactory. Services for Jody have not yet been scheduled.
All three boys were on the wrestling team. The other wrestlers will me be meeting with Coach Kandel during lunch in his room.
Several counseling resources will be available today. Please send students who are in need of those services to the counseling office or call the switchboard for an escort.

Different activity groups were forced to raise money for their activity. Coach K scratched his head for money making ideas for the wrestling program. He felt pretty stupid walking around the neighborhood with a box of pizzas on his shoulder, knocking on doors and saying, "I'm the Liberty High wrestling coach. Would you be interested in buying frozen pizzas?" CK thought he'd done stuff like that when he was in high school and that his job was to coach, not fund raise. Since he thought his job was coach and not fund raiser, he approached the parents of the wrestlers and asked for their suggestions. Turns out they agreed to fund raise.

A junior Angel volunteer, Kevin Hawg, an aspiring photographer, approached Coach K in the halls one day. He'd gotten word that the coach was considering producing an activity calendar featuring athletes, musicians and drama kids as a fund raiser. Kevin was willing to take the pictures and since Coach K had a local print shop in mind, he told Kevin, "You capture individual and team shots and we'll get 'er done."

But wait. Coach K had NOT gotten the permission of Mr. Usels. Hold everything. Seems Principal Usels fumed to Coach K that he was getting phone calls from other schools requesting Hawg take pictures for them so they could have their own activity calendars. Bottom line, according to Usels: "You have to stop taking pictures and forget the calendar." Seems other coaches had seen some of Hawg's swimsuit photos and wanted their own!

Teacher Concerns

Could counselors alert us before pulling students from our classes?
Should a principal who transfers a failing English class senior to PE and given a passing grade be fired?
Thoes who can, do. Thoes who can't, talk.
Study halls are a waste—students wander the halls

Mr. Runberg listed the following ad in the school bulletin: "HELP! NEEDED—Carpet remnants, easy chairs, beanbags, cheap, like preferably free. See Mr. Runberg in E 42."

Seems he stirred up the Prince Pal again because he got a prompt note from Da Man: "Mr. Runberg, are we re-furnishing the room? Let's discuss during your conference period on Monday at noon."

Faculty Lounge

Bully hollered across the lounge, "Hey, Runberg, did you get those classroom furnishings you wanted for E 42? Sounds to me like you were scraping the bottom of the barrel...for free even. That's okay, you'll adjust to Liberty in time."

Inter-office Memo

To: Liberty Staff
From: Mrs. Wilt Jones
RE: Wilt WDP Jones
Letter from Wilt's mother

Dear Liberty Staff and Students,

Although we are out of state at the closest medical facility and hope to bring Wilt back soon, I wanted to apprise you of his condition and health status.

As you know he was severely injured by a blow this face which resulted in his falling. When he hit the ground, the back of his head struck a concrete curb, completely knocking him out and paralyzing him.

Fortunately persons present had the wherewithal and presence of mind to call 911, resulting in a rapid trip to the hospital and subsequent transport to this facility.

Wilt and I want to convey our gratitude to you and to thank you for your concern and your prayers.

It has been very difficult for Wilt but he's a fighter and fights every day. His traumatic brain injury has been a wakeup call for all of us. We are so thankful that he is with us. Even in his condition we have hope he will return to his former lively self. He went from 180 pounds to 112 pounds since the accident. A week ago we were able to give him food by mouth after twelve weeks of IV feeding.

He cannot talk or walk yet but the prayers keep him going daily. He can now sit up for 30 seconds. We are so proud. Of course, I'm his biggest fan and never leave his side. I can read his emotions on his face—pain, sadness, anger—and he smiles with his eyes.

I know if Wilt could talk, he'd have a very special message for each of you. "Think! The Lord gave you a brain. Use it to guide your every move— because your actions could be taken from you in an instant. While limbs and body parts can heal, if your brain is injured, you may never think again. These are your life's best days. Don't waste them."

Mrs. Jones.

P.S. Liberty High is kind of representative of freedom of so many things like being awake, being able to tie your own shoes, attend school, able to walk and think. Please don't take these freedoms lightly.

Impressed by the letter from Mrs. Jones, Louie stated to friends, "That announcement from Mrs. Jones is a Magoo. Can't say the same for her lame 'teacher' husband."

One afternoon Mr. Timmons and a friend awaited the movie to start. Bully Bill and the school security guard approached Mr. T and his friend. Bully played his old "I got you" trick and told Mr. Timmons, "You never changed after you became a famous writer. You were a p---- before and you're still a p----."

Timmons had no respect nor fear of Bully, looked him in the eye and said, "Thanks, Bill. Have you ever considered your AKA name Elohssa? That's the backward spelling of a body vent." Timmons made his point, didn't await an answer then he and his friend went into the movie. Don't think Bully Bill had many people get in his face regarding his immaturity. And he never bothered Mr. T again. (Much later, however, he did ask Timmons for a copy of one of his published books and bragged on Timmons that he'd once taught with him.)

Tuffy and Clancy are wrestling practice partners at 191 and 175 pounds respectively. The wrestlers had a road trip scheduled but Coach K had a serious cold, if not pneumonia. Concerned about his runny nose and eyes, he explained that he wouldn't be able to make the trip. But old Usels Box liked his power and told him "if you don't go, the team doesn't go." In vain Coach K explained that other schools had two or three teams and the head coach couldn't attend away meets with all of them. In the interests of the team, coach went, slept nights on the host team's wrestling mat, did so-so in the tournament and stopped on the return trip so wrestlers could load up on junk. The store manager asked Coach K if it would be okay to give the team a case of oranges because "they're the best behaved team we've ever had in the store."

"Thank you, sir."

"You betcha. Come back any time."

Marshall and Mazzie went to Punkie's Parlor for root beer floats and music. The parlor was a throwback to the 1950's soda fountain scene with music selections at the tables in the form of flip chart jukebox tunes. They talked about their growing up years when Marshall admitted he didn't get a whole lot of exposure to Dr. Seuss but rather the Walt Disney classics *Pinocchio*, *Little Toot* and *The Ugly Duckling*. And, of course, Hans Christian Anderson and the brothers Grim and *Grim's Fairy Tales*. They remembered their grandparents talking about the changing times from the 1950's and 1960's and the idea that even if retro things like bobby sox, hoop skirts, saddle shoes and Motor City music vs. today will never be the same.

Don't you know?

Before he left Liberty, Mr. Timmons periodically asked students what he needed to change and whether they'd advise new students to take his class. I've listed a few comments from students.

Change:
Nothing. LS
Take:
Sweet guy, doesn't favor anyone. AM
You will learn a lot. He tries to help every student. JB
He's a cool dude! Gives his students respect! It's been great having you. KC
I love this class. 99% of those in it—even those failing—love it. He's the sweetest, kindest and funnest teacher in the school. SC
You're the best teacher and friend I ever had. You "learned me good." LS
He is a caring teacher who is genuinely interested in you as a person. WG *
Mr. Timmons understands kids. JR
* **Later both WG and JR became principals in Liberty's district*
Do not take:
You'll die laughing. JV
If you lack self discipline, you'll have trouble. Mr. T does not push; you gotta push yourself. Bob G

Parent-Staff Message

Coach K,
I understand that wrestler loaf cake with Kandel's Klowns written on it with frosting got thoroughly devoured by those starving wrestlers. Congratulations. Wilda Price

Inter-office Memo

To: Mr. Kandel
From: Mr. Wild, Liberty Principal
Subject: reading selection
L.L.,
Received a parental call last night referring to a reading assignment about the dehumanization of athletes. With all the other fine literature that exists, dad was concerned as to how this fell into the realm of sports literature. Both parent and I agree that it is not necessary to call attention to this type reading. You are correct that some athletes are dehumanized, but...

Stop by if you feel a need to discuss it.

Mr. Wild

To: Mr. Wild, Liberty Principal
From: L.L. Kandel
Subject: response to your dehumanization comments
Mr. Wild,

I appreciate the concern of both you and the father. However, *Meat on the Hoof* vividly portrays the colleges' throw away mentality toward athletes once their eligibility is used up. If sports literature exists besides this book, I'd love to have either you or the parent suggest a title. Until then, I'm trying to expose students to reality.

Thank you.
Kandel

Parent to Teacher

Dear Mr. Kandel,
Before Bill left for school this morning he said, "I like Mr. Kandel." It caused me to realize that you are the reason he enjoys going to Liberty.

Keep up the good work!
A happy parent,
Ginger Newsome

Student Writing

Guys focus:
Get money
Get car
Get Gas
Get girl

Girls focus:
Get money
Get dress
Get date
Get guy

Student Comments

I remember Mr. Kandel with his black, horn rimmed glasses, wool stocking cap, fanning his Swingline stapler six-gun in his leather mittened hands. What a goof. Probably one of the reasons so many kids loved him is because he wasn't afraid to be himself. Remember when he got new glasses and told us he only wore them for sex appeal and gave us his home phone number, 345-BABE...or STUD...or HUNK? I remember a few times when he stuck a thumb tack into an entire orange or apple peeling and hung it from the bulletin board. He usually left it a week or so, not long enough for it to mold. And he always put up a bulletin board with his report cards and tattoed-scarfaced drawings kids put into his suggestion box over the years.

March-May

Before the first daffy-yodels of spring peeked above their earthen cover and pines turned knotty, Liberty's thin clads showed up at the circular oval ready for the track season—runners, hurdlers, jumpers and hurlers.

As they've done all year, Marty Niemi and Benjie Konrad were ad-getting for the yearbook Heavenly. They take turns driving "old Staff's" car around town after buying a large, brown paper bag of pop corn and soliciting ads every day. Up to that time in Liberty's history, they'd earned more money than any previous ad-getters. By year's end they'll likely set a record.

Marshall and Lu Lu engaged in their ongoing discussion about ethics and religion.

"You know, Lu Lu, you're no dummy. You know that good intentions don't get things done. Good intensity does."

"Yeh, Marshall. I know that you know that I know. And?"

"We have talked about this in the past. It's not my job to change anyone. It's not anyone's job to do that. The only person I'm supposed to change is in my skin. I agree with you that Christians are hypocrites. But we've got to start somewhere. Name another religion where God seeks man. When a Christian becomes aware of his failings, he can ask forgiveness. I plan to follow the Gospel until something better comes along. But I'm not expecting that to happen."

"Okay, Marshall. I can't argue with that. I'm kind of in the same boat."

"Well, I hope you keep rowing, pardner, and you find your Skipper."

Inter-office Memo

To: Mr. Wild
From: Mr. Rose

RE: parking lot activities

Mr. Wild,

During my third hour conference period today I noticed at least 2 couples participating in "pre-parental" activities in the Clarkson van. It appeared that all were naked and fully engulfed in a blue haze of smoke, which flowed from the passenger side window. Might be time for security to check out the van.

Thank you.

Mr. Rose

After reminding us that "you can judge a kid by the candy wrapper he throws onto the floor," Mr. K explained the protocol for proper etiquette in introducing folks. Generally there are several things to consider. For instance, make eye contact, speak clearly and loudly enough to be heard, state the name of the person you wish to honor first by saying something like "I would like to introduce" or "it pleases me to introduce" or "please meet," name the person being introduced and last provide some information about each person.

Normally you introduce the younger to the older, the male to the female, the person of lower rank to the higher ranking person. Copy the examples on the board and keep in mind the techniques we worked on earlier to correct them using dialogue, punctuation, quotation marks and capitalization. If you think any of the examples are incorrect protocol-wise, please indicate them.

grandmother i d like to introduce you to my friend j b tanamount

it gives me great pleasure aunt sarah to introduce you to a classmate of mine john pepet

coach jiminez it's my honor to introduce you to the student body of liberty high school

During a weekend wrestling tournament, wrestling cheerleader Megan, maybe in a moment of weakness, depressed and drunk, arrived at the gym. Discouraged over a recent battle with a friend and a boy's rejection, she wandered away from the gym, into the woods and snow.

Somewhat confused, her thoughts were ajumble. "I stood behind a cage. I could not get out for they would not let me. My best friend Mary was on the other side of the wall, separated by misunderstanding and confusion. I felt like I would burst. My life is ruined. I have nothing left. I will be out of the honor society, my teachers won't like me, my acceptance into a good college will not be possible. I have hurt so many people I want to die. I've been so stupid. There is no hope for me. I have no right to live and cause so many people so much pain. The only way out of here is to run.

"As I heard my heart beat fast, I left my cage. The woods beckoned, almost with arms spread wide. Down the bike trail I fled. I will be undisturbed there. I hope no one will follow me, worry or care. I jumped off the bike path into the deep snow which cut my legs. After how I had treated people, pain didn't matter. Before long I collapsed from exhaustion."

Disoriented emotionally, she lay down in the snow, thinking about dying—for the most part oblivious of her situation.

"Looking toward the sky, I saw trees towering over me (parents?): 'We have raised you with the right values, with love and trust; why do you hurt us?' The voices of the past continued, 'I was upset with you and called you a bitch, but I did not mean it. I like you too much to hate you,' John had said to me."

Watching the windblown clouds, Megan's mental journey continued, "I felt light as a feather, my thoughts drifting with the clouds. Love is like the wind. It travels high in the air, low through the valleys and way over the tops of the mountains. Wind lets nothing get in its way, like a tree or a wall. It carries things like leaves which flip and fly, dropping where they will. When people love, they flip and turn, become confused while they soar. When love is gone, they drop like a leaf…lying motionless. Soon buried beneath the snow. The wind plays with everything but nothing plays with the wind. One is either caught in love or waiting for a breeze to pick them up and let them fly again.

"The love clouds floated by and I felt the cold touch of death, like a leaf that falls to the ground. Although I felt love out of reach, I still could feel the power of a small breeze within me which gave me warmth.

"As the warmth eased away, the cold settled in. And I thought of those I'd hurt, those who I needed to be loved by, those who I loved. I had recently left my friends in search of new happiness. They would no longer except me, so I kept searching. When I became troubled, I found one of my friends to be true. He held me, shared by concern, said he would always be there.

"I'd hurt my parents, ruining their trust in me, again. I began to shiver though the fear of the cold death that was sweeping through me. Help! Somebody! Help. John! Mom! Dad!

"I struggled to move, unable to feel my hands or legs from the knees down. I stuck my hands under the sweater. I tried to sleep, but my teeth did not stop chattering. When my legs and feet hurt so violently I knew I wasn't dreaming. I dragged myself across the snow and discovered I was lost. I screamed at the top of my lungs.

"Was that a voice? It was so far away. It came closer. And then I was lifted up by John. He carried me back to the gym, to its warmth."

Although diminutive in size, Megan emerged from her experience gigantic, like a boss. After her hospital stay and recovery, she returned to school, with a different outlook. She confided in herself and her diary, "I will be much stronger than ever before. I made a bad mistake but I am not a bad person. My mistake was something I did, not something I am. My outer shell is not who I am, my inner self is. I will focus on reality and improving as the person I know I am…not conformed by peer pressure to be something I'm not."

Student Writing

"Why Can't we be Ourselves?"

Everyone's always telling you to be like someone else but no one ever tells you to be yourself. Perhaps most famous is mother telling her son to eat his vegetables so he'll grow up to be like his father. How many people have you heard telling their kids to be themselves? None!

We aren't old enough to stand on our own two feet so we have to be like someone else? We can't form our own opinions or ideas on anything because it might conflict with our parents' or teachers' opinions—at home you get parental pomp and at school you get teacher talk. Therefore you grow up thinking and being what they want you to be.

So, we don't form your own ideas until we leave home and school? Why wait that long?

Darlene Randall

Circular File

Bitch

My name is Meredith Elizabeth Scott. Most people just call me Bitch. Right now my hormones are going wild. I can't control them. I want sex all the time. My needs are never satisfied. I think some day soon when I'm having sex I'll explode with pleasure. My life will start making sense and sex will be my career. I won't be a hooker or a call girl. I'll just be there to please, but I'll always be known as the Bitch

One night at Lover's Roost, Marshall, who carried himself somewhat like Cyrano carried his white plume, engaged in a philosophical discourse with Mazzie.

"I think I love you. But there may be a catch. Do I enjoy holding your hand…kissing you…want to jump your bones? Affirmative in the first two and I think yes on the third.

"Do I want to change the TV channel or change a diaper? *Hmmm*. Not sure. Real love would deny itself for the other. I'm not sure how close to that real love I am.

"I want to touch you intimately, to hold your hand. To kiss your lips. To massage and feel your body. To engage in physical intimacy. But more than that I want to touch your heart, your soul…to become a gentle, caring, kind person to cherish you for you and forever.

"We've got to save ourselves from ourselves and for ourselves. We need to pray to the Big Guy for self control and minimal hormonal activity. You agree?"

"Yes, Marsh. I do. We are committed to each other, plan to go to college, graduate, marry and have a family. In that order. No hanky panky in the meantime."

"We know where we're going and we know how to get there."

Wall Talk

"Tuffy, did you hear about the time Myrna Melons got some upset with Coach K?"

"No, I didn't Clancy. What's the deal?"

"One time I passed her in the doorway to the classroom. It was a tight squeeze, if you know what I mean. She was some upset by his quote on the blackboard which read 'In this world of give and take, there are few men who can give what it takes.' She was adamant that he add *women*.

"Myrna explained that Mr. K always said men should respect women. 'You said men should treat women well and not hit them, but now you're degrading them.'"

"Clanc, do you think she was serious?"

"Oh, yeh. Coach tried to explain that *man* meant humanity, that it was the generic term for mankind…that the quote meant there are few folks who achieve. Figuring he needed to end the discussion and start class he asked Myrna, "Would it make you happy if I added *women* to show I'm not a misogynist?"

"Myrna was twitterpated and said, 'Yes, it would.'"

"Mr. K walked to the board, picked up a piece of yellow chalk and added three words… 'and fewer women.' The quote became, 'In this world of give and take, there are few men who can give what it takes…and fewer women.'"

"Myrna was livid."

"BDK said, 'Lighten up. I'm joking.' I don't think she spoke to him after that.

"I have to wonder how she'd react to the woman who recently pleaded to remove the word *man* from our planet. Where would she be today without *man*?"

Corner of the Shadow

The little theater stage gets a lot of action when no adult is present. Is some adult responsible for locking the little theater door…or are the violators adults? *Hmmmm.*

You are being upstaged.

With reluctance and suspicion Coach K had watched Tuffy begin the wrestling season. He was surprised that the team selected Tuffy as one of three team captains. Halfway through the season Tuffy was unscored upon. Coach was somewhat surprised and credited Tuffy for some kind of turn around.

At the state wrestling finals coach instructed Tuffy while rubbing his shoulders and back preceding the championship match. "Okay, Tuffy, this is the only guy to defeat you this year. Both times he caught you in a cow catcher and flipped you onto your back. Like we've discussed all week in practice, you either shoot your double leg with your elbows at your sides or you fake a shot on the takedown. I don't care if you fake it for a whole period but do NOT shoot your double with your arms out."

Turned out Tuffy shot several near double leg attempts that were strictly fakes. He did not get caught in a cow catcher. And in spite of the fact that the Cossack's father promised him a Mustang if he won, he did not get the Mustang. Tuffy prevailed with a giant smile and both index fingers pointed skyward as he left the center of the mat.

Although it was a party night, Louie chose to attend the tournament. When each of his Liberty Angel classmates won the championship in his weight class, Louie shouted across the gymnasium, "THAT'S A MAGOO!"

Angels' Halo

Time Out: 4 for 3 in 2 By John Wakefield

If a Most Valuable Athlete of the Year Award is presented to a Liberty student, then it should go to Tuffy Bidar. In his three years at Liberty he has won four different letters for three different teams in two different sports. As a sophomore and junior he lettered for the Huskies, whose team broke a three year nineteen game losing streak.

As for football, this was Tuffy's big year. He lettered for the Angels but, more importantly, he made the All-Conference football squad on both offense and defense. It seems that three letters and a couple of all-star awards would be enough but not for Tuffy.

Drafted by wrestling Coach Kandel, Tuff indulged in an untried field of his personal varsity career at the 191 pound division. Seems any guy who could wrestle running backs to the turf could wrestle also. At least try. The only teammates his size were Clancy Fitzsimmons at 175 and the heavyweight Ray Wycoff, 50 pounds heavier.

Tuffy took to wrestling almost as a duck to water, but slower. He started at the bottom. Rumor has it that the Princpal Usels told Coach K that if Tuffy got tossed from any more matches, as in DQ'd or disqualified, the principal would kick Tuff off the team. Say, what? Since when does a Prince Pal have that authority?

Coach K told Usels that he was teaching Tuffy moves AND the rules at the same time. Tuffy didn't cotton to some opponent's diving toward his legs and returned the move with a forearm shiver!

With a win-loss record of 3 and 7 no one thought Tuffy had a chance at state—except Tuffy and Coach K. And they were both right.

Later Coach K apologized to Tuffy for being so tough on him when school began. But Tuffy told coach it was a shock, that he wasn't sure the coach would even allow him to try out but the state champ speech awakened him and spurred him on. It was for his own good.

Suggestion Box

"Ah, but a man's reach should exceed his grasp or what's a heaven for."   Miss Quote   **❝ ❞**

If I said your class materials are boring, that gives you too much credit.

                                       TNP

When a girl ceases to blush, she has lost the most powerful charm of her beauty.

Literary Jeanie 

I swung in to see you on Hollywood and Vine.   *Tarzan*

Old Movie Guy

What is the meaning of "The greatest among you will be the least"?   *Miss Quote*

Do we really have a choice in our birth?

A to Z

Mr. Kandel, We want your body.

Secret Admirers

Did you know that not all dragons are physical?

Dragon Slayer

Circular File

I was angry when Mr. K said he wished we all got VD. What? Are you crazy? Then he explained VD was virgin disease. Okay, Mr. K, you're excused.

Inter-office Memo

To: Mr. Wild
From: Mr. Kandel
Subject: Student decorum
Gene Beaumont and Terry Sloane were in the west end of "E" hall. It appeared Terry was standing lookout while Gene tugged at the bottom of a locker in the area of "E 53 to 57, pulling it outward in an effort to get into it. Suddenly four students appeared running toward them from the gym area. Gene rose quickly to his feet and they walked casually toward me, where I identified them.

Security Guards

Security checked out the blue van from which pot smoke poured and four naked teens were inside doing more than smoking. What's going on, they wanted to know? Why don't they stake out Mr. Wiggles' camper cause the antenna is always wiggling during lunch...with under aged girls no less!

Locker Room

"Hey, Darrell, let's make it with the seniors next week, senior skip day."

"I feel ya! Let's make it happen."

"We'll need to get passes or skip class."

"I'm pretty sure we can get passes through the office. Let's plan on it."

The following week the four guys set out to party with the seniors, knowing they'd have to come up with some bucks for booze from the keg. When they got to the party, Greg paid for a pitcher and he and his three pals began to swill. The weather turned sour so the guys sat in the Blazer and drank pitcher after pitcher, maybe a dozen pitchers split four ways.

The other three had to leave so Greg sat in the truck as they left him in the face the mounting wind. For some reason he stayed in the parking lot. About five minutes passed when people came up and told him someone had rolled a Bronco. At that time he left and came to the scene of an accident, the Bronco on its side. The car looked familiar and as Greg ran to it, he noticed an ambulance and he looked inside. He spotted one of his pals. He told his friend, "It's gonna be okay, Darrell." The officials told him to exit. And he did. But he got into a serious one way conversation with God.

Mr. Nozall sat with the chairman of the science department. "Hey, Leo, I think that rookie teacher referred to as Mr. Rose, because of his clouded idealism and rose tinted glasses, is about to be launched into the stratosphere."

"Why do you say that?"

"Haven't you heard? He confronted the boss about the in-service scheduled to teach us how to properly teach kids. He actually wrote a note telling the Prince Pal that 156 hours of in-service was a waste of time and costly to the taxpayers...that it would be better to select those teachers who wanted or needed the training and allow them to do so. He actually said he was 'extremely adamant' and would not attend."

"Wow. He must be looking for a transfer to another school, district or job."

"Well, Mr. Do Gooder told his class he wanted them to know he loves them...that if he couldn't get that across, it didn't matter what he taught them.

Pretty funny, huh?"

The boozer boys were always on the lookout for beer truck pirate activities. Two guys scored a keg of beer on the way home from school one day. When they spotted the truck with the back open, Dick pulled up and Greg jumped out, grabbed a keg and hustled it back. Zoom! They split.

Another day on the way to Shakey's Pizza for lunch, Looney Louie spearheaded a plan to abscond with some of the contents of a beer truck, should they be so lucky. He told them to keep their eyes peeled for a BAH wagon, Barley and Hops. Before they reached the pizza joint, Lu Lu shouted "beer wagon!" Their antennae went up and they initiated a swift plan. While Lu Lu went to the back of the wagon, the three awaited his signal, planning to grab whatever they could carry and split.

They agreed to return with the goods, no ifsandzerbuts.

They heard, "Oh, my God," figured it was Lu Lu and headed for the rear of the truck. One yelled to the others to grab imports only. They ran to the truck, dropped their loot and returned to the wagon.

About that time a guy exited Shakey's and hollered, "Get outta there!" He went back into Shakey's. Dale took off leaving the three. They split in different directions, having agreed if they weren't caught, to meet at Mc Donald's.

They made their getaway and Dale showed up and took them to Greg's place where they stashed the booze in his bedroom.

Guess you know what Lu Lu said? "That's a Magoo!"

Mr. Rose and retiring Mr. Muzzleton talk.

"So, Muzz how long have you been here at Liberty?"

"Seems like forever but it's not."

"Obviously you have a ton of stories."

"Yes, I do. Some pleasant, some not so. I've had students within the law and students outside the law. Among others I've had students in my classes who were murdered, students who murdered…students who were raped, students who raped…students who were robbed, students who robbed."

"You could write a book."

"I'll leave that to another. Maybe our claimed former English teacher Mr. Timmons."

"He was a published author?"

"Yeh, he retired. We lost a good one. He was loved by everyone."

Student Notes

BDK, You took the time to notice me when something was wrong, like my absences. You didn't look down on me about some of my prior events. I really appreciate that. I won't ever forget it. THANK YOU.

Mr. Kandel makes it fun. I hope that when my little sister is in 10th grade she can have him.

Mr. Kandel's sophomore English class was the most fun I've had in my entire high school career. He was a blast. Besides his humor, faces and walks, it was the way he taught.

Mr. Kandel is the greatest English teacher who ever lived.

Everyone loves coming to this class. It's the best class I ever had

"I saw a chick jogging on my drive home yesterday. She looked like she had two dogs, Fi and Do. Actually it looked more like a lady dog and two joggers."

My cousin was home from college and told me about a weird student in the dorm room next to his. He'd caught a chipmunk, put string on its neck, walked it to class, fed it and after a time let it go. Stranger still, the same guy rescued some blackbird chicks. Baseball bat swinging students had literally brained the parents which dive bombed them. This guy fed the chicks chopped liver and milk. They repaid his kindness by dooh doohing the walls from the flags he had pinned up. College student? Hmmmm.

Pam and Marcia attended a Youth For Christ camp for a week, their counselor was nicknamed Puke Buster because he was a reformed drunk. On their way home to the farm, they were chased by a car load of guys but evaded them and got home safely.

Teacher Concerns

All strangers must report to the office
Dress code for teachers would improve student attitude
Deal with student rudeness
Principal K needs some direction from his co-prince pals to insure consistent discipline.

Suggestion Box

Have you seen any Happy Trails?   Roy Rogers, Dale Evans

Old Movie Guy 

Ask me how I really feel about Mr. Kandel.
TNP

What's the relationship of global situations—past and present-and the Biblical view?
I B American 

When robots take over the world, will people exist?
I B American

Real courage is when you know you're licked before you begin, but you begin anyway and see it through no matter what.
Literary Jeanie

Who said "You are my sunshine, my only sunshine"?
Miss Quote

Do you think Myrna Melons has visited Mr. Wiggles camper?

Mr. Query-us   Mr. **?**-us

Statistics say all who have a sex change have psychological problems later. Therefore isn't it possible they had psychological problems before the operation?
A to Z

Multi-colored posters covered the hallways. It was that time of year for students running for student government to get their posters made and posted. Some of the more daring, and/or rich, availed color print brochures asking peers to "vote for Smot" or "Win with Quinn."

As the year progressed our Angles won some and lost some. It wasn't normal for the teams to come home on wounded wings, but sometimes it happened.
Hustle muscle. Do or Die!
Let this be our battle cry.

We can do it. Yes, we can!
If we follow Coach's plan.

Let us strive to overcome
So that we will be the one
Who takes home the gold today...
It is better we than they.

Parent-Staff Message

Mr. Kandel,
Dear Sir, Mr. Kandel:
Thanks so very much for your praise—must say I was surprised to hear from a teacher, and especially from Liberty High. I'm Debbie's Grandmother, Betty R. is her mother.
The girls all know and admire you.
There is a problem at that school, let's say many of the students are a problem. And the lack of discipline doesn't help. Seems to be in all the schools. Thanks again for your support and good luck.
Mrs. Lindy Rondell

Honor Banquet

The honors banquet was held in May with fifty students in attendance, all administrators, some teachers, parents and/or close family. The honors group had selected Mr. Kandel to be the speaker and he talked about getting MAD, making a difference. It was another milestone in the students' road to the future.

Student Concerns

Leave gym open on weekends
School should pay for rifle team's ammunition
We need more and varied lunch time sports opportunities
We have poor class selections
Dislike new policy not allowing students to change classes

At the end of the year, preparatory to next year's classes, Mr. Kandel told his students, "At the end of my first year teaching, I asked students to evaluate me, telling them to 'take a sheet of paper. Don't write your name. Imagine your brother or sister is coming next year and write whether you'd recommend me or not. And the reason you'd do so.'"

Student Writing

Kandel
It's been a great year.
I've enjoyed being here.
I know there were times when you
Thought I didn't listen;
But I want you to know I heard
Every word you mentioned.
You taught me how
To look at things from a different view
That's something that I never
Took the time to do.
Yet, there were times I thought
Of you as a preacher
But I still thank God you were
My English teacher.
Now the year is through
And I want to tell you
I appreciate the things you do.
Patricia Monet

Don't compromise yourself
playing someone else!
Anon O. Elf

Angels' Halo

Retiring teachers and principal.

Four teachers and a principal retire this year from the hallowed halls of Liberty High.

The teachers include two from the department of English, one from art and one from math. Mrs. Angel Wallford has taught at Liberty for twenty years, had three children and plans to retire to reading and gardening. Ms. Jewel Sanders taught twenty-one years and leaves with her eye on travel. Art teacher Josh Mattel will move with his wife out of state and focus on making a name for himself in the art community. Although Donald Muzzelton was victimized by his math students—seniors took his furniture into the courtyard and hauled his Volkswagen into class, he took it in stride. Mr. Muzzleton, known as Muzz, and one of our finest stated, "Every kid is different. Each has something to offer. He should retain his uniqueness to blend with the whole. Each student counts and we teachers should count it a privilege to work with each one."

Activities Principal Mr. Prentice Usels, leaves Liberty to return to his home state of Arkansas.

One of the highlights of the Yearbook Heavenly is always the senior centerfold—featuring all of the seniors in two full pages.

Wall Talk

Jody says, "That BDK is a MAD teacher."

"No, he's not," came back Billy, "he's a cool dude. He's the raddest teacher in the school."

"That's what I been tryin' ta tell ya, he's MAD— MAD stands for Make A Difference. And he's a teacher that makes a difference."

Angels' Halo

Some senior predictions:

Jason Quimby becomes construction supervisor and builds warehouse large enough to contain his larger than life ego.

Myrna (Melons) Garfield owns-operates a clothing line that provides her form-fitting undergarments as she continues to blossom.

Clancy Fitsimmons graduates college with degree in auto design and builds the Fitzmobile, an unparalleled hot rod.

Tuffy Bidar moves from semil-pro wrestling to MMA and captures the world title.

Mazzie Mc Kenzie marries Marshall Perry and raises a football team of chillun.

Louie Ellis goes on stage as stand up comic, internationally known, House of Humor named after him.

Senior fun day

Blue skies beckoned, temperatures hovered in the 80's and seniors, many of them of the rowdy nature, attacked their final fling of the year, except for graduation... and, of course, any clandestine activities of which the adults were unaware.

Nearly 100% of the seniors participated in the senior fun day. Chaperoning teachers arranged for subs to cover their classes, buses were loaded and proper safeguards were established—especially for those wishing to swim in the lake. Seemed like all the bases were covered. And, as usual, the event went off without a hitch.

A follow up evaluation of the students allowed them to comment on what they liked best, least, what was accomplished, its worth and other comments. They enjoyed the music, dancing, sports activities and free caps and T-shirts. Accomplishments included being free of school work, visiting with friends, it's possible to have fun without alcohol and showed the classes' maturity. It allowed a parting goodbye for friends who may not see each other after graduation. "It was great. Make it more than one day!"

At the end of year Mr. Kandel collected books:

"Okay, Sean, I need your book."

"Can't have it. I'll have to pay for it."

"Why's that, Sean?"

"Remember that freak snow we got last year? I had to use that book for traction in the parking lot."

"Well, at least the book came to good use."

And another kid:

"I'll have to pay for the book, Mr. K."

"You lost it or the dog ate it?"

"Worse than that. A black lab at the bus stop used it as a fire hydrant. I didn't have the spine to pick it up after that."

"I understand. Sorry I have to charge you for it."

Corner of the Shadow

Since when did counselors become administrators? I refer you to those in the counseling department who have seized the power to remove students from classes at will. And to change their recorded quarter grades.

You are being disconsidered

Inter-office Memo

To: Mr. Kandel
From: Mr. Wild
Subject: Appropriate dress
During the last week of school, as I indicated in the faculty meeting, I intended for the entire week to be take up with regular class activities and testing.

I am not sure that your dress could be called appropriate the day before school ended. If all staff members dressed in a similar fashion I believe the attitude of the students would also change and we would not be able to continue on a serious fashion.

I would like to discuss appropriate dress with you at your convenience.

Mr. Kandel met with Mr. Wild and explained his rationale. "The recommendation is laudatory for the general staff. I did not leave my room the entire day. Since my students know me and my standards and respect me and those standards, your recommendation is moot in its relevance to me and my classes.

"Were it the beginning of the year and standards had yet to be established, I could agree. However the day before school ends, when I've concluded my class work, collecting books and chose to be light hearted, I can't agree with you.

"A fellow teacher told me recently 'I've been wearing Levis and T-shirts every day, waiting for an administrator to tell me not to wear these, but no one has.' I wore the wig, headband and T-shirt as an end of the year celebratory statement: I hope you enjoyed our class and have a good summer. Had I worn a tuxedo, I'd have had the same results."

Mr. Wild had no response.

Summer school was never much of a hit with students who needed the credit. It was a 6 week course condensed into concentrated work, hoping to compensate for the failing grade of those who signed up. It ran from 7:30 a.m. to 1:40 p.m. Monday through Friday and would begin in early June. Courses offered were English, math, science and social studies. The student had to sign the contract and could be removed for any number of violations, including drug use, stealing, fighting or not working to his ability. Should the student miss five days, he was withdrawn.

Graduation

The big night arrived and the seniors were in top form. They'd practiced the evening before and were ready to face the world—freedom at last.

The seniors arrived with family, dates and/or friends and relatives. This was their big night. As the school band played, they marched in two single file lines from opposite sides of the stadium, long gowns in school colors—ivory and blue, of course—flowing floorward.

The initial priorities took place—National Anthem, prayer, introduction of honored educators including the superintendent of schools. Then the honor speaker was introduced followed by a faculty member, chosen for the occasion.

Marshall Perry was the honor speaker who addressed the seniors in a serious tone, planning to keep his speech brief but to the point.

"Mr. Superintendent, administrators, family and seniors, I am honored to be with you tonight. On behalf of our graduating class I thank you all for what you have provided us.

"Almost without regard to the 12 year excursion into life, we discuss 'commencing,' a beginning. We're at the end of the beginning. We survived. Some thrived our 'schooling' *per se*. It may be the end of organized education for most. We've managed the battleground of high school—that, in and of itself, is a victory. Now we sally forth, not unlike Don Quixote and his windmills, preparing for what lies ahead. I challenge you, and me, to pick up the gauntlet of life and to carry ourselves with pride into our futures.

"We may have fallen in battle, but regardless of our color or gender, we all matter. We need each other and choose to rise…to continue onward.

"The past twelve years of school trained us to sift out, to seek and to find. We've been given tools to research, opportunities to stabilize a moral-ethical base for decision making and the understanding that for every decision there are co-relating circumstances.

"We have been given direction in our quest for happiness. Happiness is not something that we attain by pursuit. Happiness is a by-product of our endeavors to excel and to become our very best. We achieve happiness while serving others, by fulfilling our gift to God. Whereas what we are is His gift to us, what we become is our gift to Him.

"Setting those things aside that may distract or divert us from our search and attainable goals, let us commence."

The faculty member spoke about character and challenged the students not to compromise in order to attain fame, popularity, power and/or money. He reminded them that "the best you can do is the best you can do." His speech was interrupted by the traditional beach balls sailing around—uninterrupted by security…and the commencement ceremony ended.

People gathered after the playing of "Pomp and Circumstance," took pictures, gabbed and enjoyed the merriment. Then the stadium emptied and custodial personnel made their appearance.

Marshall found his parents and they zeroed in on Mazzie and her parents. Heartwarming chatter ended with the "we'll see you later, actually tomorrow morning since we're going to the Youth For Christ all-nighter." Both teenagers told their parents "I love you" which their parents returned and Marsh and Zie drove off.

After graduation many seniors headed for the pre-arranged party. It was well known that Frank Maloney's mother provided booze during the year and that night was her crowning moment. The booze flowed and incapacitated kids filled chairs, couches or the floor. The bulk of the guys had departed for Alford Creek where they'd continue drinking. About thirty-five guys joined the game, playing king of the mountain, trying to toss each other off a ten-foot dirt bank into the creek. Two dozen cars parked nearby avoided most of the mayhem until Ray Elder, in a borrowed suit, tried unsuccessfully three times to go through the barb wire fence, before clearing it in a very tattered suit and climbing onto Jack Neff's newly restored and painted Grand Am. There Ray tap danced a tune in his discombobulated head until the roof gave way under the strain.

Meanwhile Lu Lu, having spent so many weekends at his uncle's homebrew residence in the country and somewhat immune to the effects of booze, fetched one after another from the creek before they were flushed into its mouth at the river. He helped get them into cars in a sitting position to negate suffocating on their vomit should they hurl. He was Mr. Responsibility.

In the process he thought about his own drinking. It was painful watching his friends in their condition. When he'd done about all he could, Lu Lu decided to find Marshall and tell him about his decision to quit drinking. He told a partier, "I gotta go. I'm going to head to the YFC all-nighter to talk with my friend Marshall Magoo. He can straighten me out. I've seen the light and have a fuller picture of the Big Guy. I want to see Marshall for some input."

The YFC all-nighter featured a number of events such as bowling, wallyball, golf driving range and fleeceball. Fleeceball was new to the group but highly enjoyed. It was a modified game of softball workup, played indoors. The batter swung until he hit the ball, a round sponge covered by thin leather. He had to hand off the bat to the person stationed between home plate and first base. If the bat hit the floor, the batter was out. There were no fouls and the ball could be played off the walls or ceiling. For instance, if a long ball bounced off the wall and someone caught it, the batter was out. And the catcher went to bat. Everyone got to play and the game moved right along.

As the night of darkness gave way to the light or day, Marshall and Mazzie decided it was nearing time for the FCA breakfast in the school cafeteria. With goodbyes to friends, they got into Marshall's car and headed for school.

Tuffy and Clancy and their dates followed the couple in their cars.

While dawn increased visibility, Marshall and Mazzie, happily talked about upcoming summer plans and college goals.

"Marsh, wasn't that a blast tonight?"

"It sure was, Zie. Guess we're done with YFC high school overnighters though."

"Yeh, we're about to experience the three-months of summer activities. We'll do so much together. It will be awesome."

"Before you know it, we'll be off to college to see what kind of challenges that presents and whether we'll be the champions of the world."

The whole time they drove, Mazzie's left hand was on Marshall's right knee. They were truly in love and had the world by the tail…expecting great things for their combined future.

By this time it was nearly full daylight and they neared Deadman's Curve, known by students as The Zipper. There were so many accidents at the curve requiring stitches, thus the nickname.

Suddenly Mazzie screamed, "Look out!" Marshall had a split second to react to the lurching vehicle ahead. And then a resounding collision of metal and flying glass.

Tuffy's headlights picked up the brilliant red tail lights of Marshall's car, indicating he'd hit his brakes. Not unusual on The Zipper. But this was different. Those lights glared danger, if not death. *What's happening?*

In the next second Tuffy made out smoke, dust and flying debris as two vehicles met head on and their rear tires lurched from the ground simultaneously. A cloud of dust remained in the air as Tuffy turned onto the shoulder.

Marshall's car floated in what appeared slow motion onto its top.

Clancy saw Tuffy pull off the road onto the shoulder and followed his example. Running toward the carnage, he yelled, "Tuffy, what's going on?"

Instantly Tuffy ran to Marshall's overturned car and looked inside. No movement. On the driver's side Marshall lay inert. Tuffy kicked in the driver's side window and leaned toward Marshall. "Marshall! Marshall?" He looked across the seat at Mazzie who lay motionless, crumpled and unmoving.

By then Clancy had arrived and helped Tuffy grab hold of Marshall's arms and drag him from the vehicle. While Clancy checked Marshall for a pulse, Tuffy ran around the car and kicked in the passenger window. Clancy reached Tuffy with the bad news that Marshall was dead.

Together they maneuvered Mazzie from the wreck and checked her pulse. None.

The buddies then ran over to the other car. Louie Ellis's. He was very relaxed and moaning. His passenger door was sprung open and they dragged him from the wreckage.

After dragging Louie to safety, they checked his respiration and quickly returned to Marshall and Mazzie. Just as they arrived, a fire broke out under the hood of Marshall's car. The guys tugged at the bodies of Marshall and Mazzie, getting them safely away from the fire, which turned into an inferno.

By then the faint sounds of emergency vehicles grew louder. Someone had called 911.

Before long first responders showed up. A couple of officers set up flares and orange cones and began directing traffic. An ambulance arrived. The task of moving Marshall and Mazzie was overwhelming for Tuffy and Clancy. Two classmates gone. How could this be?

While the red rescue wagon carrying the sweethearts lumbered away, silently disappearing into the night, responders loaded Louie into an ambulance. Red and blue lights flashed in unison and the screaming siren trailed off into silence in the distance.

Whereas a shadow of darkness reigned over Liberty Heights with the loss of two of its brightest lights, pleasant memories of Marshall and Mazie prevailed. In the end light overshadowed the dark. Even Lu Lu's decision to change brought a change he could never have imagined. His recovery was rapid and his guilt slowly dissipated.

The Perry's and the Mc Kenzie's were devastated with the news of their model children. Were the previous eighteen years of their lives for naught? The parents wrestled with the thought. No more sweethearts. No more children. No hope of their marriage, no children. The pain was monstrous. The two couples met and discussed their dream *poof* into a nightmare of nothingness. But then they decided to turn their tragedy into a triumph.

They acknowledged that Marshall and Louie had been best friends forever. Ever since Lu Lu became the notable class clown in junior high with his staccato-like humor and personality on steroids. Even when Louie began drinking and they differed in so many ways, Marsh and he remained good friends.

Both the Perry's and the Mc Kenzie's attended the same church along with Louie. They'd shared events, picnics, buffets and so on though their philosophies were not entirely similar.

Ultimately the parents chose to forgive Louie and, somehow, move on with their lives. Lu Lu had been released from the hospital in good condition and attended the memorial service where he sat in great remorse the entire time.

The keynote speakers were Mr. Perry and Mr. Mc Kenzie, supported totally by their wives.

Mr. Perry spoke briefly.

"In a time when we are bombarded with the modern view of success and victory, I am happy to say that we can snatch victory from the jaws of defeat…even death.

"When Jesus Christ died a humiliating crucifixion, people said he lost. He didn't lose. He sacrificed himself for all mankind. He did the hardest thing any man ever did—he gave up his will for the benefit of mankind. He chose to love rather than to get even. Whereas he was viewed as a loser, time has proven the opposite.

"In a his own, small way, Marshall reflected Jesus' teachings, always putting others first and considering their importance. Each person in this scenario is important and counts. Each had a life. Marshall. Mazzie. Louie. You. My wife. Me. Who am I to accuse anyone?

"It is our hope that those who learn about this tragic event will learn from it…and live a better life."

When it was Mr. Mc Kenzie's turn, he reminded the mourners how much his daughter Mazzie and Marshall enjoyed life and each other, how much effort they expended to brighten their world…and how much he and his wife knew the effect the two young adults had upon that world."

It was a jam packed year—filled with trivia, tenderness, trauma and tragedy. Would the next school year be any different?

Yo, Gomers!

Part II
Dawn

"Not all adults are insensitive to problems…"
Oct. 6, 1992 *Anchorage Daily News*

Dear Ann Landers:

I am 17 years old and as far as I can tell, I am a normal depressed teen-ager. I have several scars on my left arm and hand, all self-inflicted knife cuts.

I have never wanted to kill myself. If that were the case, I would have blown my head off with a shotgun. I only want to HURT myself. This may seem strange, but the mental pain I go through every day is so hard to deal with that physical pain actually makes me feel better.

An adult's first reaction would be, "You must stop doing this. It makes no sense."

Teen-agers today need help in life, not more money or things. We need someone who will listen not condemn us. Allow us to make mistakes without reminding us that we screwed up again. We know when we're doing something wrong and often we do it to get attention. Nothing is worse than being ignored and made to feel like a non-person, and there are a lot of us out there. I am just—One Voice in the Crowd in La Grande, Ore.

Dear Voice:

I contacted Dr. William J. Pieper, a Chicago psychoanalyst, and here is his response: "Tragically, many teen-agers mutilate or kill themselves because they have written off adults and believe physical pain or death offers the only relief from their unbearable emotional pain.

"They are unaware that all adults are NOT the same and that a competent professional can provide a positive, non-judgmental alternative—namely, a healing relationship—to the bleak choice between emotional and physical suffering."

Dear Abby:

Nothing in this world seems to interest me anymore since I broke up with my fiancée. I was so upset at the time, I wanted to commit suicide, but because I have my parents to support, I couldn't bring myself to end my life.

I cannot seem to get over the hurt of ending my relationship with what I perceived to be the perfect woman. We were so happy together and she seemed so right for me, then shortly before we were to be married I discovered that she had been a prostitute before we met.

Please advise me.

Not Healing

Dear Not Healing:

It's not where we came from that's important—it's where we're going that counts.

Jesus forgave the prostitute. ("Go, and sin no more.") Should you do less?

The Son rose for Dawn; will the sun rise for her?

Dawn signals the arrival of a new day…will the sun rise for each of us…and will we capitalize on the dawning of the day be the most we can be?

Startled awake by someone near her. On the edge of the bed. It was her step-father. His hand moved beneath her nightgown. Then she felt it inside her panties. Her 6-year-old mind wondered *what's he doing?* She tried to believe it wasn't happening. But it was.

"What are you doing, Sam?"

"I'm loving you. You're old enough to play love. You will understand as you get older. And I will do this more as you get bigger. It's a father-daughter secret so you can't tell anyone. If you do, they could get hurt. Especially your mother. She wouldn't understand. We won't tell her."

Dawn was stunned. *Was this real? Was it really love*? Did her friends do this with their fathers? She felt trapped.

For years nights became a nightmare. *Will he come tonight? What will he do?*

In time she noticed the thing between his legs was not like hers. It was soft but then became bigger and rigid. *What's that all about?*

Dawn regretted her mother's absence. When she was working the night shift her step-father's visits became more regular. Always playing the love game. Whenever he climbed off her, he took a balloon off his thingie which appeared soft and wet. He always pulled his shorts back up and left without saying a word.

One night her step-father came into her room. Dawn feigned sleep. She thought she heard something. Before long her mother's head peeked around the doorway.

"What's going on?"

Dawn gasped.

Her step-father grunted.

A scream shattered the stillness of the night, followed by a dull thud. She sat straight up in bed. Moments later she shook, wide eyed, scared, gut wrenching as she stared at her mother on the floor. She strained to get up, knees shaking, pushing into the wall and rising slowly. She looked at her husband who stood over her, his fists clenched at his sides. "You son-of-a"… she began before his left fist smashed into her mouth.

As I lay there wondering what to do, my step-father left the room, swearing and muttering to himself. I jumped out of bed and whispered "mother." Wanting to help her, I reached under her arms and was able to help her rise. My mind went wild, wondering about deceiving her all these years and how she could ever forgive me. I seemed caught in a nightmarish mess. *What now? Will she understand? How could she forgive me? Will she know I'm telling the truth? How will I be affected by the secret…now and in the future? Will it ever be worth living? Will I ever get over it? How can I ever make it up to her? I can't. I'd be better off dead. She'd be better off if she never saw me again.*

After months and a messy divorce which threatened Dawn's school work and her mother's health, the divorce was final. Mother and daughter took it one day at a time.

A couple of days before school began, some hallways were being re-tiled. A former Liberty student worked till lunch then sat on a pallet of tile near Mr. Kandel's room. Coach K carried his lunch pail from his room and joined the worker.

"Hey, Mr. K. We had some bodacious times here in the hallowed halls of Liberty, the B.G. for the ages, didn't we?"

"We sure did, Bill. I always enjoyed watching you thread the defense and drop one through the hoop or nail one from the corner. You were a great shot."

"Thanks, Mr. K. Whatever happened to the worst history teacher I ever had, Mr. Usels?"

"Oh, a few years after you graduated, he became a counselor."

"Really. That's bizarre."

"You think that's bizarre. After that he rose to the position of activities principal."

"You're kidding. Really?"

"Yeh. One situation he would like to have a do-over on was the transfer of a student from another school. He told her folks she couldn't play at Liberty until she lived in that area for a semester. Her father told Usels that the district changed the volleyball season from spring to fall. His daughter was innocent of the scheduling change. Usels wouldn't have any of it. So, when his daughter went to state as a hurdler, her dad and teacher took a day of professional leave. While he was there, he talked with the secretary for the state association of high school activities, explained the problem. The association guy told him to drop by his office on Monday. He did. Problem solved. The bad news, almost hilarious, was last spring before he retired, Usels called the teacher into his office and told him "you went behind my back." Teacher had a three word reply, "Yes, I did."

Wall Talk

Clay: "Okay, who thinks being seen in your sparkly, new machine is more important than being yourself, letting others know the real you?"

Quinn: "So, you're saying there is no pot of gold at the end of the rainbow…that the quest supersedes the wealth…maybe that the quest IS the reward?"

Clay: "Well, maybe the rainbow isn't what it seems. Yes. Maybe the pursuit is actually the reward."

Quinn: "That kind of throws a new light on the idea that instead of 'You're the story of my life…You're the life of my story.'"

Clay: "And one other thing…following a rusty rainbow won't lead to happiness."

Freddie: "You guys. This discussion is weird and a little heavy for me. I'm heading for class."

Almost before Coach K knew it, the cross-country season began and the Angels were off to the races, no pun intended.

Coach tried to vary practice, always including warm up and down, fartleck, interval and distance. Sometimes he divided the runners into two equal teams to complete—the number 1, 3, 5, 7, 9 runners against the 2, 4, 6, 8, 10, and so on. They had a destination where coach usually had a treat stored—apple, banana, candy bar—and each runner had to return with evidence that he'd reached the turn around point. A couple of times the team stung coach with candy wrappers he had not left…or fruit of the same nature.

Dawn had never attended a X-country meet. While awaiting the beginning of the race among a relatively small crowd of spectators, she could almost feel the warmth of the birch and quaking aspen trees, golden-orange leaves waving slightly in the breeze along the race trail. Everything about the venue pleased her…the tinkling brook stair-stepping into rolling hills and back dropped by rugged mountains.

Dawn heard the race starter, "Runners to your marks." And before she knew it, *Bang,* the starter's .22 blank pistol rang out and the runners were off.

Cheering fans either ran to another spot where they could watch the runners' progress or stood around visiting. That's when she noticed a tall, athletic and attractive girl on the sidelines.   Dawn approached the tall girl.

"Hi. my name's Dawn. Not to be rude but are you new? I haven't seen you before today."

"How could you miss someone as tall and beautiful as I? That's a joke. No, I'm not new. I've been out of town all summer at different events. My names Victoria. My friends call me Tori."

"That's a beautiful name. Love the shortened version too."

"Thank you. Do you come to these races often?"

"First time. I heard there was a race after school and decided to check it out."

"Do you know any of the runners?"

"Not to my knowledge. None of them looked familiar."

"Cross-country is one sport that gets very little glory. I've seen races later in the fall or after a rain where the runners come across the finish line red-legged, mud splattered. It's common for them to have mud and snot covered faces. They must love their sport to endure that. And no one sees them. It's not like football or basketball where everyone in the crowd sees the entire game. These runners get no glory."

"Well, I've yet to see the snot nosed runners but this may become a habit."

"You have probably heard that some people want to win at all costs?"

"Yes, I've heard that. The statement applies to life as well as sports."

"Yes, it does. There was a coach in the state who was lauded for his 300 victories but any number of his players over the years came from out of state. He recruited them via relatives here. How do you think that affected those players? Didn't do the coach's rep any good either."

"You make a very good point. One we'll have to discuss further should our paths cross."

"Speaking of crossing paths, here comes the first runner. Yell for him."

After the race and subsequent hubbub of the parents and other supporters, Victoria told Dawn it was nice meeting her and if she couldn't drop her anywhere. That's when Dawn watched her drive off in a Mercedes.

Rumor has it—some cross-country guys said—that BDK didn't have a clue about the sport. He told them at his first practice the year before that he knew runners ran into the woods and out of the woods but he didn't know what they did in the woods. He told them the athletic director asked him if he'd like to coach the team. He didn't. He told the AD he'd only heard about cross-country. So a couple of days later the athletic director gave Big Daddy a whistle.

BDK told the AD, "I'll coach the team until a real coach comes along or someone who knows what he's doing shows up. It's only fair to the kids."

It had to be humiliating to the coach and team as they met the reigning state team in a dual meet a few weeks later. At the start of the race, the legendary opposing coach stood atop a wooden spool, baseball cap perched atop his head and stop watch in his hand, awaiting the appearance of his orange clad harriers. It wasn't more than a blink of the eye when thirteen silk clad runners appeared. Since his team had no uniforms because it was a new school—they wore T-shirts and cutoffs, Big Daddy kept waiting to see a white T-shirt. Those orange-clad lads hadn't lost a race in six years. That's the day he told himself he wouldn't quit coaching cross-country until they'd beaten the orange guys.

Obviously Big Dad didn't know at the time that within three years they'd own the state running trails...and even better, a new-experienced coach came to Liberty. That was when Big Dad turned over his whistle and clipboard to Lynn Roumagoux who built a dynasty in cross country running, skiing and track. Yeah, Coach Roumagoux!

The first week of school Mr. Wild sent Coach K a note. Wild wanted to see Coach K after school. No subject. Just the note. Coach took it as a command. So when the final bell rang, he took his lonely briefcase to Wild's office. When he entered, Wild gruffly stated "the others will be her shortly" before he turned to his desk. Hmmmm. Coach sat down, opened his briefcase and began correcting student compositions.

Before long the athletic director and activities principal showed up and Wild had them sit while he closed the door. He then handed Coach K a paper delineating his misdeeds as the head wrestling coach with the order to "sign it." Both the AD and activities principal gave each other looks of surprise, if not shock, apparently ignorant of Wild's intentions.

Coach K quickly skimmed the document which accused him of recruiting a wrestler, suggesting wrestlers have cheerleaders and his comment to an opposing wrestler the previous year. Hmmmm.

He told Wild he was guilty of some of the "offenses" but not all. He explained the hockey team had cheerleaders called ice warmers and it seemed more student involvement was a good thing because it would be a plus for both young men and women to engage in mutual support. He also said he had apologized to the other team's wrestler and his family the year before. And then he asked, "Don't you find it somewhat strange that you've accused me of recruiting a wrestler who was here two years before I recruited him? What's with that?"

Wild had no answer…only that next season there would be a different coach.

Coach K told him his contract necessitated his presence until 2:30 at which time it was…so "I'm leaving. If you intend to fire me from coaching, make sure you have a good reason."

At the season ending wrestler banquet, a senior emcee announced that coach had appreciated the young ladies who had supported the team. In the way of introducing the young ladies, the emcee mentioned they were active "athletic supporters." That got a muffled hoot from the audience…some probably didn't get the double entendre.

Turns out Coach K's replacement, if you can call him that, was immensely disliked by wrestler parents. On top of that, he went deer hunting during Christmas break, found it so exciting he called his wife and told her to call the school to inform them he'd gone to attend a family's funeral in another state. Total scam. He got a slap on the wrist, but was not rehired to coach.

It probably didn't even occur to Prince Wild that during Coach K's wrestling tenure he invited wrestlers to his house a couple of times during the season to reward those who had pinned opponents. Wrestlers who'd pinned an opponent the fastest in a match received a steak; others who'd pinned opponents received a hamburger. And Coach K operated on a slim, single family income.

Suggestion box:

Mr. K, how about having discussions regarding:
Parents: they do too much for kids; they don't do enough; they don't love their kids; they don't understand their kids…
Teachers: don't know how to dress; women show too much flesh;

many are ugly…etc. Why do teachers try to teach something they know nothing about/they're stupid. Why are classes so boring? Positive reinforcement works. Why aren't teachers educated to understand kids? Why don't teachers put as much time into their students as they do their week ends…or their boring classes?

They don't know how to dress;
Women show too much flesh.
Men attempt to be brave,
Really fail to behave.

You might say our teachers were of the black hat and white hat variety. Bad and good guys and gals. And, of course, some gray hats— those who had both bad and good qualities. Most kids managed to tolerate the black hats. The kids reveled in the teachers who wore white hats.

Some teachers were intellectually gifted but they had so few human skills or were so inept at working with students that their classes were saturated with non-learners, bored students or hopeless scholars.

Karen Denton was one of the good ones. She taught English and poetry. Kids loved her. She was well educated and got the material across along with a caring for the kid attitude. She was a published poet, chairman of nearly every English group in the state—state council of teachers, nationally, etc. She edited the state newsletter. She was positive, thoughtful and helpful. Never a negative. Gave great support to the sports groups, cheerleaders, teachers. A truly wonderful woman and teacher.

She told her students, "My job is to teach you English writing skills that lead toward productive compositions and/or poetry. But my mission is to help you achieve success by knowing the difference between fiction and fact. If you know what matters, that's what matters! Emphasis on KNOW."

Ms. Denton was missing. Seems she had some physical problems with her knees. She was embarrassed to teach from a wheelchair. After a few days of coming to school after her operation she left notes and disappeared.

Mrs. Harriet Solvertan called all the English teachers one Friday, wondering if they'd heard from her.

"Have you heard from or seen Karen Denton? Some of us in the English department are concerned because no one has heard from her. As you know, she was in a wheel chair the first few days of the week but called for a sub from Wednesday on."

"Yes, I know she was wheelchair bound because of her arthritic knees. That she was embarrassed that others, especially students, saw her that way. No, I haven't heard from her."

"If you do, please let me know. I'll call the others. We have a telephone tree. We've contacted the police department. A couple of us went to her apartment and found multiple notes written the past few days and addressed to different people."

"Okay. I can join the search if you let me know where to look."

"We've already checked out the highway south and the one to the north. There are arterials we need to check. The state police are also involved."

Turns out the troopers found Ms. Denton in the foothills. She must have taken pain meds. Maybe was disoriented. Maybe took other meds. Anyway, she was dead. Exposure.

There were mass people at her memorial service. Mourning the loss of a great teacher.

Student Writing

I think you are one of the few people in this world with lasting success. To have lasting success, a person needs to be happy and to have peace of mind within. There are very few men who do not drink smoke, chew, do drugs or care about their families. Very few. But you are one. And you try to uplift others, all the time.

Corner of the Shadow

Welcome to my world. Ha, ha. We, the teachers, are the ones who oil the engines. But we are the last to know. Are we not members of a union that expects us to be honored and to whom we should be communicated?

You are among the untold.

Dawn was no stranger to sadness, her life had been fraught with pain and sorrow. Yet her smile could awaken the morning sun. She was lonely and considered her options. One day at school, somewhat confused, she approached Tori and told her about her English teacher.

"Tori, Mr. Kandel had all his students fill out a sheet of paper listing their favorite things, like fragrance, food, music, movie, actor, magazine. He told us he would put these little vignettes showcasing our lives on a big poster the months of our birthdays …a different batch each month. And that if we didn't want them on the wall, to draw a large 'X' through them. I put a huge 'X' on mine.

"Guess what? He will be bringing cupcakes made by his wife every month for kids with birthdays that month. He calls these kids his Birthday Babes. Is that too much or what?

"Seems like every year some class gomers try to convince Big Dad that they had a birthday every month. Ha, ha."

Angels' Halo

Dear Bucky
I'm dating a guy who treats me like crap. He keeps saying things are going to get better. I love him and don't want to lose him.
What should I do?
Wanting Out

Dear Wanting Out,
Letting go, walking out, is hard. But it sounds like your friends and your heart are telling you it's time to say au revoir.

Circular File

One day a friend, my mother and I talked about life. She told us the hardest part in life was knowing where to draw the line…here, here or here. My friend said, "Or you don't even have to draw the line." And mother said, "True. You can omit the line on a date and stand in line at the clinic."

Eight to ten Liberty teachers and one principal meet each Monday morning before school in J-7 to pray for students, school and community. I asked one of them, my science teacher Mr. Wisel, about the fifteen minute sessions. He told me the prayers were similar to:

"Dear God, we come before You today to ask You to help us love our students and to help us present our subjects in an understandable fashion. We know that some of these kids are hurting, that their confusion and pain is so great that it is hard for them to concentrate on their class work. Many of them are in a survival mode…in an atmosphere of chaos. We pray for understanding, that we can avail ourselves to their plea for help. We ask that our school staff reaches out in unison to these kids—each one is important. We want their success and best health. Thank You. Amen.

"That pretty much is the theme and the essence of our prayers for the students and staff," responded Mr. Wisel.

Corner of the Shadow

Are we being led like lambs to the slaughter? Have we no voice regarding the tardy policy? Are we to believe that the administrators know more then we?

You are being dumbed down, lambs.

Student Writing

Jamie crouches quietly. Tears streaming down his face, he wipes at them, smearing through layers of grime. "Jimmie!" his mother screams and his eyes widen with sheer terror. She follows the trail of pee to the cupboard and throws open the door.

Although he is completely potty trained, he doesn't talk yet. He whimpers and pushes back into the corner.

She grabs his tiny arm and drags him from his shelter. Even at three-years-old he has learned not to fight.

His mother, jobless and on welfare, is an alcoholic. He's never met his father.

Jimmie's steeled himself to her angry, drunken words, "You stupid kid! Why can't you piss in the d--- toilet! Are you dumb? Talk to me, boy. Why don't you ever talk? Answer me, boy, are you stupid?" She slaps him. Then hits him harder with an open hand. "Are you paying attention? Are you?"

She drags him by the arm to the dingy, filthy bathroom and points to the toilet. "That's where you do that, stupid kid! Why can't you learn?"

Jimmie's thin little body is covered with bruises and scars. He has never lived without hunger.

His mother shakes him and slaps him again, resulting in a pool of yellow on the floor. She screams again and slams Jimmie onto the toilet. In a rage she doubles her fist and slams it into his face. His head smacks the back of the toilet. Too much for him. His eyes roll back and he falls to the floor. His mother watches, stunned. She is scared this time. And she should be.

Joan Garner

"Phantom of the Ages "

Over the fence. Across the water course. Onward. Relentless hounds nipping at its heels. As a blushing bride on her wedding night, its reddish hair seeks the solace of shameless security.

Onward. Unrelenting. Baying hounds bouncing behind. By day's end, ghosting away as if into thin air. The phantom fox Approval escapes its pursuers to run another endless day.

Peapickin' Larry

During one of their serious talks Marshall and Zie broached approval. He commented, "High school provides the perfect opportunity for acceptance. You can be yourself and be accepted or not. Peer and adult pressure demand a choice. If drinking alcoholic beverages, doing drugs, driving the perfect car or truck, wearing the proper clothes, being the right person, attending a party or getting laid, are requirements for acceptance, I'm unacceptable. I will not sacrifice myself, my beliefs, my standards in order to be accepted because of some mythical belief system. I'll stay true to myself and either be accepted or not accepted. That's my choice."

Class Discussion

Approval or security. BDK asked the students if there were a difference between approval and security. We discussed and determined that approval was a means of gaining security…after all we all want security and it seems it comes in part from gaining approval.

Student Concerns

Student lockers should be private and not broken into
Lunch hour is too short
Smoking rules not enforced
Parking lot smokers defy you to hit them with your car

Angels' Halo

OPINIONS

What's the big idea? Who ever heard of locker searches until this year? Come on. What's with our privacy rights? I'm not gonna complain; I'm complaining NOW!

Our new disciplinary administrator is all over the new policy: "Lockers may be searched for the purpose of locating weapons or firearms…" blah, blah, blah.

Mr. Copper says, "We need to do everything under our democratic precepts to insure student safety. In my private opinion locker searches will be a good thing in protecting our students."

If that doesn't sound like a politically correct answer—"In my private opinion"—what does?

And here's another politically correct batch of BS. Mr. Johnson, the reigning school board chair, implied over the phone that high schoolers are stupid.

If the searches are conducted before and after school—when the students are NOT present, what's the point? How does that insure safety?

Moron (get it)—more on—this later.

It didn't take long for Dawn and Victoria the reunite. One day between classes they crossed paths. Tori was talking to a really good looking guy with just the right tightness in his Levis and buffed out shirt with bulges in all the right places. *Wow* was all Dawn could think without shouting. Dawn didn't want to be rude but wanted to talk with Tori.

"Hi, Tori. I don't want to interrupt but wanted to say 'hi.'"

"Not a problem, Dawn. This is my friend Matt. Matt this is Dawn. We met last fall at the cross-country race."

"Hi, Dawn. Nice to know you. Maybe we'll meet later but I'm late for my geology class. See you later."

"Okay, Matt. Bye."

"'S'up, Dawn?"

"I just wanted to say I'm looking forward to doing more with you and wonder if you might have the time."

"Sure. I can definitely work you into the school daze schedule. Know what I mean? Let's plan some outrageous stuff."

"Okay. See ya later."

Faculty Lounge

One of Liberty's pilots asks a colleague, "Do we tell the new teacher we have a system…or should we keep it among ourselves? You know, the situation involving a discipline problem where we send the kid on a wild widget chase? You know what I mean?"

"You mean when you give a kid a hall pass and send him to me and I send him to Ferris and Ferris sends him on and on looking for the widget or the widget wrench…till class is over?"

"Roger that."

One day Mr. K asked kids how he could best help them, since so many of them were not reaching their potentials—"so many D's."

One girl raised her hand and said, "You don't make us work."

"I don't make you work. You mean I don't demand, browbeat, stand over you with a whip and force you to meet my expectations?"

"Right. Other teachers do that."

"Well, let me explain that situation to you. Part of my educational philosophy is that students should have the opportunity to fail before they reach college. That they should not spend their freshman year in college wasting their parents' money partying, having fun, goofing off and discovering their error at the end of the year.

"Also, students need to learn discipline—how to be accountable for their responsibilities. Every semester I provide each student a front and back sheet of paper with the essential activities per day. Obviously we do not adhere to it 100% but it's sufficient to apprise you of your responsibilities: spelling quiz every three weeks on words you misspell on compositions, vocabulary every week, composition each week during the comp section, biographies on Americans who have shaped history—including the two Japanese who led the naval and air attack on Pearl Harbor. Sprinkled among those activities are sessions on sentence structure, grammar, parts of speech and how they are identified.

"Perhaps the most telling argument for my teaching style is that I won't be here in ten years to wipe your butts. If you're going to make mistakes, as in fail, this is the time to do them."

Mr. Kandel's comments were met with some affirmations within a few days, in his suggestion box, his mailbox or under his classroom door:

From T.V.   I learned in this class that you need to get your assignments done and turned in…yourself. You aren't the type teacher who holds students' hands. Everything is on the students. If they don't understand, they can ask you. Other teachers push us but we're not kids anymore. We need to learn discipline and accountability. Thank you, Mr. K.

From G.S.   Your class is made up of responsibility and maturity. You put the responsibility on us to do our work and some of us just don't have enough responsibility to wake up and realize the real world without being pampered. I really enjoy your class Mr. K. You're a great teacher.

From C.H.   I really enjoy the class but feel pretty stupid because I didn't do anything. I'm sorry you went to all the work to teach and I didn't do the work.

From J.V.   Thank you BDK. Your class helped me realize if I'm going to make it in life, I need to take responsibility and do the work.

From C.T.   Mr. K, You always do all you can to help all your students. I've done terribly this year because I didn't apply myself. Please, please don't change a thing. If I'm in here next year, I promise you, I'll shape up.

From M.P. Mr. K, I just wanted to say thanx for being a great teacher and making class interesting enough for me to listen. I've learned much about the real world where I'll be living after college. Thank you.

From P.H.   Mr. K, Thank you for what I learned in your class. It was my favorite class. You taught us well. I learned to apply myself and it has paid off.

From C.L.   I liked this class because you didn't bitch at me when I didn't do the work. You are my favorite teacher.

From D.S.   You teach in a manner that makes the students feel important. You help us become individuals.

Suggestion Box: For BDK

Get new glasses.
Retire.
We will be nice to you because it's be nice to animals week.
It's people like you that are starting the downfall of pencils. You accept only ink.
You are a man of many faces: ugly, ugly, ugly.

Locker Room

"Have you ever wondered about the results of rejection? Have you ever heard of Ted Bundy, Robert Baker, Gary Ridgeway? What do they have in common? (Besides serial rapists-murders, they share numerous characteristics—torturing animals, bed wetting, rejection, pyromania). Is it possible had they had different childhoods their outcome would have been different?"

"That's a serious subject. I have heard of those guys. Yeh, you probably heard about Mike and Spike Arnold, the younger brother was praised and the older son embarrassed?"

"I heard Mike dusted his old man."

"Yeh, Mike was born first. Not a great specimen of 'manhood' as he grew. He was slight of build and a bit timid.

"On the other hand Spike, two years younger, started shaving as a ninth grader while Mike still had peach fuzz."

"I hear their old man was an abrasive and dictatorial man who put down Mike in front of guests at every opportunity, praising Spike and belittling Mike. That the dad was a wimp himself."

"Yeh, the boys stuck to a rigid curfew, to be in bed no later than 10 PM, in their rooms by 9. They were not to come downstairs for any reason. A couple of times they were late getting home and the old man wore them out with a willow branch. The late arrival was punishable but not worth a beating."

"Mike never complained nor resented Spike. He realized his father was the immature, if not bully, family member. Thought his dad had the little man complex. His disgust with his father grew. One night it reached a boiling point. Some endure the boiling point, even the breaking point. But Mike was not one of them."

"When Mike thought he heard a disturbance after he and Spike had gone to bed, he sneaked to the head of the stairs to investigate. What he saw astounded and outraged him. A number of naked couples formed a daisy chain in the living room. That was enough for Mike.

"The next morning at the crack of dawn he took his deer rifle, a pump action, and waited for his parents…who appeared within minutes. Mike pulled the rifle's trigger once, pumped a fresh round into the barrel and touched the trigger again. Then he called the police to turn himself in. In court the jury found him guilty on two counts of pre-meditated murder and sentenced him to life in prison."

"Do you think parenting matters?"

"Yeh. Life for death."

"How many of our peers have parents who abuse each other, especially the old man who beats his wife like a punching bag on a regular basis?"

Teacher Concerns

No close contact between students in the building—no kissing, etc.
No romantic displays between students
Counselors need to share information about students in order for teacher to assist student
Consider instituting hall monitors to keep student traffic flow moving
Monitor student assembly behavior

Faculty Lounge

"I'm always amazed that teachers go on strike and cross the picket line because they want more money, smaller class loads and more time off. Maybe they shouldn't have taken up education as a profession."

"Did you hear about Chad Wickers who saw a kid smoking a joint in the parking lot? He went out to confront the kid who took off but Wickers ran him down after a mile. Guess the kid didn't know Wickers was a college distance runner."

Next time Dawn and Tori met, Dawn related a story she'd heard about a little girl subjected to abuse. Dawn thought it might set the stage for her plans to give Tori her poem. Dawn had decided to breeze straight through the story before allowing Tori to comment.

"Tara, was raised in Akron, and was three months old, when her father Peter Cook divorced mother Linda—Tara, her sis Chris 2 stayed with mom. When Tara was three, mom re-married, adding 13-year-old stepdaughter Nancy then a boy two years later. Though Tara and Nancy became very close, Tara was bounced back-forth between mom and relatives for ten years.

"Peter lived with Rose Yuko's three kids ranged in age from 11 to 15 and she convinced Peter they could raise Tara and Chris. Deputy sheriff Papa Peter wore his weapon at home, frequently pointing it at his head, cocking it and pulling the trigger.

"In time Rose changed from nice to monster and began hitting. Chris was rescued by children's services…leaving Tara behind…to became the house servant…severely punished for improper work. Tara seldom received more than a sip of water and was told she'd have to earn her food.

"After Rose found her in the kitchen stealing a couple of candy bars, Rose kicked and beat Tara and Peter handcuffed her to the railing overnight. Rose's oldest son installed a lock on the 3x3 foot closet into which Peter and Rose kept Tara, a rag stuffed into her mouth.

"Rose often punished Tara by leaving her naked inside and outside the house (in the snow) for hours—telling her she had to earn her clothes. Tara's bruises and injuries often kept her from school. Rose told Tara that she was bad and the parents were making her good.

"When Tara missed a month of school, the nurse visited. Rose said that she was not home. The nurse contacted children's services and the police but Tara fell through the cracks. On one of the days Tara attended school, guidance counselor Joey Bratt saw her and noted the difference in her attitude—from self-assured to meek with dark circles under her eyes and bruised left cheek.

"Although Rose continued to lie about Tara's school non-attendance, Joey arrived with a police department community worker and took Tara to school… Joey never gave up. He orchestrated a truancy hearing—even after failed and repeated efforts Joey battled Rose, Peter and children's services.

"In the midst of body failure and in panic Rose took Tara to Marymount Hospital in Garfield Heights, Ohio…where they took the 35 pound girl. Her body temperature was 80 degrees and covered with hundreds of infected sores and burns. One ear was nearly bitten off; one side of her face collapsed from beatings. Her gags and bonds had worn the skin away from her face, arms and ankles. No hospital staff who knew of her expected her to survive the night.

"The examining doctor described her loss of blood pressure, infected heart, lungs and spinal fluid and her condition as 'Horror.' Evidence abounded that she'd been beaten, tortured and starved.

"Even though she stopped breathing that first night in the hospital, she regained consciousness a week later and it took months before she could digest gelatin. A blood vessel broke in her head causing a stroke and she could not straighten her legs. It was two weeks before she talked.

"Her father and Rose were arrested and charged with child endangerment, felonious assault, kidnapping and attempted murder...convicted of 12 to 45 years in jail; Rose sentenced to 18.5 to 55 years. Tara was recovering, though emotional and physical scars will likely last her entire life, and studying at U of Akron in criminal law, wanting to reach child abuse victims."

Tori was spell bound and asked Dawn how many teens she thought were subjected to the same kind of treatment. "Did you ever wonder how many kids out of 100 are genuinely loved by their parents. How many parents love their kids unconditionally…without pressure to perform? Perhaps they had no time for love. Maybe instead of wondering and conducting a poll, we should discuss with our friends and see what we can do to bring them to the point of our wondering…of realizing that we can make it even though we feel unloved."

During their discussion of child abuse and its wake of mental anguish, Dawn asked Tori to read her poem.

"Hi, I wrote this poem a few years ago. It speaks of putting yourself before family and possible disastrous consequences.

"I feel kinda like we're soul mates so to speak and I'm really interested in your thoughts about it. Maybe you can read it and next time we meet, you can give me your interpretation of it."

"That would be cool. You want me to look at the rhyme scheme, the message or both?"

"Rhyme scheme is okay, but I'm mostly interested in what you think of the theme. I wrote it when I was13-years-old and titled it 'Breaking of the Dawn.'"

"I'll do it."

Tori took the poem and read it later.

It was the breaking of the dawn that I had loved so dear,
Yet the breaking of the dawn is what I'd learned to fear.
It was the breaking of the dawn that each day brought new life,
Yet the breaking of the dawn had filled my days with strife.
It was the breaking of the dawn that brought new hope each day,
Yet the breaking of the dawn chilled me where I lay.
So, I wonder, is it wrong or is it right,
Shall I see the dawn, or shall I see the night?
What will be my plight?

Suggestion Box

When you assigned American biographies, why did you include two Japanese—Isoroku Yamamoto and Mitsuo Fuchida—the first week in December? They're not Americans.

Why are some kids so obsessed with being popular?

Where did you get your Lamborghini poster?

Why do you always tell us your car is a Lamborghini with a Suburban body?

Class Discussion

Let's review the subject of love. We'll begin with a definition of the word. What say you, class?

"Love is when you like someone so well you can't live without them."

"Love is getting what you want."

"Isn't love when you get a girl pregnant, you marry her?"

"I think love is wanting something so bad, you'll do anything to get it."

Mr. Kandel listened, as always, then asked, "How many kinds of love are there? You've hit upon a couple of them. Have you heard of *eros*, *philia*, *agape*? Do you know the differences?

"All three are words from ancient Greece. For instance Eros was the god of love, identified with the Romans as Cupid. That love is sensual or identified with sexual desire. Probably 'doing anything to get it' may be self love. What most kids think of romantic love is more than likely *eros*.

"On the other hand, *philia* equates to brotherly or friendship…where we care about our neighbor.

"The most difficult and purest form of love is *agape*. That's a denial of self, where one loves unconditionally…say a person forgives another instead of accusing and holding a grudge. A great description is in First Corinthians chapter 13 of the *Bible*.

"All too often when teens talk about love, they often mean the word that starts with "l" and ends with "t" and has US in the middle. Just remember, you can take the perfect man, the perfect woman, put them under a perfect roof and have a perfect problem. You have two people from different perspectives moving in to live together. If they aren't willing to adjust, they will have a very rocky road.

"Too many girls find the guy with the white horse, but he can't find the saddle."

Wall Talk

"What's the difference, if any, between an acquaintance and a relationship?"

"When, if at all, is it okay to go by common sense instead of going by the book? How about some examples?"

To: Mr. Wild
From: Mr. Nozall
RE: student decorum
Mr. Wild,
I was walking down the hallway between the two offices when four Black male students erupted from the office doorway and into the hall inches in front of me; with them was one white male student.
The boys were Lance Conner, Lane Savage, Ron Tolt and Larry Burns. Ron Bowie was the white boy. I was disturbed by their deportment from the office and into the hall as they were running recklessly.
I was concerned they weren't in class. I looked at their class schedule cards and asked Mrs. Hayes about their presence in the office. She said

the Blacks chased Bowie into the office where he picked up a ski pole for defense. Since no administrators were present, I continued down the hall.

In a short time I encountered the Black students and asked them why they weren't in class, indicating they were just goofing off. One replied, "We are goofing off. We're gonna get you Whitey's, we're gonna get Bowie."

I assumed they were clowning around but made a point to follow up and let you know.

Respecfully,
Mr. Nozall

Student Writing

Suicide…
A bitter sweet revenge,
    So many ways
    To take the plunge.
It's a way to get even
    A way to attack.
Sure, they'll be sorry
    But you'll never be back.
Too many ways
    To do the trick—
    Guns, rope, poison, pills
    Just take your pick
Or maybe a knife?
Take careful aim
    Because if you don't
    There goes your fame.
They'll be sorry
    So sorry they'll be
    They need to understand
    There were no signs to see.
But unaware of what would happen
    To the loved ones left behind,
    We take with us, a part of them
    And keep it until the end of time.
        Tamy Stolt

Class Discussion

Dating was a regular topic of discussion. Sometimes normal, sometimes dicey...such as: Mr. K, did you ever want sex on a date? Were you a virgin when you married?

What's more important whether the date is attractive or trustworthy or sweet.

What about personality...where does it place in dating?

I get along well with guys but I've never been asked out on a date.

Do guys want to marry the same type girl they date?

Wall Talk

Lane: "Did you hear about Coach G, over at Riverdale High?"

Blake: "No. What's new? Did he recruit another ineligible wrestler?"

Lane: "Worse than that."

Blake: "He finally got caught letting his wrestlers use diuretics?"

Lane: "Keep guessing. You'll never get it."

Blake: "Okay. I give. What then?"

Lane: "Looks like he's going to the Gray Bar Hotel. Knocked up some chick in his last school, a 15-year-old. Statutory rape. And he paid for her abortion."

Blake: "Holy smoley."

Angels' Halo

Dear Buckwheat,

A step-brother and step-sister from one of my mother's many marriages sexually abused me when I was 4. I've never told anyone and have been able to block this out until recently when memories keep resurfacing. I need help.

Bucky says:

First, the trauma you feel is not your fault. You need to share this with your mother as soon as possible and to report it to our local health facility that deals with this situation. It may be helpful to share your situation with the school nurse, counselor and trusted staff member... who will no doubt refer you to groups who deal with this issue. The Division of Youth Services may also be a step in the right direction. Please keep me posted.

Faculty Lounge

"One of my students asked me if I were a Christian. Knowing public sentiment about religion and school and planning to elaborate, I said, 'Yes, I was born in America.' She said that wasn't what she meant and she asked me to define 'Christian.' I told her many people think all you have to do to enter Heaven is to die…that a Christian is a follower of Christ, not someone who knows about Him. Somebody who walks hand in hand with Him daily. And that just because you die doesn't assure a spot in His kingdom."

Detention

One day Rudy Johanson, whom BDK had nicknamed TDOW for Tall Drink Of Water, came late to class. Mr. K told him he'd have to bring coffee and donuts to stay in his class during lunch the next day. Of course, that was Mr. K's way of making Rudy feel good about himself.

Tall Drink did not disappoint. More to the point, he brought a thermos of coffee and a dozen donuts for Big Dad. Was Mr. K ever surprised! "Okay, TDOW, you've awarded me for your tardy. Thank you. Does that mean I'm a gonna hafta come ta yer basketball games?" And they both laughed.

Bully Bill stopped counselor Ms. Ritchie in the student center, eyed her up and down and suggested he engage with her in some adult activity. She responded bluntly and to the point, "One a------ in my panties is enough." I think he got the point, no pun intended.

The process for choosing a new coach is laughable. Really. Get this. The administration wants a coach from the district or outside who will conform to district policy. Prospective coaches may pick their staff contingent upon administrative approval. And, of course, he must be hired for his qualifications, not some politically motivated reason. Administrators, athletic director and coach applicant should be honest. Really?

So just how did that process work for Coach K, the guy who "recruited" a wrestler who had been there two years? And how did that process work in replacing Coach K with one the parents and athletes hated and who later lied and was slapped on the wrist?

So much for the coach hiring propaganda.

Angels' Halo

Exchange students

This year the Liberty Angels host three students from foreign lands. Please welcome them and see what you can learn from them. They will definitely be learning from us.

Mitsuo Minoko is from Japan. Mitsuo is a 16-year-old junior who attended a co-ed school in Japan. He plans to play on our Angel basketball team.

Claire Johnson hails from New Zealand. She is a 17-year-old junior who attended a Catholic girls school where uniforms were required. She's on the gymnastics team and taught aerobics in her homeland. She finds our school to school competition more fierce than her former school.

Donald Boucier comes to us from France, where he attended school from 8 AM to 6 PM five days a week and Saturday mornings. He had no after school sports or other activities and finds Liberty High a huge change.

Suggestion box (Mr. Kandel received more personal messages)

Are you free tonight?

I love you. You're cute, kind and sweet.

We love you Mr. Kandel—your secret admirers.

We want your body.

Where did you meet your wife? Where did you go on dates?

Class Discussion

Why do some guys feel a girl must do something sexual with them because he spent money on her? Doesn't he want the pleasure of her company?

Why does a guy try to get as far as he can with a girl on the 1st date?

If you have arguments with your boyfriend all the time, what should you do?

Why do some girls think some guys are out for sex?

When a guy you really like wants to go too far, do you satisfy and keep him...or don't and lose him?

Victoria met Dawn and told her she'd read her poem and wanted to discuss it with her.

"I read your well written poem about the dawn. I assume you're referring to the part of day when it's getting light. The tone of the poem was that you loved dawn but feared or had concerns about it. And that those concerns were great enough for you to consider what the dawn might bring. Is that right?"

"Yes. Tori, I know we hardly know each other but I'd like to run something by you and see if you have any thoughts. I was sexually abused by my father for ten years. My mother caught my dad with me and divorced him. I don't know how I can live with myself because of the years of deception toward my mother."

"I'm so sorry to hear both those issues, Dawn. Incest and guilt. I'm at a loss to understand a man's action towards his daughter. Surely your mother doesn't blame you. Surely she is supportive."

"Yes, she is. But I still have the guilt…and the nightmares. I think I'll always have them."

"Dawn, sometimes 'always' never happens. It's kind of strange that you'd talk about your problem. I have one too. You see the car I drive… you see the clothes I wear…I'm pretty well groomed, right? You talk about a man's action toward his daughter. I talk about being unloved by my father. We're very much alike."

"What do you mean? How are we alike?"

"We're both victims of parental misguidance. Your father did not love you. My father has not loved me. I have been forced to excel. To win at all costs. It's hard to be a parent because it's on the job training. Unless you had some good mentoring or examples, you do the best you can.

"I know when you go back a few generations, life was tough for those people. Many of them grew up with a strict parent or two and carried on those family ways. Generally it seems people have mellowed. But some still have the strictness or some unpleasant characteristic."

"That's terrible, Tori."

"Yes, it is. But it is a reflection of one or two generations past. Like I said our forefathers had it pretty tough. Their parents were pretty much no nonsense."

"Well, maybe we can discuss this later and try to make sense of it."

"Okay, Dawn. You can count on me."

Inter-office Memo

To: Mr. Wild

From: Mr. Runberg

RE: English proficiency

Little Johnny Q. Public's adventure times twelve started when mommy and daddy dropped him at school his first day. Somewhere along his first year in the public schools his big adventure ended. He was below his classmates in achievement. He was stamped, labeled and programmed an underachiever. He continued to achieve less than his peers, learning little except to dislike school, question teachers, trust them less and get by on the least amount of work. BUT HE NEVER FAILED.

Although unable to master the 7th grade English skills, he managed to skim by to the 8th grade. He hung in there, turned in enough work—even though he didn't understand it—to make grade 9. But he didn't learn much about English. Ninth grade was a breeze because all he had to do was read a couple of plays and stand up in front of the class and give a couple of speeches. He squeaked into the tenth grade.

The big day dawned when Johnny had to take the tenth grade English proficiency test. Adventure times twelve misfired and Johnny was sent back for editing. Adventure times twelve would have to be rewritten.

Quotes from proficiency classmates:

I was in reading intill 7th grade. I hated English. The teachers never had time for me and they weren't very good to start with.

Grade 11 boy

I think that test stuff can eat s---. They should have told us in the 7th grade.   *Grade 11 girl*

In ninth grade I only got three cridets the hole year. I had to retack ninth English.   *Grade 11 boy*

They kept taking me out of English and putting me in reading in 7 and 8. English is usllay a distar for me.   *Grade 11 boy*

7th—I was in reamideal reading; 8th-10th— I just couldent understand it; 11—here I am.   *Grade 11 girl*

Conclusion:

Having taught this class two years and realizing nearly all students herein were taught little, if any, English in the 7th and/or 8th grades, rather transferred into reading, it seems prudent to review the curriculum. It also seems prudent, if not necessary, to evaluate their English skills much sooner than the 10th grade. Each student's progress should be noted and passed on to the next English teacher who can then provide more salient teaching. Of necessity and in the best interests of students, principals will evaluate each English teacher for proficiency. And students having trouble in English must be addressed way before the 11ᵗʰ grade.

This entire proficiency test and follow up skills class is in serious need of evaluation. Our students deserve better. It is my earnest desire to do whatever possible to alleviate problems in this area and to be informed what can and will be done to remedy it.

To: Mr. Runberg
From: Mr. Wild
RE: English skills...
Mr. Runberg,
In the privacy of my office I reviewed your most recent memo and comments about English proficancy. Regardless of your efforts the class was sanctioned by the school board and administrative office at the school district office. Although you've provided clear and certain needs in your conclusion, we will continue with the recommendations of the administration office and the school board.
Let us carry on in good faith,
Principal Wild
When Runberg received the memo, he thought Wild is saying in essence my efforts and those of others on behalf of the students suck. Another typical administrative maneuver. How do these "administrators" expect us to respect them? Is it any wonder so many teachers submit to the status quo...bury their heads in the sand and look forward to retirement? Guess what, Mr. Wild? I refuse to join them!

Liberty Heights Journal

Letters to the editor:
Dear Editor,
I was totally disgusted and outraged by the action of half the team that hazed a freshman. These lads should have been kicked off the team for the season. The reaction of the administrators and nitwit parents really gets me. Pressured by parents, the administrator turned the 9-day suspension into 2 days. Meanwhile parents griped that the suspension would hurt their poor babies' grades. Too damn bad! If you had raised your kids properly in the first place, they never would have acted as they did. If the victim had been a girl, would you consider it funny?

Don't expect victims of hazing to come forward. They've seen no action will result.

Dawn told Tori, "When BDK handed me back a test, I told him, 'I know I failed. I didn't study for it.'"

Kandel said, "Well, you didn't pass the English part but you aced the art part." And he walked away.

She couldn't figure what he meant, thought about it till next day and asked, "What did you mean when you said 100% on symmetry yesterday? I failed the test."

He said, "You walked through the 50 questions and answered them *a, b, c, d* or *e*…ten times. Your symmetry is excellent."

Dawn told Victoria, "Mr. K told me about my art pattern on the test and alluded to symmetry. I think he's playing games with me."

"Why would you say that? Mr. K does not play games. Yes, he's funny and goofs off a lot, but he has a serious side that is almost cunning. He knows exactly what he's doing. You'll see."

"Well…"

"I heard one time the school star hockey player got wound up in his class and challenged Mr. Kandel. Mr. K accepted the senior's challenge with one of his own, 'You want to go outside?'

"Mike answered, 'Yeh.' And Mr. K said, 'Go ahead.' The class laughed, Mike smiled and accepted Mr. K's humor. Case closed."

Not long after that Dawn asked Big Dad, "You commented about my symmetry a while back. What did you mean by that?"

"Dawn, you marked the test in symmetrical sequence. If I divided the fifty questions into groups of five, you had exactly ten of each letter starting in order with a, b, c, d and e. Very symmetrical. I assessed your symmetry and considered a number of the compositions you've written that deal with peaceful streamlets, butterflies, birds chirping and pastoral settings. I'm guessing those are masks for something you're hiding."

"Mr. K. You're right. I have some concerns. Have had for some time. I've heard you have helped kids in the past and wonder if you might listen to me."

"Dawn, I'd be honored to listen. I might even talk if that's okay. Do you want to have me listen on a specific day?"

Circular File

In my hands are paper and pen. In my head is life. In my heart is death. I'm gonna kill myself. Black lives matter. Yeh. What about any life matters? How many times will I write "I'm gonna kill myself" before I get the nerve to do the deed. Why don't I matter?

I'm as worthless as you know what on a you know what.

You'll find me with the used sanitary napkins at the garbage dump. You can catch me on the local nightly news. I'll be there. Then my parents won't need to tell me how worthless I am again.

Dear Parents,

My English teacher, the special dude that he is, Mr. Kandel, who is dedicated to learning me the goodest English he can, informed the class today this is the last progress report of the year.

My grade looks like this: I have completed 34 of 35 assignments. My third quarter grade was 2.1; my current grade is 3.09; my semester average is 2.59 or "C+" to "B-."

Love always, your almost perfect child, Candice Burnett

Home Ec Teacher

Ronda Hill taught a class of home ec for boys. They had a blast and learned a great deal from her but her next door teacher thought they were noisy and turned her into Prince Wild. She got a little reprimand. Probably a serious mistake by the drafting teacher. Ronda didn't forget. When the first opportunity arose, she sneaked into his room and borrowed his personal note pad. Mrs. Hill wasted no time in writing most every woman in the school a love note. Yes, she forged his name but the down side was printed at the top of the note was "From the desk of Ricardo Ramos."

She and her best pal, the art teacher played many a trick on the staff as long as they remained at Liberty. One of her greatest tricks was to have her home ec classes launder the uniforms of the athletes. She took delight in perfuming the wrestling singlets...seemed like she grooved on goofing off and having fun, but was a great teacher with a terrific sense of humor.

She and her art teaching pal taped pubic hairs (blonde and brunette)

It had come to the attention to Mr. Kandel that students loved his class discussions. They were always no-holds-barred-take -no-prisoners and totally uncensored affairs. Tell it like it is. First Amendment, freedom of speech. Let 'er rip. They gave the kids a chance to relax from regular English, an opportunity to speak their minds and, as one student told him, "It helps to know there are some adults who care."

Mr. Nozall talks with another teacher about Mr. Rose. "He's pretty uppity. Told his department chair that he was not interested in teaching a remedial English class…that basic fundamentals of English could be taught successfully with existing knowledge."

"Bet that went over well with the chair."

"It didn't end there. The chair forwarded the note to Prince Pal who reprimanded Rose, telling him he had no choice in the matter. In other words, teach the class or look for a different school…or livelihood."

Linda Lahardesty asked one day if her fifth hour class could have a social event. BDK said, "No. We don't have social events in this class."

"Oh. Well…"

"However, if you want to have a party, that would be okay."

"You mean, it's okay to have a party."

"Yes, I'm not much into the euphemism of 'social event' which means party. This class is so deserving that I'm willing to grant the group a party."

When word got out, which was inevitable, that Mr. K allowed a class to have a social event, a student asked him, "Why does your fifth hour class always have parties?"

Mr. K provided a totally honest and forthright answer, "Because they ask. Hint, hint."

It was kind of weird because no other class asked him if they could have a party.

Secretary Concerns

All adults should monitor halls and lunchroom

Teachers should not expect a student to have a pass from the office if the teacher sent the student without one

Circular File

Too big. Too little. Too hairy. Too hairless. Too old. Too young. Too tall. Too short. Too skinny. Too fat. Too smart. Too dumb. Where will it end?

It's sad that so many parents aren't parents. Why don't parents know they can help their kids more if they try to understand them?

If they're real parents, they draw the line. They hold the line.

There are specific advantages to being identical twins. My friends Phoebe and Polly, unless you know them well and spend time with them, you can't tell them apart. Phobe is really good at math and Polly excels in English. Therefore whenever one has a math or English test, the better one subs for the weaker one. It's as normal as sunrise for Phoebe to take two math tests—hers and Polly's—and for Polly to take two English tests.

Phoebe told me it was common for the math teacher to say, "It's an open note test, not an open mouth one."

Class Discussion

So many people hope to be famous. We've got Handel, Mozart, Houdini, Shakespeare, Knute Rockne. Maybe all these greats bloomed where they were planted and achieved through their efforts. We can all become masterpieces in our own way. We need to make the most of what we are and hope to become….speaking of which, the real masterpieces were their mothers. They deserve the most credit—whether real or wishful mothers—they have sacrificed and given unconditional love and support to their children. How many famous people are there without those kinds of mothers? And how many of you will be as famous as the masters?

"Mr. K, why would God allow my friend to get pregnant?"

"Oh, was she sleeping with God?"

"Mr. K. No, she was sleeping with her boyfriend."

"I understand. She's sleeping with her boyfriend but God impregnated her. Right? I'm always amazed when kids accuse God for their friend's death…or for letting her get pregnant. Sometimes when you add one sperm and one egg, you get three humans. Why don't kids credit God for saving most of them for the good He does in their lives. Sleeping with someone may not result in pregnancy but the activity is pregnant with consequences."

Don't you know?

Student Writing

Exodus

I didn't want to cry.
I didn't want to die
But no one seems to care
Or want me anywhere.
Since I can not excel,
I feel I am compelled
To pull the plug today.
That's all I've got to say.

Make sure that everyone
Knows now that I have won.
Goodbye. See you later.
Less than a Common Tator.

Having experienced one of his major band scenarios, Sott Davenport, asked Mr. K, "Did you call the cops on me over the weekend?"

In true standup fashion BDK answered his neighbor, "Scottie, you know whenever cars are lined up on both sides of the road as far as I can see in front of my house and our house is vibrating from the music in your garage, yes, I did. I assumed your parents were not home and didn't know when they'd be back. I guess I should have just walked over the half block and checked with you."

"OK. Thanks. No worries."

One of Coach K's students dropped by to pick up the FCA schedule for the year. It offered a variety of activities, including going to Coach K's for hot choco, cake, etc. :

Fellowship of Christian Athletes Activities

The following monthly activities are scheduled for the dates listed. Twice a month during lunch we will have an activity (if you wish to attend).

The first Wednesday we will see a movie and the third Wednesday we will hear a speaker.

October 25 ——— Video night/gym night; get acquainted
November 9 and 10 lock in/potato party
December 20-22 ——— Weekend retreat (with two local groups)
New Year's eve ——— party and sledding, snow day (next)
February 7 ——— bowling, potato party and homemade ice cream
March 3-7 (spring break) ——— hike, camp out TBA
April 19 ——— softball w. local FCA group TBA
May clamming ——— Date depends upon tide TBA
June ——— rafting TBA

At their first meeting, Coach K had asked them to list any that interested them in order to plan for the following year. He said those with most "votes" would be offered for a vote later. Activities listed were: archery shoot, bowling, camp out, fleeceball, football, gym night, hike, ice skate, lock in, potato party, sledding, snow day, softball, video night, volleyball, weekend retreat, whirly ball, other.

Student Concerns

Suggest satisfactory sponsors who are interested in kids
We have frivolous classes that do not pertain to life situations
Need more occupation-oriented courses
Teachers need to base grades on performance rather than personality
Vandals should be punished with fines or forced to repay for damages
Teachers should be given more authority to curb vandalism
Patrol bathrooms

Janitor Concerns

Teachers leaving early and their apathetic attitude toward their jobs—failure to discipline

Teacher Concerns

Even out class load
How about a pat on the back for teachers once in a while?
May I have desks in good shape, books for all students and a roof that doesn't leak?
Please explain the excessive numbers of students in the halls during

class. Thank you.

Mr. Sumpter chewed out his archery class one day, explaining their shooting had devolved. "So far more arrows have missed the target than during the first week. And another thing—one guy was standing three feet behind another guy and shooting. He could have shot the guy ahead of him.

"We've got students clowning around, pushing others into those people who were shooting. You trying to get someone killed?"

As previously agreed, Dawn and Victoria met with BDK in the school library. He knew they had become friends and commended them on that friendship and its importance.

"Before we get too far down this road, I want to share a brief story. I had a good friend in high school. My mother didn't want me to hang with him. Basically I told her he had no friends and I wanted to be his. So, she tolerated our friendship. Ray became my hunting buddy, mostly for pheasants, quail and ducks. He was the best shot I ever knew. He could hit a pheasant flying at ninety degree angles with a .22 rifle. We usually hiked from town, through the orchards, filled our T-shirts with apples and spent the day hunting.

"On this particular day one of our mothers—can't remember which—dropped us off at the aqueduct. We were actually on the asphalt near a stubble field and we headed for the aqueduct which brought water into town from five miles away. It was a 5-foot wooden tube with leaks, providing some water puddles for game. As we hiked toward the pipe, we flushed a pheasant and he blasted it with his shotgun. It was so close the wadding from the shell was in the bird,. We dressed it, built a fire and ate it before moving on.

"Anyway, we were buds. But two months after I left for college my mother called me to let me know that Ray was missing. I heard it on the news. Seems he went hunting mulies with Dave Franklin after Jerry dropped them near Troy, Oregon, on the Rattlesnake, planning to rendezvous at the Snake. Ray and Dave floated roughly fifty miles hunting mule deer, dropping and loading two into their inflatable. They reached the Snake but their ride wasn't there.

"Dave told the rescuers that they were tired of waiting for Jerry and they decided to head downstream to town and keep an eye out for him as the road paralleled the river. They didn't know he'd had a flat and took a while to change. Downstream six miles later at Captain John's rapids the inflatable took on water and turned over. Ray wore hip waders and a bandolier of shotgun shells around his neck. And he didn't know how to swim. Dave made it to shore but Ray didn't.

"A month after my mother called, they found Ray."

Tori showed compassion in telling Mr. K that his portrayal of friendship was appreciated and that she was sorry about the loss of his friend. "Mr. Kandel, Dawn and I have a major situation in common. We'd like to see what kind of advice you can give us."

"Okay, Victoria. Where do we begin?"

Dawn interjected, "We feel we have been unloved our entire lives…or at least not loved to any noticeable extent."

Tori took up the dialogue, "Mr. Kandel, we feel our parents either intentionally or unintentionally have failed to love us."

Again Dawn spoke, "Remember when we had the class discussion about love? My take away was that unconditional love was what we were to have been given. But I was abused physically and Tori was emotionally. We both feel unwanted and have talked some about suicide. After all, who needs us?"

"That's where you're wrong, Dawn. People commit suicide for a number of reasons such as family problems, rigid rules, pregnancy, feeling they're misunderstood, drugs, school problems. Kids think parents spend too much or too little time with them, don't listen to them or don't understand. You girls fall into some of these categories but you have every reason to flaunt your lives in confidence. To overcome the problems of the past and to achieve fantastic lives.

"I had a former student who wrote about his experiences in Detroit. He gave me permission to share with teens if I thought it might help. Here's what he wrote. I'd like you to take it, read it and tell me what you think about it tomorrow."

"The girls looked at each other, Dawn's million dollar smile crossed her lips and she replied, 'Okay, Mr. K. We'll read it together and get back to you. Thanks.'"

I had three friends who killed themselves. Saul always had something going on—a party, fighting, trouble with the cops. Wherever he was trouble followed. His father worked in a convenience store and one night three Puerto Ricans blew him away with a shotgun. Saul's mother moved him into a run down one room place with eight people living there. He didn't like it, moved in with a couple. Turns out the guy was a drug dealer.

Two of Saul's buddies were older than me but they kinda took me under their wings and we enjoyed the good times. One night we heard about a fight, couldn't find Saul so headed for the action without him.

BDK told Dawn and Victoria, "When you think you're hot stuff, you usually get burned."

Suggestion Box

Security Guards

A female student Tent shared with a female security lady, reporting…

Student: "I've experienced sexual harassment several times. In the hallways where there are no teachers, guys make vulgar comments and touch girls. I've experienced this."

Security: "Have you reported it? Can you identify the boys?"

Student: "Yes, I can identify the guys. It's almost always the same ones. I have not reported it."

Security: "Why haven't you reported it? They could be punished."

Student: "Not likely. I know girls who have reported the abuse. They have even struck back with whatever was in their hands. They got suspended…not the guy. Even with witnesses sexual harassment is hard to prove. Guys lie for each other. And they go unpunished."

Security: "Well…"

Student: "Some day some guy is going to get hosed by a boyfriend or killed. What will it take to wake up our administrators?"

Girl Talk

"Sally, did you think much about the close call we had the other night… at the party…when we escaped the bedroom scene?"

"I know, Veronica. Kinda like the glow of the back seat could have other ramifications, whether your motivation is love or 'I need to do it because everyone else is.' Let's say what if the pill doesn't work?"

"Or what if the other contraception fails? You're fourteen. What if the big wham becomes a tiny whimpering baby?"

"They strip to the naked noodle and his magic marker messages her greeting card."

"Yeh, the big share becomes a big nightmare. The ongoing headaches, hunger for dill pickle and peanut butter sandwiches. The constant irritability and grouchiness. Let's say the chick timed everything right. She's not having her period. She's using preventative measures and she's safe. *Whoops!* She skipped a menstrual cycle. Now it's two periods? Time for the drugstore pregnancy test. Oh, oh!

"Right. What do I do now? I'm two months pregnant. Let's see. How do I tell my boyfriend…or one of the guys at the party? How do I tell my parents…I can get an abortion. Or, I can have the baby. What other options are there?"

"Yeh. Your love nest turned into a bastardnette instead of the bassinette. Even though, euphemistically speaking, the "bastard" has been replaced by "love child." Why would anyone label an innocent baby a bastard? Your friends quit being your friends because you won't party. You can't afford a baby sitter. Your parents don't want or support you. You get a job and ride the bus to work. Who babysits for you? What do you tell your grandparents, friends, teachers?

"It's a gen-you-whine mess. Why doesn't the sex ed class teach you some of this stuff. And they could throw in a little bit about budgeting and morals. Fortunately me and you had at least a little bit of morals and avoided the sex-cessful efforts of those drunk dudes. And we got away before things went south."

"Though our hearts were pounding, we escaped because our heads were listening."

Why are girls so dumb that they think a guy's going to love her if she gives up her virginity to him? Are they so stupid they think their surrender is going to keep him faithful? Is surrendering their virginity more important than "being chicken"? Come on!

Yeh, she can give it up and be labeled slut, whore or bitch. Or she can say "no" and retain her reputation, self respect and be a "chicken."

Student Writing

Comey wants a pardon.
China wants wheat.
Someone wants a war,
    Now ain't that neat?

The Senate wants some action.
The House is bored.
There used to be Chrysler
    And now there's still Ford.

Everyone wants something
    Almost every day.
Here's your poem.
Now I want an A.

Debra Tillerton

Angels' Halo

Watch for CC in our next edition of the paper. She's the explosive shortstop playing for the Liberty Angel softball team. And she's one of the best athletes in the state. Her real name is Christine but in respect for her Native American heritage, we call her CC, short for Chippewa Christine.

Inter-office Memo

To: Mr. Wild, Principal
From: LLK
Subject: Staff comments

Mr. Wild,

Not to be a tattle tale, but you might be interested in the following comments made by staff. And, then again, you might not:

"I hear Mrs. Logan is leaving, going to another school."   "I can't blame her. All she does is referee all day long between the students and the teachers. That wouldn't happen if they'd clamp down here."

"I just close my door and hope the crap doesn't creep in, the lack of discipline."

"We need a tighter ship."

"You're fighting a losing battle."

Some people will balk at the suggestion of being told what to do, but you are the boss and we can either comply or leave. I request that you allow a group of volunteer teachers to work with you to establish some solutions addressing these concerns. Some have told me they'd volunteer in this effort.

Respectfully yours,
Mr. Kandel

To: Mr. George Donald, Superintendent Liberty District
From: L.L. Kandel
Subject: deception

Yeh, yeh, yeh. I get it. I won't even bother writing a 2 page letter to the superintendent because I'll get a CYA response, if any. My intent would be to ask about his fabrications to the faculty the other day and his hidden agenda to bring our school on line. But, save my breath.

Sincerely,
LLK

To: Mr. Kandel
From: Mr. Sundair
RE: activity communication

Mr. Kandel,

You are right about the failure of the office to communicate the recent student activity.

And you were right in not allowing students to attend without proper passes. We have entirely too many students ducking out of classes on a whim in order to avoid those classes. More teachers should follow your example.

Carry on.

Mr. Sundair

Mr. Phillips gave extra credit to those who carried a ten pound flour sack for a week, to emulate a child. If they were separated from the child, they had to pay $3.00 an hour for a sitter.

Other students could carry the "child" if the parent knew who it was. There was a kidnap caper in which one student tired of carrying the "child" and hid it in his locker. When he returned to the locker, it was gone. So were his extra credit points. Some kids who dropped their "child" also lost points when the flour exploded the bag on impact. By mid-afternoon the second day, two "children" had expired. The funniest part was that the student who stashed his flour in his locker found a plate of chocolate chip cookies and a note that read "thanks."

Student Comment

Years ago BDK taught a class called Involvement. It was for dead-end kids, those destined to drop out, druggies or the like. My older brother fit the bill and was selected for the class. The class purpose was camouflaged, tagged a fundamental English class to improve reading and language. But it was really to get kids to come to school, to class, on time…and to stop skipping.

BDK used *Hot Rod*, similar car and motorcycle magazines as bait. Seems his goal was to give the kids some kudos, give them a chance they'd been denied in the system, to give them some self esteem.

He kinda tricked them. They went on a field trip with flat paint, brown, beige and gray. Small spray paint cans. Each kid had a couple. Their mission was to spray paint over and camouflage the graffiti that had previously been sprayed. He kinda got the last laugh because he figured they were probably guilty of putting the graffiti there to start with. My brother and friends thought BDK was cool.

About the class? They showed up, but it wasn't until they got a pool table that they were on time. Seems one kid challenged him one day…"there's a pool table at an alternative school, why can't we have one?" BDK said, "Why can't we?" The kid was floored. Next morning BDK spotted a pickup with a pool table on board backed up to the outside door. The table went into BDK's room.

Only one problem. The principal, Mr. Wild, showed up demanding BDK remove the table. BDK told the principal it was brought by students, used by students before and after school or during lunch. And "we've had no tardy students since it came to the room." That shut up the Prince Pal.

Those kids must have approved of BDK because when he told them he was building a cracker box on the outskirts, they provided him septic tank plumbing, a kitchen stove and fridge, and a washer and dryer. He never asked them where they came from.

My brother loved him. That's the reason I took him. And I'll always be grateful.

Liberty has great musical tradtions. The Angels have abank, jazz band, choir, swing choir and orchestra. The marching band has majorettes and flag twirlers. Some awesome musicians and great music teachers hang out at Liberty. We have everything from individual honky tonkers to long hair musicians.

Student letter to parents

Why can't you treat me like a 15-year-old? I don't need you nagging me all the time and living my life for me.

I'm writing this in order to get the whole load off my shoulders. It seems like every time we have a discussion, it's two against one and I always loose. I've been a sissy too long and it's time to clear the deck.

I know I am not perfect but no one else is either.

Because I've seen abuse of drugs, alchol, and parents, I've chosen to never be abused in any way. If someone hurts me in any way, I'm going to do something about it. If I go on like this, I'll end up killing myself. People think they can dump so much on me at one time and that I can handle it.

If I were old enough to leave home, I'd be long gone by now.

I'm going to have a very hard time for the next three years because you won't treat me like a young woman.

I have dreams and pride. I'm proud of my abilities and I'm going to be somebody special one day. I don't want to be just another person in the world. I want to make a difference. I want and will get a quality education in order to fulfill my dreams. I am self-motivated and don't need threats or nagging.

I really don't need people trying to lower my self-esteem any lower than it is. Give me a chance to prove myself.

Mr. Wild made an executive decision. Mr. Smithers had a senior hockey player failing his English class so Mr. Wild transferred the jock into a P.E. class and gave the kid an English credit so he could graduate. Saved embarrassing the kid and passed him. Public education at its best. Maybe that's part of what Mark Twain meant when he said "Don't let schooling interfere with your education."

Wall Talk

Penelope: "Why do you think guys are so obsessed with lettering in sports?"

Lynne: "I think part of it is the status. Part of it is approval. Part is self-esteem."

Penelope: "My boy friend told me about some of the initiations. Seems pretty gross."

Lynne: "Yeh. I know. I've heard about guys being blindfolded and walking off the high dive at the swimming pool, not knowing completely what they were doing. And I've heard about the nastiness of searching through the toilet in blindfold and finding fortunately…overripe bananas."

Penelope: "Guys. What makes them tick!"

Teacher Concerns

Wonder when the book publishers will introduce a scratch and sniff sex manual?

Please fill out the poll in your mailbox: Is it the head shed's plan to bring this school down?

How many principals does it take to screw in a light bulb? One. but they're all out to lunch.

If it will save you any time, skip my evaluation of you this year, Mr. Prince Pal.

Kids used to come to school to learn; now it's for a party map.

Whose idea was it to put condom dispensers in the restrooms?

Kelly invited Dawn and Tori to a Fellowship of Christian Athletes Monday night activity. A group of kids met regularly for games with a brief sharing time about halfway through the evening. That usually amounted to a short reading from the *Holy Bible* or a student's sharing about his faith. The girls enjoyed their evening and thought about going again, though Tori's sporting activities took up a ton of her time. They even considered attending one of the FCA monthly events.

Dawn found herself drawn closer to Matt after he invited her to view his rebuilding project. He lived with his grandparents because his folks were killed in an accident. Matt related to most things aviation. His grandfather had been a Certified Flight Instructor with a hangar and strip in the nearby field. As a tribute to his parents, Matt took on the plane project. It also had something to do with his grandfather's influence. He had actually taught Matt to fly and Matt had logged 200 flying hours since obtaining his pilot's license.

Matt explained to Dawn various terms related to the airplane: empennage, elevators, stabilizer, rudder, flaps…and told her "you don't steer with a steering wheel but a stick." He told Dawn, "I never got over the thrill of flying with my dad who was a Cub pilot and guide in Alaska. I decided I needed to get into the sky."

Matt got airplane parts from his grandfather or his grandfather's flying friend.

Matt's grandfather liked Dawn and during a heavy conversation gave her some serious advice. At least two of his comments gave her some things to consider: You get out of life what you put into it; don't short change yourself. If you are going to succeed, YOU are going to succeed…no one is going to succeed for you.

Suggestion box (Weekend highlights):

My sixteenth birthday. It feels great.

I quit drinking. It was my 2nd weekend I didn't touch alcohol. My boyfriend bought me a diamond opal ring.

My weekend didn't have a highlight.

I had a splitting headache and hinted to my mother that ice cream was in order as I tackled my homework. She complied and ice cream saved the night and the homework.

My weekend highlight was having my two month old niece puke on me.

Going to the football game.

Hang gliding off the World Trade Center and landing in a sewage treatment plant, over and over.

Did you know that BDK is a real dragon slayer? Dragon Slayer

"Roz, why don't you run away or something? Don't you know anyone you could live with till graduation?"

"No, I'll hang in there and after I graduate, I have a plan."

"Doesn't it suck being treated like crap and your brother is treated like some holy person? Is your family very close?"

"Peg, you know better. We're not even close at all. But I like it that way. It works out better. Won't be long and my family will be a memory in the rear view mirror."

Over the years Mr. K received his share of gifts and cards, all wishing him well. He proclaimed his favorite non-nutritious "food" was Cheez Its, so he frequently found a box on his desk. One year he received a note which read, Mr. Kandel, "We respectfully request your presence at tomorrow's assembly. You are a finalist in the 'ugly' Teacher Contest! Congratulations!"

And he was. He received a Certificate of Award proclaiming him the 1ˢᵗ runner up at the 1ˢᵗ annual "Ugly" Teacher contest.

Don't you know.

At the appointed time the FCA kids met at the sledding hill, knowing afterward they'd be going to Coach K's for hot choco and pizza—probably made from scratch by his wife.

A couple of dozen vehicles roared into the parking lot—everything from Jeeps, Hummers, 4 doors and vans. Nothing special, just vehicles.. Young men and young women of all shapes and sizes tumbled from the vehicles and geared up with their winter coats, hats, mittens and muffs.

A fresh foot of snow had fallen overnight so the proverbial snowball fight ensued, snowballs flying in all directions. Twenty-eight degrees welcomed the sled, inner tube and snowboard riders.

Many remembered the previous year's event when Lu Lu was up to his legendary self and called some of the girls snow hounds. When questioned, he admitted he didn't mean hounds in the sense of dogs, nor girls who savored Purina. He said the young women were real honest-to-goodness snow lovers as in snow hounds. But some wondered because he had that Looney Louie twinkle in his eyes and the Lu Lu smile on his face.

The worst part of the event was a couple of near misses when sleds or inner tubes crossed paths. The funniest part was when Matt failed to secure his feet properly to a snowboard and when he hit a significant bump, his board went in one direction while he went in another. The best part was that there were no injuries and a couple of hours later when they left, everyone was hungry.

The drivers made way and room for each others' vehicles at coach's. When they transitioned from their vehicles, their olfactory senses recognized the wood smoke and they saw blue-gray smoke tendrils creeping skyward from the chimney.

Coach K's wife had the kitchen and living room fireplaces blazing and the crackling dry wood mesmerized the kids. Among others, Dawn and Victoria jumped in to help with the table settings and food.

The kids ate pizza, drank hot choco and were surprised when their dessert consisted of home made ice cream.

Mr. Greenbaugh had a mini-meltdown which resulted in Lynda Hamlet's suspension for two weeks. Seems she loaned her friend a magazine. She had finished her assignment and saw the magazine on our table. Greenbaugh was "patrolling" the room, walked by our table and grabbed the magazine. Lynda asked him politely to have her magazine back. He told her since he didn't know whose magazine it was, he was taking it to the office.

Lynda tried in vain to persuade him that it was her magazine but he continued to state that he didn't know whose it was.

The fifth time he passed her table, Lynda grabbed it and placed it under her books and papers. She refused to give it to him, began putting her books away and he turned and threw her books across the room.

Lynda jumped up and began hitting and kicking the man. Some students cheered her on while others tried to hold her back.

She stopped and began retrieving her things from the floor...before walking to his desk and pushing everything off onto the floor.

She exited through the back door, James the narc apprehended her and took her to the office. She screamed and called Mr. Greenbaugh names as James tried to calm her.

She was required to see a psychiatrist before returning.

Seems to me, Greenbaugh should have had a psychiatric evaluation... and/or fired. We actually pay those kinds of people to "teach" children?

Time flew by and Matt's plane project involved more and more time with Dawn. She became engrossed in him, not his plane. And in time her thoughts of betraying her mother faded, along with her nightmares.

Corner of the Shadow

Is it ethical for a principal to transfer a failing student whose English grade is required for graduation into a P.E. class and receive English credit?
You are being conned

What kind of pressure was applied to convince Mr. Wild.
You are being Wilded

Inter-office Memo

To: Marla Frankenship's teachers
From: Julie Melenkamp
Subject: Marla's condition

You may already know that Marla Frankenship was involved in an auto accident this weekend and is at Liberty Hospital. I wanted to let you know the details as many rumors are circulating.

She was in intensive care but has been moved to her own room today. She had a cut over her eye and has had surgery for that. She is wearing a bandage over it but will regain full use of the eye with no further surgery. Both legs are broken and the doctors have inserted metal pegs. They anticipate no more surgery for that but she will be in a wheelchair for a while. They do anticipate full recovery on the use of her legs. She has lots of bruises and swelling, but they will heal.

The doctors anticipate that she will be in the hospital two to three weeks.

If you have questions, stop in. Thanks.
P.S. Her birthday is Tuesday 1/17.
Julie M.

BDK talked to Victoria about her high level of athleticism.

"It's remarkable what you've achieved in soccer and volleyball. I'm proud to be in the same school, our little corner of the world with you. I'm proud of you and happy to know such a fine young lady."

"Thank you, Mr. K. But I'm not sure how long this will last."

"What do you mean?"

"My athletic abilities are one thing but my emotions are another. I had the ability from early on. Dad took me to tumbling where I was the only third grader competing with sixth graders. I excelled in gymnastics but he let me try soccer and volleyball. Pretty much all my achievements in sports are due to pressure from my dad. He's driven. Works in the pressure cooker world and hasn't adjusted. He works on the principle of production, not relationship. He believes in 'produce, produce, produce.' I can hear him now, 'Nobody wants your autograph until you're famous.'"

"I understand. Children suffer loss of their childhood…so much emphasis is placed on achieving in sports, music, acting, etc., that the children miss their childhood.

"When I was a rookie coach and knew pretty much nothing, I wanted to help athletes succeed. Wanted to learn what it takes to help athletes improve, so I took an independent study course which I called "Anatomy of a Winner." I actually interviewed Olympic athletes and asked their suggestions on what it takes to succeed in sports. I boiled it down to external and internal factors which amounted to blood, sweat and tears. You can succeed with much effort if that is your goal and you have the ability."

"I understand that Mr. K. But that's part of my problem. My heart's not much in it. My dad continues to pressure me to succeed. Even though I've achieved all kinds of awards including MVP and even top twenty ranking in the nation as a hitter in volleyball, he's never told me how well I've done. It's always 'you could have done better' or 'that's not good enough.' I'm never good enough, whether it's my sport or my grades. Maybe he doesn't understand that producing positive people goes a long way toward production."

"I'm sorry to hear that, Victoria. It's probably pointless for me to tell you about the paper I wrote comparing "Anatomy" with victory. A dozen years after completing "Anatomy" I did a paper comparing success with victory. Whereas success resulted from hard work, victory resulted from surrender. Anyone can succeed BUT a victorious person must learn to surrender."

"I'm not sure I follow you."

"Obviously you know about not giving up. But let me highlight an experience I had with wrestlers. What might have been our best year ever, three wrestlers quit and one threatened to quit. All of them had potential to become state champs. Although I suggested the first two hang in there—one got a girl pregnant and wanted to work to support her and the other lost a match 1-0, they quit. The father to be had commendable motive. Later that season the young man who defeated our guy by one point was killed in an auto accident. The third boy was undefeated in junior high and couldn't take losing as a freshman.

"I told him he was too valuable and had too much skill to quit because he lost a match. I told him he was only a freshman. Because he lived out of town and the school bus was long gone, I drove him home every night 17 miles one way. But within a couple of weeks, he quit.

"The fourth wrestler told me after being pinned two nights in a row and with tears running down his cheeks, that he would turn his gear on Monday.

"I was surprised. He was a senior with no wrestling experience. He had been selected all state on defense and offense in football. A big kid, 190 pounder. I knew he had to be hurting badly because guys like that don't cry for nothing. So I said, "You could be a state champ. But in order to honor you, I'll take your gear on Monday."

"At practice Monday he told me, 'I won't quit. But I'm never getting pinned again.' And he didn't; he was a state champ. I tell you this because you are already a champion. You need to choose what you're going to do about the pressure from your father."

"Wow, Mr. K. You've given me a lot to think about."

"I guess I'm saying if the reward is great enough, the sacrifice is worth it. I hope you don't overstress…but that you consider your great achievements and what's left for you to overcome and to do. You might consider the example of the Man who lived and rose from the grave. Jesus was the ultimate victor."

"Thank you, Mr. K. I will give it much thought."

"Tori, you've got to start where you are. You are special…because when you're gone, there will never be another you. Even if your friends oppose your best intentions or if you have to care what your friends think, they really aren't your friends."

"Thanks, Mr. Kandel."

"You're welcome. Keep your chin up." Then with his disarming and charming humor, BDK added, "it's actually a delightful chin."

Having received praise from her friends and support from Mr. K and others Victoria confronted her father regarding doing better.

"I've never told you that you could do better. I've never said what you've achieved is not good enough. That's all I've heard my whole life. You've never complimented me on my successes. I've achieved unparalleled achievements and awards. Have I ever told you that all your money was inherited? That you did nothing to earn it? No, I didn't. I've spent seventeen years trying to please you. You can read it. It's a note expressing my pain, anguish and plans to commit suicide. But I'm not going to follow through with it. I've had it in my hope chest for months. However a number of situations have taken place to show me that I matter. That suicide is not an option. That suicide accomplishes nothing, not even for the victim. . I'm ranked among the top twenty players in both sports in the nation. From now on I'm going to pursue my goals. I can continue or I can quit. But whatever I do, will be my decision. If I choose to play volleyball or soccer, it will be my choice not yours."

After Victoria and Dawn spoke with Mr. K about the suicide note, they agreed that suicide is not a solution—too many are left hurting because the dead person chose to leave. Tori told Mr. K, "I'm going to try this God thing we heard about at FCA. It couldn't be any worse than what I've experienced the first eighteen years of my life. I think Dawn and I have decided to spend as much time as possible celebrating life. Since we love infants so much, we're going to start a Kid's Outlet. We can collect or buy children's items and drop them off at the Kiddie Drop. We can start there and see what develops. Right?"

Flashing her smile, Dawn agreed, "I'm in, Tori. Let's flourish."

And Victoria proclaimed, "We're moving from Success Boulevard to Stardom Lane."

Part III
Save the Dogs

They came K-9, but they were not pets. This pack roamed at will, destroying what they could—resembling a wild wolf pack—killing not just for food but for fun. At first this band of dogs gone wild was merely somewhat of an annoyance. They were few and merely somewhat aggressive. But in time that changed. Like a cancer the German shepherd, mongrel and Doberman pincher group swelled to include at least three pit bulls, an additional couple German shepherds, three more Dobies, a couple of lab crosses, a great Dane and a wolf. And did I mention a couple of coyotes?

Initially the feral pack targeted lone cats or dogs...but the pack started attacking and eating large animals—horses, cows, sheep. The feral tidal wave assailed the area...taking whatever they wanted. They were here to stay. Or were they? The death and discovery of this missing iddy-biddy infant could well be the catalyst for action against the growing pack of domestic dogs gone wild. Maybe now those who protected the killer dogs would admit the danger those dogs represent to the citizenry.

"Tain't purdy," grimaced old-timer Tad Newcomb. "Sheriff, ya know it never is when ya eyeball a dead 'un. But this is worst. Here I seen a iddy biddy or what some critter left of a infant child. Just a skull, skeleton and some bones. Purdy near makes a growed man cry."

"You found an infant?"

"Yeh, sheriff. Maybe that splains the missin' child...lost but found. Seems we gotta get word out ta th' folks hereabouts...keep a eye on thangs... try ta figger out what done this mean trick."

"Tad, thanks for coming in. For letting me know. I'll follow up and see what's next. First thing I'll do is inspect the scene. It shouldn't be hard to find based on your information. Then I'll put out the word, get it on the radio and television, maybe a reporter will do a piece and we can track down the beast that is responsible. I'm going to contact the folks at the Double K; they can probably help spread the word since they've been here the longest. Thanks again, Tad."

It wasn't pretty. A ravaged human body never is. But this was worse. This was a child...or the remains of one. Nothing but a fleshless skull and skeleton...with shredded and scattered clothing nearby.

Grandparents

A tree lined, bubbling creek passed below and behind the house. The semi-circle drive directs folks to the front door. Off to one side in back is the barn. Twenty feet in front of the kitchen sink window is a tree with a heart that grandpa made years ago. Made from a 4x8 foot plywood panel the valentine reads "I Love Rose." Initially it was red with white letters, but time took its toll and Gramps made another which is white with red letters.

He calls his Rose "my Hunky Dory" and they've been married for a ton of years, long enough to have a child who fell in love with horses, married and had a daughter named Cimarron Rose. Of course, the Rose came from grandma's nickname.

Grandpa learned to drive at age 10 on a Massey Ferguson tractor. One day, knowing his grandfather was gone, he walked by grandpa's house, started the tractor and took it for a spin...cutting doughnuts in the neighbor's field.

In high school Gramps worked on his grandfather's farm in North Bend, Washington. When the clock struck 4 AM, it was time to round up the cows from the field—mostly Holsteins with a Guernsey or two. They milked till 7 then inhaled a huge breakfast of bacon or ham, eggs, waffles and real milk and cream...back in the day when folks drank milk cold and right from the milk house, even before the cream was skimmed off. Then it was clean the barn—shoveling out gutters and hauling the wheelbarrow up the ramp and dumping the load onto the pile on either side before spreading limestone. Usually after that it was either naptime or eating lunch before an afternoon nap, then rounding up cows and milking again before dinner. Bed time came early...most nights around 8 PM because milking was twice a day every day, same time morning and evening.

Other duties included helping neighbors with hay, mowing and raking the hay into windrows for baling or loading as loose hay, hauling the hay to the barn and stacking the bales or using the hay hooks above to move the loose hay into the loft.

Most days he worked from "can't see till can't see."

When his earnings at the end of summer amounted to $100, a railroad watch and a .410 single barrel shotgun, he thought he got ripped off. Grandpa now realizes that the watch and shotgun were lasting because he still has them.

Grandpa brags about seeing two hot chicks walking in front of the college library on 68th in Portland. He decided to marry the one in the red and white plaid wool skirt. They fell in love after their first date to Mt. Hood. His sister Laura Lee and her husband Les had invited him and a date to accompany them and his niece Kelly. Surprisingly, they made the round trip in a 1952 Studebaker.

Her grandparents had grown up in the Northwest—Gran on 112th in Portland, Oregon, or, more specifically, Park Rose, on the Columbia River. She wanted a horse. For some time she kept asking her father for a chance to move to the country. She actually rode with her friend Marlene whose father cared for Trigger, Roy Rogers' horse, during the Rose Festival activities. Gran even got to ride Trigger once.

A neighbor lady divorced and gave Gran a 17-hand high Palomino that she had fed carrots whenever she could. Gran was ecstatic when they moved to a 559 acre farm a few miles north of Dayton, Oregon. She was a tough tomboy. She often swept her room, hiding the particles under a rug then went riding her horse. She rode the property and atop her horse, shot mistletoe from oak branches. All she wanted was to ride Duke. Maybe some day be married and have a family

When her parents insisted she attend college, she told her high school counselor she didn't plan to study much. She wanted to have fun and find a Christian man to marry…get her MRS. Degree. She was one of the most dated co-eds on campus but Gramps snagged her—he says he chased her near four years before she caught him!

Gran and Gramps have their heads on straight.

Sheriff Moss made his rounds, stopping first at the Double K. Gran and Gramps welcomed him and invited him to coffee and a dessert. After a brief stay, he informed them about the infant-child discovery and headed out to spread the word, hoping the community could help address the situation.

Teacher quotes

Small minds worship big boobs.

Mr. K reminds his students "the three R's still exist—Reproduction, Rock and Roll."

I don't know, I'm just a teacher. Teachers don't know everything—they just think they do.

If you want your parents to have a heart attack, offer to do the dishes?

Student Quotes

He wears rip-stop Levis to keep the girls and pervs away.

After the party Josh experienced the Rainbow Yawn again. He never learns.

My first thought when I saw her was "make up covers a multitude of sins."

God and me are gonna party.

Some people say the more things change, the more they remain the same. Maybe.

People come and people go…kind of like the ocean tides. Even though Liberty Heights is the same old town with the same old faces, we have new faces with new developments to consider. Even though the school is still the same old Liberty High with the same old faces, we have new faces with new approaches to learning.

BDK remains a familiar face though he's starting to show age. He proclaims "You kids can laugh at me. Seems the world has passed me by. Sometimes I feel like I'm doomed to failure. I've never smoked marijuana or snorted coke. I wear no nose ring nor have I a tattoo. I feel like a failure because I'm married to my first wife. All I can claim for success are three wonderful children and some coaching success." I remember once he said, "I will say and do things that may you not agree with. I want you to think—to seek the truth. Truth is the only thing that lasts—you cannot have life without it." He kind of sounds like Grandpa T.

People often refer to the "good ol' days." To an extent, they're right. However some of those good ol' days weren't so good. They entertained good memories but bad memories also existed. For instance think about the old saying "When Johnny breaks the law, Johnny law goes after him." That brings us to Mr. Wiggles. He eventually collected some lonesome days in the Gray Bar when cops visited his camper in the Liberty High parking lot. The antenna wiggled and the cops busted the perv. The under aged teen in his camper netted Wiggles the hammer, three hots and a cot. So Mr. Wiggles' wanderlust waltzed him to the waiting warden.

Another new and unwanted face in the community belonged to the development of mysterious and evolving predators. Some folks suspected the bunch of feral dogs seen of late. Some reported their chasing domestic animals on farm land. Might be time to interview some of those folks to compile a prospectus.

Wall Talk

"Even though a girl is desirable, her attitude may desire something. Like, the most beautiful woman in the world may not be attractive."

"Yeh, Black Knight, she's a fox with a pit bull's attitude."

"Speaking of dogs. That brings up the subject of their food source…or another name we can call them. How about Roofer or Barker…or we could refer to them as Purina Gobblers or Friskies Fans."

"Yeh, some of them have a real nostril problem…real stuck up."

"But some are total oinkers, as in oink, oink."

"Where the dogs are concerned just dial 619-mutt, or 619-ruff. Not to be confused with 619-foxy, eh? And when we give them our phone number, it's 619-hunk or babe, right?"

"Now yer soundin' like BDK who always told us his phone number was 345-stud."

"Well, we could do worse, eh?"

Grandpa T calls Will Boston to tell him about the sheriff's visit and the discovery of the iddy biddy.

"Will, I hear you just returned from a deer hunt up in the Blues?"

"Yeh, me n Roth's kid took our wheelers into a foot or more of snow out of Pine Ridge. Beautiful day. Lots of tracks. Saw some does but no bucks. Just got back."

"I wanted to let you know that Tad Newcomb discovered what appears to be that missing Morgan child. The good news is that the boy was found. The bad news is that it wasn't pretty. Actually pretty ugly. Appears the child was eaten. I'm guessing that pack of dogs is guilty. Tad reported to the sheriff and we got wind of it. I thought you'd want to know since those dogs have chased livestock."

One night Cimarron re-read an earlier post in her diary. She's written in great length in order to remind and to encourage herself.

Dear Diary

I keep being reminded lately on how far I have come in the last five years. I was going into the 5th grade when I lost my mama. Coming home one night we were rear-ended by a guy who was distracted. He assumed we'd go through the red light but mama stopped on the amber.

There was a huge metallic sound and we both hit our heads on the back window of the pickup. The truck received a scratch on the metal bumper. We weren't so fortunate.

We appeared normal but a couple hours later mom asked Grandpa T to take us to the emergency room at the hospital. We were told we were okay. We weren't.

Several weeks later we learned we had traumatic brain injuries and we began medical care, including chiropractic and supplements to replace needed nutrients. It all helped but it wasn't enough because a few months later mama died from a misdiagnosed blood clot in her head.

The loss of my mama was very difficult for me, in so many ways. My father has always been there for me, loving and understanding and my grandparents are very supportive. Now we live as a family unit.

I had to do a lot of adjusting, including not being able to ride my horse for more than two years...I couldn't even take care of him that first year without assistance. My schooling suffered, I couldn't even read for very long. My situation was not ideal by any stretch of the imagination. However I hung in there, hoping that things would return to 'normal'.

Multiple times I almost threw in the towel and said I couldn't do it anymore. I hated the physical pain. I hated the emotional pain. I felt helpless. I was not me. My world was turned upside down. Friendships and relationships where strained. I was slandered behind my back more times than I would care to count. All the plans I had where shattered. The passions I had in life where put on hold.

Somewhere in the middle of all this, Gramps gave me a book, *The Power of Positive Thinking*. At the time I could only listen to how this book saved his life, and read snippets here and there. The book goes on to explain how important it is to have a positive outlook on life, and most importantly, a relationship with Christ. It is so true. While I have not read the book from cover to cover, it has been an excellent reminder for when things get hard, quitting is not the answer.

No matter what life throws at you, never give up, never give in. Seek support from trusted friends and family. Pray to God. No matter how hard it may seem now, it WILL get easier. It's taken me several years to feel that life is getting better, but looking forward, it was worth powering through.

But perseverance is key. I encourage you to keep your head above water and swim on. Take one day at a time and each day dig a little deeper. You may be surprised what you are capable of when you put your mind to it. And if you don't like something in your life, change it.

Work towards bettering yourself and letting God shape you into the person he want you to become. As time progresses, it will get easier. Live the life God wanted you to have. Don't put a false expiration date on something that was supposed to stay around much longer.

Because Mr. Kandel loved language, he shared that with his classes, giving them some interesting take home assignments. He wanted us to understand the changing language and gave us half dozen phrases to ask out parents about their meaning or experience with them. I suspect part of his reasoning was to get us to interact with our parents…and for our parents to understand he was trying to help us. I think he was pretty sneaky.

The first five phrases were:

      getting down to brass tacks

      naked as a jay bird

      smooth as silk

      chew the fat or chew the rag

      shake a leg

He gave us a list of phrases to consider for the year. (Appx. 1)

Student Writing

Out of all the mistakes I've done
I think theres only one
That I seem to regret
A mistake that I will never forget.
My mistake was that I set you free
Telling you that your love wasn't for me.
I guess you'll never know
The real reasons why I let you go.
At the time it seemed the thing to do.
I never thought of how much I'd miss you.
If only I could go back in time
I'd change things to where you'd be mine.
I think its to late.
Now I guess I'll have to dwell on my mistake.
Although time has past and the feelings for me have faded away
The thought of what could have been in my mind will always stay.
Mandy Fortuna

Suggestion Box

Did you hear about the little kid in Sunday school when the teacher asked if anyone knew the name of Mary's husband, Jesus' father? A little boy raised his hand and said Virg. When the teacher asked how he came up with that, he said, "The Bible says the baby's parents were Virg 'n Mary."

Yore Lore

Grandpa told me the story about when he and his older sister Laura Lee went to the Coast to Coast store empty handed and came home with a smile. He totted a huge Jeep under his arm and she held a doll. Their mother marched them back to the store with an iron cord warming their behinds and told them "we don't touch what isn't ours."

Another time grandpa got egged by his grandfather. His papa was returning from the hen house, saw gramp's mother on the porch cutting his hair. Papa chose a rotten egg, tossed at his daughter who ducked. Yep, Gramps caught the egg with his forehead and got egg all over his face. Totally true story.

Cim's dad

Cimarron thought a lot about her traveling father. Seemed he was on the road all the time. Traveling to Dallas, Phoenix, Seattle, New York. Sometimes her grandparents drove him to the airport but as often as not he left his vehicle in long term and picked it up on his return. He repped major corporations as an advertising exec. He was quite the driven man. Got to produce.

Cim thought he'd be around more after her mother died…that he'd help make up for her loss. But he had to put food on the table, as they say. The good news is that her grandparents helped make up for his absence. Gran helps her understand women ways. Gramps tries but admits "I ain't no woman." Nevertheless, they make a good team and are good for Cimarron.

Having grown up on the farm and in the outdoors, Cim is fully capable of outside activities such as running a chainsaw, including dropping, bucking, splitting and stacking tree rounds, horse work and all it includes.

Sig Olson was a good friend and neighbor of Grandpa and Grandma T's. He was shocked one morning to discover dozens of slain turkeys in his raising pens. Myriad tracks in the pen identified dogs. He assumed they'd jumped or climbed the fence. Many of the birds were merely killed as if for the fun of it. Some were partially eaten but most were merely dead. He called Grandpa T to report and to ask if he'd seen any of the curs.

"H.J., lost several turkeys last night. Looks like the work of some dogs. Have you seen any recently?"

"Sig, I haven't seen any lately. Heard they were terrorizing folks' animals. I know Sheriff Moss was informing folks about them and looking for them. It might be time for a town hall meeting to get to the bottom of this…maybe set a bounty."

"Well, you know some folks are not going to take well to that idea. Too many bleeding hearts. I sp'ose it would be good to get it on the city council agenda though. Might do some good."

"Let folks know about your turkeys. I'll spread the word. Maybe we'll get some traction and remove those beasts."

"Okay. Thanks, H.J."

Class Discussion

"So the subject today is the meaning of life. What say you, class?"

"I think we were all put on this earth for a purpose. Everyone has a special purpose, some don't know it, but they do. They're supposed to live up to that purpose."

"The meaning of life is to get by and make a difference or just get by or party hard and die young!!! Just depending on social status or your beliefs, but me I don't need an excuse I'm not religious. I don't care."

"The meaning of life is simple. It is a test…a series of problems that we have to solve. When we are finished with our test, then we get a grade. Either you pass or fail."

"Mr. K, what is, in fact, the meaning of life…and what came first, the soap or the soap opera."

Teacher Concerns

We work hard but get no acknowledgment as to our efforts.

How can we best deal with the friction between teachers and administrators?

Instead of posting teachers at every doorway between classes, how about one or two in the hall?

We're a non-functioning "team"—how about some unity between staff and administration?

Teachers need instruction on parking in non-fire zones.

Student Concerns

Disallow smoking
Allow to smoke anywhere in the parking lot
Large hall groups make it hard to pass
Longer summers

Circular File

Take your brain for a walk. Get it some fresh air. Give it some R and R.

You can miss somebody without loving them; but you can't love somebody without missing them.

Suggestion box

What's the greatest thing you can give someone...shoes, smile, hope, job, money, religion?

Do you know that all men who wear white hats are not necessarily good men?

Dragon Slayer

Within a day or two Cimarron took her grandmother on a shopping trip to town. Cim talked about school's being a disaster. She told Gran that even high school kids couldn't read. She said her English teacher told a concerned mother whose son had lousy penmanship that "in spite of his penmanship, he's a reader and that will create new worlds for him." At least Mr. Kandel had his finger on the pulse of education.

Gran answered with one of her great one liners, "Yes, Dearie, you can get real messed up if you don't have the right path to follow."

On the way home they spotted the feral pack chasing a horse. Looks like the horse outdistanced the dogs after striking one with a rear hoof and crippling it.

A short time later Grandpa T learned of another neighbor whose calf was taken down and eaten by the pack. By now it had been labeled the Lobo pack because of a wolf that appeared to be leading it.

It almost seemed unsafe around the place any more, not knowing when that bunch of dogs would appear. One morning at breakfast Gramps prayed for the hearty breakfast: "Lord, we're sure enough thanking You for what You've helped us put on our table. Thank You for the chickens, potatoes, hog, cow and for all grandma does to fix it up fit for us to eat."

Then he asked Cim if he'd told her about his "downfall" at his Uncle Walt's while growing up near Everett, Washington.

"No, Gramps, you haven't shared that one.

"Well, I guess I was a lad about four or five. We had a little building at the end of the path behind the house where we did out business…no indoor toilet. I was in a bit of a hurry since Ma Nature was calling pretty sudden. Problem was my older sister was inside. If I'd known then what I know now, I could have used the bushes. But I didn't.

"Seems those who positioned the outhouse dug a hole larger than the parameters and the hole was large enough to accommodate a small child. As I ran around the outhouse, I found the hole. Not on purpose, mind you. Next thing I knew gravity took over and I fell into the basement of the outhouse."

"Come on, Gramps. You're kidding, right?

"Actual truth. Cross my heart. God's Gospel."

"This didn't really happen, Gramps."

"Oh, Little Darlin', it happened. On one of my trips around the 'house, *boom*…down I went. Into the basement."

"That's disgusting. What happened?"

"I really don't remember. I just know that I was rescued."

Boomer and Sir Checkmate shared the barn harmoniously. It was fun to have the horses, Trinity and Mr. Darcy, Cim's service dog, in playful moods as they all got along just fine. Cim's calico cat Trinity roamed the barn and thought she protected the horses. Cim didn't tell her otherwise. And Cim enjoyed her new pup Nellie. On occasion while proudly riding Boomer on the Double K Cim had a visit from her friend Oiseau, a Kestrel she rescued, treated and released after its broken wing healed. It often shadowed her and landed on her shoulder.

In the past Gramps trailered the stud to those wanting his services. Later Gramps opted for artificial insemination to save on travel, safety and so forth. Since purchasing the stallion when he retired, he expedited his business, using it to supplement his teaching retirement until he has completed the great American novel. His loyal and competent veterinarian Joel Wrangler handled Grandpa T's artificial insemination and transport arrangements.

Darin Parsons finished his chores and reminded his mother that she had promised to drop him at his favorite fishing stream. She agreed and he eagerly gathered his fishing pole, stringer and some bait and jumped into the pickup with her. Before long they were at the bend in the stream upstream from the bridge where she would pick him up at 5 PM. He waved goodbye as she pulled away from the shoulder of the road.

Darin figured he'd catch some rainbow and cutthroat trout while fishing downstream to Martin's bridge. He baited his hook, tugged a couple of yanks of line from his reel and he gently lobbed the line to the head of a hole. Boom! A strike. Darin subdued the scrapper to shore, delighted with the foot long rainbow.

He hop-scotched his way from hole to hole, collecting several fighting fish in the 12-inch to one pound class. While moving to the next hole, he spotted kind of a rolling ground tornado moving across the field. An admixture of brown, black, tan and white. Then he realized it was a living thing that turned out to be the dog pack folks had been talking about. The closer the "cloud" came, the more it seemed he was their target. He assessed their gait, heard their barking increase and reacted, almost automatically. Looked like pit bulls, German shepherds, a great Dane, Dobies, a wolf and a couple of lab crosses. Darin dropped his stringer of fish, set his pole on the ground and climbed a tree, barely ahead of their arrival. Several jumped toward him, teeth bared, slavering from their mouths. He climbed a little higher to make sure he was out of their reach. A Doberman and a pit bull, slashing and slobbering, teeth bared, lunged upward toward him. Some of the dogs scented his catch and devoured it, gobbling fish from the stringer and fighting over the morsels.

He knew dogs can't climb, at least not those kind. But he was concerned about the passing of time. He needed to head downstream in order to rendezvous with his mother, so she won't think something has happened to him… if he weren't at the bridge. He kept waiting, trying to think of a solution that wouldn't get him decombobulatged.

Some dogs sat on their haunches leering at him. Others milled around. Shortly a large Herford bull and a younger one approached the stream. When they saw the dogs, the bovines charged them as one. The younger, feistier one tossed his head toward a couple that tried to dodge. One leaped at the bull's neck but by then the old timer came to the rescue of the younger bull,

142

butting the dog onto the ground and stomping it with its front hooves. The younger bull bawled and charged into the midst of the pack, scattering them. As they fled, the two bulls approached the stream, drank from it and crossed to the other side.

Wondering if the dogs had left and wanting to meet his mother without delay, Darin descended the tree and, eyes on a swivel, hastily made his way downstream to the bridge, hoping the dogs would not re-appear.

Within a short time his mother's pickup hove into view and he jumped into the truck. Almost before she could ask him where his fish were, he blurted he'd been rescued by old man Carmen's two Herford bulls.

"Rescued? What in the world do you mean?"

"Mom, remember when I was in dad's logging camp for three weeks last summer? I saw my first bear behind the cook shack at the garbage pit one night. I went to the cook shack whenever I woke up and the cook made me whatever I wanted for breakfast, fixed me a sack lunch and I fished all day? Remember that?"

"Yes, I do, son. Why?"

"Remember dad said I was probably imagining hearing a bear? I told him after he dropped me off from his truck that day part way up the mountain so I could fish my way back to the camp, that I thought I heard a bear. I considered scooting into a culvert, the ones they were replacing the old ones with. Instead I got up my nerve, grabbed some rocks and climbed a tree… ready to take on any bear. I did that three times. Then dad showed up with a load of logs bound for the mill. I got in his truck for a ride back to camp.

"When I told him about it, he said I probably heard the donkey on the mountain or a truck…or, maybe I was imagining it. I thought about that while I was in the tree with the dogs below me. Believe me, I did not imagine those dogs. They were real and they were vicious. I'm going to go dog hunting."

"Son, you're not making sense. Slow down. What are you saying?"

"Mom, while I fished that pack of feral dogs rushed and treed me. Only old man Carmen's bulls chased the dogs away and I was able to meet you on time. I'm going after those dogs."

"Okay. I understand. You were treed by dogs. I'll have something to say about that big time at the next town hall meeting, But first I'm going to contact the sheriff, pronto."

Student Writing

"Dirty Jeans" *

She meant well. Maybe she just didn't know about little boys and bugs and worms and rusty nails and fish.

Maybe it's because she grew up with no brothers.

Maybe it's because she wasn't a boy.

Maybe it's because she was used to a clean house.

Maybe it's because she didn't like the smell of fish.

She was startled when she saw the boy's pants on the floor—they were moving. When she finally got nerve to approach them, she jiggled the jeans and a frog fell to the floor and hopped across the room.

When the mother came home, the babysitter explained the mystery of the moving pants, asking the lady about the bugs, worms and rusty nails she'd shaken from the holey and dirty jeans.

"Oh, you had a normal day. He's always coming home with critters and odds and ends in his pockets. When he plays outside, he usually goes through at least two pair of pants a day. What with his trips to the fields, the woods and the pond, he's a one man expedition.

"In the beginning I didn't know how to deal with him. He was always dirty, full of energy, bringing home stuff. He was often cut or bruised. And did I mention…hungry? He's a boy. That's what boys do. Dismantle stuff. Bring home things you don't want in the house. They grime their bodies.

"At first I didn't understand.

"I complained to my neighbor Cy. Told him my little boy was a mess. That he was always dirty, bedraggled or bleeding. He didn't like baths. He preferred dirt to soap.

"My Little Guy brought home fish and asked me how to 'fix' them. I didn't want them in my kitchen. I didn't know how to 'fix' them. But I learned. I asked Cy. He showed me how to clean and cook fish. Then I taught my son.

"Cy told me my son was experiencing the blessings of boyhood.

"I didn't want to deny my son those boyhood blessings. I learned that it wasn't MY kitchen. Even more important, in his wise, old way, my neighbor showed me that there was something more valuable than my kitchen. And I told my boy to bring those smelly fish into the kitchen whenever he wanted. And he did, along with the rusty nails, bugs and worms."

--Little Pea Pickin' Larry

*Sub title: The Kitchen or the Boy

How often do we marginalize those we love...perhaps assuming we'll have them forever? Or how often do we place more value on stuff than we do on people? While contemplating these ideas, I thought it would be nice to take a closer look…at a boy, a babysitter, a parent and a gentleman whose decisions were based on their experiences. I wanted to portray the benefits of knowledge… and to show that personal relationships are more valuable than things—in Alaska and beyond.

Faculty Lounge

"Get this. I got a note from a mother for Caden. I assume she's perfecting her satirist writing skills. Here's what she wrote":

Dear Teachers,

Caden has sprained fingers on both hands. Although we tried training him to write with his feet, we found he was useless in this capacity. Please allow him to use a tape recorder rather than a pencil until he heals. We would like to avoid prolonging discomfort from this injury so he can resume household chores.

Sincerely, Mrs. Sandy Motahl

"How's that for a missive from a mother?"

Speaking of writing, Mr. K never assigned an essay with a specific number of words. He told the kids a single sentence could be as powerful as a book. He reminded us that "if I assign a 350 word essay, you'll be doing more math than English…as in, 'I only need 5 more words.'" And he focused our attention on writing.

Every year when working with descriptive writing, he read the class half dozen paragraphs written by amateurs or published authors Twain, Steinbeck and Dickens, had them assign a grade to each and determine whether or not the author was a professional writer or a student. The class always gave student papers a higher grade.

One that he read was my favorite, written by a student:

"Coghill"

The early morning sun reflected off the waters of the bay. Pinkish-red of the sunrise shown through the fog as it slowly lifted off the marsh. In the quiet, early morning the shrill cry of an eagle and the whistle of duck's wings broke the silence. In a river not far away, spawning salmon splashed in the pools and seagulls cried over the choice fish stranded by the tide. Far out on the bay a crab boat moved through the mist, its wake shimmering like threads of gold reflecting the sunrise. Far away came the sound of honking geese, their music growing steadily louder and then trailing into silence.

Grandparents

Cimarron always loved hearing about her grandparents. She never tired of their stories. They were two generations earlier than she and she was curious about the 1940's through the 60's. She'd heard about sock hops; Princeton and flattop haircuts; Afros and bee hive hair styles; peg legged pants with white socks as well as bobby sox and Viet Nam.

Having been born in Deer Park, Grandpa lived all over Washington. He and his two sisters bounced around the state. His parents raised rabbits and one day after stealing a pack of gum and sharing it with his friend in the barn, they discovered the "gum" was laxative and they were busy for a day or two.

In Duvall when the population was 236, he and his older and younger sisters sat outside the tavern in a 1941 Buick between drinking hours awaiting their mother's presentation of potato chips and bottled soda. Their day's activities were capped by nightly brawls where their mother was beaten, subjected to fists, rope, knife, car. That's where his mother took him as a third grader to the sheriff and turned him in for shooting out street lights with his BB gun. He also learned to swim in the Snoqualmie River and refined his love of peaches by sneaking to the neighbors summer place and stealing quart jars of peaches. Uuummm. Until he exited their basement one day into the backyard full of people. He hastily blended into the woods, never to return to the cellar.

He loved the aroma of evergreens but had a strong dislike for nettles. He and his sisters cut bark from cascara trees, dried it in the barn for sale, filled gunny sacks and sold it for $.29 a pound. He graduated high school in Clarkston where he swam the Snake River between Clarkston and Lewiston before the dams were built.

Janitor Concerns

I understand the need for monitoring bathrooms due to those who do not leave their waste in the toilet, but shouldn't the bathrooms be open until after the busses leave. I had two girls who needed to use the restroom but I was forbidden to open it. They dropped their panties and peed right in front of me. Guess who got to clean it up?

One day Cimarron looked out the kitchen window just past Gramp's "I Love Rose" tree valentine, Cimarron noticed Boomer acting strangely in his round pen—running back and forth, looking to the southwest beyond the barn, whinnying. She said to grandpa, "Gramps, I'm going to check Boomer.

He's acting up. Just to be safe, I'll put him in the barn."

Cim left the kitchen and Gramps grabbed the Model 94 Winchester lever action .30-30 that leaned near the corner cabinet at the back door.

Cimarron's concern was realized as she barely had time to get Boomer into his stall, close the door and skedaddle into the barn. She grabbed the barn .22 and climbed the stairs into the hay loft. As grandpa walked onto the porch, several dogs yapped and snarled at the barn door. Quicker than the proverbial "drop of a hat," before the hat hit the floor, Gramps jacked another round from the magazine and began warming the barrel.

Almost within seconds Cim heard the roar of her Gramp's smoke pole. She joined the event and fired rounds into the pack below. Almost before it had started, it was over. The remaining half dozen dogs fled.

Cim climbed down the ladder, settled her horse and opened the door. After peeking out cautiously, she walked toward the back door of the house and met grandpa in the yard.

"Well, Little Darlin', looks like we ventilated a few of those mangy mutts. They won't be bothering anyone else's livestock. Let's hope those that escaped will come to the same end."

Gramps took Cimarron's barn cat Trinity into the house and said, "Kitty cat. It's time for Gramps to take a nap. You want to saunter into the living room, hit the couch with me and snooze? Maybe a little cat nap? Hey, you're not answering me. Cat got your tongue?"

And he wondered about the community and when they might respond to these deadly attacks? The greater question remained: will the pack take down people again?

On a Saturday afternoon Cimarron rode Boomer around the property. A silver pickup passed her going in her direction and she saw the taillights blossom half block beyond her. She rode on and stopped at the truck where Mr. Newcomb and another man stood to greet her.

"Hi, Cimarron. How ya doin'?"

"I'm fine, Mr. Newcomb. How about you?"

"Just dandy. This here's ma friend. He's a visitin' from out of state. Josh Larue."

"Nice to meet you, Mr. Larue. Hope you have a good time here."

"Cimarron, I wanted ta see ifn ya've had any news about them air wild dogs?"

"Nothing lately. Maybe they've left the area. If I hear of anything, I'll let you know. I plan to talk with my daddy when he gets back. He's on a business trip. Nice of you to stop and say hi."

"Okay, Cimarron. Have yerself a nice day. We'll keep in touch."

As they drove off Tad told his friend that Cimarron was a good cook, won numerous blue ribbons at the state fair, had been active in 4-H. While he explained the attributes of Cimarron, his friend interrupted him, "Bet she could show you a good time rolling in the hay."

"Thet ain't no way to talk about Cimmaron Rose. Shame on you. You wouldn't even come close to saying thet ifn you knowed her granny and grampa. They're the best. She's a sweet tribute ta her community and gender. Not some one night stand chick. She ain't thet kinda girl.

"There's jes somethin' about Cimarron. She'd look hot in a evenin' gown or a pair a leather chaps and spurs on the heels of them air cowgirl boots of hern. She's a marvel. She's a 'get 'er done gal.' Has been since I first seen her."

Teacher Quotes

If I were in your boat and wanted to get to shore, I'd do some serious rowing.

John, come down off your vine and find a seat, please.

Sue, climb out from beneath that mask and...oh, excuse me, that's your new hair style.

Which reminds me, to play hockey, you've gotta get on the ice.

Student Quotes

Why does anyone take that teacher? She's as dumb as a bucket full of biscuits.

I heard Mrs. Williams is sick. She must have come into some bad plankton.

Faggots have the right, but they are wrong.

This is the only class I have that's important. After first hour I go home.

In time townspeople met. Papers and other media outlets carried the growing concern over the dog pack. The discovery of the Morgan child made them wonder if the pack might attack other humans.

The disturbance of the pack of feral dogs had definitely come to the attention of the town council, a subject of great concern. Some wanted to save the dogs; others wanted to remove them. To say there was a conflicted community is understatement. People were for or against the dogs, a veritable A to Z in attitude.

Chairlady Mrs. Chan: Discussing this dog situation is not on our agenda, but we could briefly entertain comments about it...as an informal introduction. We can discuss more fully at our next meeting.

Ms. A: It appears to me that it would be most appropriate to ask if there is a possibility the domestic animals reverted to their ancient instinct because of global warming.

Chairlady: Is there anyone present who could address this question from the standpoint of biological science or meteorology?

Mr. Z: Thet question's not even close to removin' those blood thirsty critters. We're sayin' they's a danger to society. Has nothin' ta do with revertin' ta instinctual habits. I'm new hereabouts...been here less 'n a year but come on!

Mrs. J: Having studied in the areas of both biology and meteorology, there might be something to Ms. A's question. However I'm not well enough acquainted...haven't actually done the research...to answer in the affirmative. Maybe we should consult with our game and fish people, even if we have to go to the capitol.

Mr. P: These dogs are not pets. They're not even renegade dogs. They're feral—gone plumb wild, blood thirsty, killing machines for the fun of it, actual monsters. If you're going to describe them accurately, don't use pets but rather monsters.

Mrs. Parsons: My son was recently targeted by these dogs while he was fishing. They chased him up a tree but some of Mr. Carmen's bulls chased the dogs away. What is going to be done regarding these beasts? My son could have been killed. It's about time someone stepped up to defend our community.

Mr. T: I state unequivocally that the feral dogs are 1) increasing in number, 2) out of control and 3) attacking with greater frequency and ferocity. They're even attacking people. On the way to my tree stand a few weeks ago, I was attacked by a pack of half dozen or more dogs. It was too dark, but I was able to fire a round into the pack which turned them. There was a flash of orange from the barrel of my rifle, some yelping mixed with snarls and barks. The pack vanished and I scooted up the tree to safety in my stand. I never saw a deer and a few hours later, cautiously sneaked back to my truck.

Mr. B: Do you think you may have hit any of the dogs?

Mr. T: I'm not sure.

Mrs. L: Are you thinking maybe your shot scared the dogs and they left the county?

Before class started one day Cim asked BDK, "Mr. K. You've heard about the feral dog pack running around. What's your opinion on that? Maybe we could have a class discussion one day.

"Great idea, Cimarron. We have some time before the bell rings. Want some class input?"

"Sure."

As might be expected, some of the students knew about the pack while others didn't...and some wanted to continue the status quo while others wanted removal of the dogs.

Yore Lore

As a child Grandpa was at the grandparents for a Sunday meal that included all the cousins and family members. His grandfather asked for the biscuits and Cousin Leslie tossed the unwrapped dozen toward grandpa. They fell short, landed in the extremely hot bowl of gravy that splashed onto gramps. Before he knew it, he was standing on a chair totally nude in front of God and everyone, being examined for burns.

Wall Talk

"Did you hear about Mr. Kandel and the identity crisis he stirred up?"

"*Nein, amigo. Como estar* and *comment allez vous*? What's the deal?"

"Toward the end of the school year he shaved his beard. Next day at school kids asked him why he shaved. Guess what he told them?"

"I give up, amigo."

"He said, 'Oh, you're thinking of Larry. I'm his twin brother Barry. I came to visit with my parents and he took them to see the mountain. I'll be subbing for him till the end of school.'"

"And?"

"Some kids thought Larry was lying, didn't believe him. And he was. Seems the yearbook teacher had teacher pictures in the book— Larry and Barry's pictures were beside each other—same suit and tie, one had a beard, one didn't. Larry taught English and Barry taught sex ed. Somehow Mr. K had his picture taken at different times in the same outfit. It was a hoot.

"That was last year. So, this year when a student didn't believe he had a twin brother, BDK marched to the school library and retrieved the yearbook with the pictures. Who can doubt a picture?

"BTW, amigo, the foreign language teacher Ms. Visher would have some problems with your pronunciation of *nein* and *como estar*, eh?"

Yore Lore

Grandpa points out the focus of church. Are we here to serve or to be served. And he makes a point on his view allocating church time, providing a perfect recipe:

Pastor gives kudos to the congregation; tells how great they are

5 minutes

Congregant gives personal testimony, tells what God is doing in his life

5 minutes

Music including a special

10 minutes

Sermon

10 minutes

Congregational prayer
> *5 minutes*
Birthday/anniversary events every Sunday
> *10 minutes*
Patriotic stuff on those days
> <u>*10 minutes*</u>
Total time   under an hour
He added that if a pastor can't get the message across in less than half hour, the message probably isn't worth hearing.

One day Mr. K planned to show a movie. He took the proper precaution and prepared in advance by sending notes home with his students. Basically he asked the parent to approve or disapprove the student's watching the television special *Devil Worship*. One mother, Mrs. Gladden, returned the note with her child. She had marked do NOT approve and sent a note: "I don't think this type of material should be shown in school. You are not qualified to answer any questions on the material." He had tried.

Class Discussion:

In his objective, knows-the-kids manner that his students had learned to respect, Mr. K introduced the class discussion and turned it over to them.

So many students salivate over getting laid. So, let's discuss the event. Why do so many see the boy as the stud and the girl as the slut...why not stud and studette? If the girl downs a half dozen or more guys why isn't she called a studette instead of being relegated to the garbage heap? If he's a hero, why isn't she the heroine? The guy gets the glamour, the girl gets the bad rap. What's with that? He's praised and she's thrown under the bus. On the board for discussion: "If an active boy is called a stud, shouldn't an active girl be called a studette?"

Why the double standard? What say you, class?

Locker Room

"Do you ever think about how it feels to be mistrusted?"

"Ever? Yeh, all the time. You mean everything you do is scrutinized… that you must measure up to someone else's expectations?"

"What about the individual? Don't his thoughts and actions matter? What about me… doesn't the person inside me matter?"

Yore Lore

Grandpa explained the idea that in some ways life is a party—a composite of the good and the bad. Kids plan and gather for a good time. Sometimes it goes well and sometimes it doesn't. Sometimes things backfire even if it's not a party. He said, "I remember numerous 'back in the day' things, some good; some bad."

They cruised the main drag on weekends. Had drive-in movies. Did a lot of hooky bobbing in the winter, or bumper bouncing as some called it. Freshmen watched their "P's and Q's" to avoid getting de-pantsed by seniors or, literally, meeting a urinal head on resulting in a swirly. In order to avoid getting a swirly, they hid in places like the library, cafeteria or little theater. Some guys managed to sneak peek above the girls' locker room but they got caught. Yes, they also had suspension.

Gramps was on his high school football, basketball, badminton and trampoline teams and was chief justice of the student court.

Although human nature pretty much stays the same, he admitted lingo changes. For instance when he was a lad, cool was another way of saying neat...as in neato. Then it kind of morphed into radical, ragin, groovy, badass and boss. Of course in the same time span man has been called man, cat, dude, bud, dog.

Even though change is inevitable. Some things never change. They had kids who tackled in football but admitted they didn't know how to tackle life...just like now. The times and culture does, but human nature remains pretty much the same. Look at our society today.

Suggestion Box:

Do space aliens have navel lint? Is it white like ours?

Why do some say some drugs are worse than others, aren't drugs drugs?

Why do teachers dress so dorky?

How do you deal with a girls over protective mother that grounds her for no reason?

To make it in school you have to be a great BS artist.

Do you enjoy being married?

Can I have a cupcake?

Grandparents

Gramps told Gran, "After our web guy put me on Facebook, I was checking it one day. Guess what? Remember that young lady who loaned me her journal so many years ago, the one who mentioned she'd been sexually abused by her father? She posted a message to me on Facebook. I'm thinking 'You're kidding, right?' How many years ago was that?"

"Howard, that was before you retired. What did she say?"

" I printed out what she wrote so you could see it. Here it is."

Mr. Timmons,

I don't know if you remember me, but I was one of your students. I got pregnant before my 10th grade year and wrote a paper on teen pregnancy statistics all the while being pregnant.

I gave my diary to my friend for you to read. She said you were concerned about what was going on. You wrote me back. This I have never forgotten! Your true compassion and concern touched me and still has from this day.

You wrote me a passage from the Bible that I used to think of often.

Jeremiah 29.11. "For I know the plans I have for you, says the Lord. They are plans for good and not for evil, to give you a future and a hope," how beautiful. I loved how you crossed all the "you" and put my name.

That really touched me.

I've never thanked you properly for you generosity. It was a tricky situation back then!

That is all over now and I have a wonderful life with 4 beautiful children.

We are truly blessed. No complaints here. It was LONG hard road but we made it.

Thank you again! You truly are a great teacher of learning, compassion and understanding!!

Sincerely,

Alana Marie Holland

Wow. How do I respond to that? It is amazing that you wrote. I was just thinking about you yesterday and wondering--as I often do--how you are doing. What a nice, make that very nice, note. The first thing I'll do is copy-print and show my wife who is my shining beacon of kindness and love and who will very likely end up in a place where I will be shoveling coal to keep her warm! Feel free to email (gezzerandgezzerette@gmail.com). I'm so happy that you have weathered the storm. If I'm not mistaken-- in fact I'm 100% positive--that I have a copy of your diary which I hope to use some day in a book. It would be so cool should that happen and

I'd have your approval. All best to you and yours. Would be fun to learn about your family.

"That's amazing, Howard. She weathered hard times, your compassion touched her and she wrote you."

"Yes, she did. I'm going to write her and invite her to visit us. Maybe we can talk her into writing her life story, to encourage other young ladies.

The atmosphere at the Double K was almost always relaxing…a kind of safe house for all. Cimarron enjoyed that. Her grandparents had no TV (never converted from analog to digital), got news from selected conservative computer sites, watched old DVD's and VHS tapes on their TV monitor. Gramps thought the IPhone was awesome but didn't think it was necessary for him. Nor were he and Gran addicted to instantaneous anything. They thought the time would come when generations won't be able to write because cursive is not taught.

Case in point regarding new vs. old. One time Cim was eating dinner with them when Gramps told a funny story about his recent visit to the bank. "I stopped at the bank. You know how they want you to input your name in order to facilitate bank teller needs? I input Trigger and the young woman looked at me like I was from another planet. I asked her, 'You don't know who Trigger is?' She gave me that blank look again so I said, "I guess I won't input Buttermilk next time I visit. She was Dale Evan's horse and Dale was Roy Roger's wife. His horse was named Trigger. You've never heard of Roy Rogers, the King of the Cowboys?"

"No."

" I told her, 'That's okay. I don't know anything about Justin Bieber either." And I went to the teller.

Gran joined the fun and asked Cim if she'd ever told the funny story about Mr. Terry and his singing. When Cim said no, Gran launched into her story. She and Gramps were giving Mr. Terry a ride when he was a freshman. He sat in the back seat of their old Volkswagon bug…and began singing. A short time later he piped up, "I bet you thought that was the radio?"

And Gran answered, "Yeh, the static."

He laughed and said it was the first time he knew she had a sense of humor.

In the privacy of their bedroom Gran talked with Gramps about Cim, "I'm some concerned about Cimarron. She's recovering from her truck accident but seems to be taking on the weight of the world. She's right. But it may be too soon for her to struggle through the crisis of the damages adults inflict on kids."

"I know, Buttercup, but she's a go getter. She has mentioned the parallel between the dog pack and adults. Her argument is more than sound. She wants to talk with her dad. I believe she will before too long because the situation's reaching a boiling point."

"Well, she's concerned about America, as she should be. How many liberties will we lose?"

"I think next time he's home, we need to bring it up.'

"Okay."

Considering the feral dog pack which Cim paralleled with adults and teens—adults being the predators, teens being the prey, she brought it up at dinner.

"I'm concerned for my fellow students and the pressure applied by adults."

Grandma spoke first, "Dearie, you have enough on your plate for the time being. Your shoulders aren't wide enough to take on the weight of the world. Why not wait a little longer before tackling those problems?"

"Well, I don't think the problems will diminish. I'd like to be part of the solution."

"Little Darlin', your granny and I know you are part of the solution. You're going wonderfully well and will continue to do so. We believe in you. Maybe it would be good to wait till your dad's back and we can have a giant discussion."

"Well, that's a possibility. But in the meantime, I'm going to research on the internet."

And she did. Cimarron started with the past…compared with the present. She reviewed age old stuff. Back in the day kids had things like mud puddles, sticks, dirt clods, Lincoln logs and legos…but as they grew older, they witnessed technological changes—typewriters, cassettes, video games, CD's, Blue Ray, cell then smart phones, laptop tablets. Most were positive, but not all.

Her minimal search mushroomed into a major research of multiple concerns, many of which she'd never heard, or of which she was ill informed.

And what kinds of things big pharma was doing. For instance what about chemicals in the form of weed killer, fluoride in our water, genetically modified stuff?

Gramps asked her about her findings and wondered about "the

snowflakes opposing the president." He alluded to the You Tube vid "Astonishing 2011 prophecy" about the election of the president six years before he even announced he was running. Then Gramps asked, "When was the last time someone opposed God and won the battle?"

Her research was mind boggling. So many questions, so little time. When could she discuss with her Daddy?

Almost before she knew it, Cimarron's dad blew in late one evening, gave her a hug and told her they'd talk tomorrow. He was bushed.

The next day after breakfast he gave her a present, which was normal on his return from a business trip.

"Gee, Daddy, what's in the package. It's too small to be the saddle you promised." She opened the small box and found a note, "To my lovely daughter, Cimarron Rose. If you walk to the car, you'll find your present."

She dashed outside, opened the car door and found nothing. Her father, following her, moments later, arrived, "You might check the trunk…your present was easier to load there."

"Oh, Daddy. You clever devil, you." There was the beautiful saddle she'd wanted for some time. "You shouldn't."

"What better present could I give my Little Angel?"

That night she wrote in her diary:

Dear Diary

Am I right or wrong? Kids are pimped by adults who sell them drugs, booze, tobacco and prey upon their youthful innocence and bodies for sex and other pleasures. Look at what MTV is selling them, and the clothing industry which shouts for their desire for acceptance with "the look." What's glamorous about deception, like cosmetics, movies, tanning booths, etc. Youth are the prey of adults.

And there's something to be said about vehicle ventures where little instruction is given regarding safety, like 4-wheelers, motorcycles and so on.

Kids need to be kids, not mini-adults. Let them grow up with curiosity, experimentation, making and being forgiven for making mistakes.

Our culture is a carbon copy society where we have to be like someone else, we can't be ourselves, have to copy others' dress, language, actions.

The next day Cimarron wasted little time in talking with her father. She expressed the similarities between Liberty High and Liberty Heights—

children braved the challenge of high school to face the reality and challenge of adulthood in town.

High school is a microcosm of life, a stepping stone to the next level, called adulthood. Both are very real. Sometimes one can be more dangerous and tougher than the other.

She told him, "We deserve better. We deserve a chance for freedom… to be individually successful and happy."

She pulled no punches in explaining the evils promulgated by adults. And she asked him how people could victimize kids.

While working his farm one day, Jack Hudson took a break when he noticed a bunch of circling crows. He drove his tractor for a closer look. Crows cawed and fluttered on the other side of the fence beyond some brush. Thinking he might need to remove some of the undergrowth, he carried a hand axe in his right hand. What he saw through the brush was a dead deer lying on the ground, missing a large portion of a hind leg.

He noted it had been dragged down by a dog or some coyotes, maybe a wolf. About then a German Shepherd nearby rose to its feet and lunged at him. Fortunately it missed his throat and he swung the axe at it. Three times it snapped and lunged for his throat before his axe struck a glancing blow to its neck, causing it to flee.

Another hunter related how while sneaking through woods to his deer stand he'd been attacked by a pack of snarling dogs. He fired as he backed down the trail, killing the lead dog and the one behind it before wounding a third dog. The fourth dog took a gun barrel to the neck in its leaping efforts to reach the hunter. Fumbling for more ammunition and reloading his rifle, he reached the safety of his tree stand while the remaining dogs cleared out.

The newspaper quoted a game biologist saying the entire farm community was overrun with mongrel-feral dogs which locals assumed belonged to someone. But none of the neighboring farmers claimed them nor knew to whom they belonged. Dogs tore up rabbit cages, removing wood door facings or ripping off the doors and slaughtering every animal they caught. The biologist said those dogs are the worst thing happening in our county. They were a danger to small animals but are now a concern to adults hereabout. The game boys are considering an open season with no limits on the dogs.

Dear Diary

Since when have adults the right to live a child's life for him? What is the solution? "Adults" need to grow up. Give their children some credit. Let the kid live his own life. Why do parents think being number one requires whatever it takes? Why can't we accept a kid for who he is instead of what we want him to be or what he has? What's with labeling kids...we pigeon hole him for his job, what he has, his past including achievements or not. He's a loser or a winner. Why? Why can't he be who he is?

Seems like we're doing things backward. Instead of trying to change the heart through the head, we should be changing the head through the heart.

Prior to the second town hall meeting two men talked about the feral dog problem. Each shared a personal experience.

"The first time I saw the pack, eight dogs loped silently and in single file following the one they call Lobo, a big gray wolf. They ran the ridgeline. Two pit bulls, one beige the other rusty brown, two Doberman pinchers with Dobie markings, a Heinz 57 and two coyotes brought up the rear...But there are other packs."

"I've read about other packs in the country. Doing a lot of damage. I had my own adventure not long ago. I silently slipped along the deer trail in the breaking dawn and within half mile of two farm houses. Was I surprised by the presence of half dozen dogs with some puppies. They were upwind of me and looking the other way. Suddenly a bitch, closer than the others, jumped to her feet, curled her lips back exposing her fangs, savagely growled a threat and with hair bristling and muscles taut in a crouch as if ready to spring, eyed me menacingly. I slipped off my rifle's safety and shouldered it. She whirled and ghosted into the brush. The others followed suit, including the pups.

"When I asked the farmer who'd permitted me to hunt his wood lot whose dogs they were, he told me he and other farmers had seen numerous packs and the farmers carried on a running feud with the livestock happy mutts."

The chairlady called for order at the proper time, the group rose for the Pledge of Allegiance and a word of prayer, then the town hall minutes were read.

City Attorney: "I don't know if you've considered the ramifications of the dog pack carousings. Who is responsible for the destruction and death by these animals...financial officer, county clerk, country sheriff, public safety, county commissioner, governor? Cost will run into the thousands if these animals kill the wrong livestock. For instance, what about the black stallion at the Double K, the one that runs around twenty grand per stud fee?

"The dogs are not as well established as the feral hogs in the southwest but those hogs damage foliage and landscape. One woman living in an association subdivision paid two times to have her yard re-landscaped, around five grand each time; and she couldn't afford the third time. But landscape pales in comparison to human injury. The damage in lost lives has not only financial but also fatal consequences. Have you thought about that?

"What about an attack on a human that results in death…how is that going to fare if family sues the county or state for wrongful death?

"I predict this dog issue is not going to sit well. You've got the dog protectors and the dog removers. You're already seeing a community torn apart because of these dogs."

Sheriff Solomon: "I'm not sure of the ramifications of dogs running wild. What kinds of things could come from the feral dog situation? I don't know who would be responsible in the event of an injury to animal or human, certainly not in the case of a human fatality."

Mrs. Parsons: "Because of the danger these animals pose to the community, I'm here to express my opposition to their presence and to seek some kind of action to remove them…for our safety.

"These dogs are probably not going to be deterred but continue their predatory ways; their pups will learn from the pack parents."

Sheriff Solomon: "We're here to protect and serve. Our priority is to public safety. We can take care of this problem internally. We will evaluate the situation and come up with a solution."

The discussion moved toward shooting, poisoning, trapping and/or snaring. But several addressed the loss of "too many innocent animals."

In the end it was decided by the local law enforcement personnel.

Sheriff Solomon: "Ultimately we'll let the law decide."

But the townspeople had a different version. That's when the 3 S's stepped in—shoot, shovel, shut up.

Teacher Concerns

Since when did counselors become administrators?
Instead of rewarding tardy students, how about detention?
Tardy policy…falling apart.
Were counselors hired to counsel or to schedule?
Shouldn't they teach in their major or minor fields. Why is a P.E.

teacher teaching home economics?

Kids used to come to school to learn. Wait. Kids used to come to school!

Strangers on campus? Will students or teachers be shot first?

School Shooting

Word got out that a student planned a shooting. He named names and selected targets. He met with BDK and admitted he was upset but saw no solution in violence. He targeted Mr. Nozall because he bullied a kid, a pervert coach who hit on this kid's cousin and a counselor who tried to put him into English skills class because he thought the kid was stupid. He actually overheard a counselor tell another person in counseling office "that kid is dumber than a rock."

Mr. K told him he used to teach that class. That both he and Mr. Runberg provided the principal information about the class. Mr. K told the boy he was sorry he'd been treated so poorly but glad that he came to him. Let's see what we can do to correct these problems.

The student acknowledged teachers would be there forever because of the goofy union affiliation and tenure. But he promised Mr. K that he would not follow through with his plan. Both he and the student went to the administration to follow up on the situation.

Grandpa T shared with Gran and Cimarron a letter from a friend in Anchorage. Seems a black bear showed up in a park in January. Not surprisingly the media, supported by the local fish and feather guys, told cross-country skiers to be aware of the bear. Gramps wondered What about dispatching it for people safety?

Cimarron remembered the summer after she drove the Alcan with her grandparents. On the way they had stopped near Dayton, Oregon, on the farm where her mother grew up, to visit her Uncle Craig and Aunt Vicky. They told her how her mother rode her palomino...shot mistletoe from oak trees with .22 rifle. Cim helped Uncle Craig buck oak limbs with a Stihl 056 her father gave him; she used the smaller 029. Cimarron identified with her buckaroo tomboy mother with lots of grit.

Gran and Gramps left her with Gramp's friend and she worked for Moose McGinnis till school started. Had a great time in the Great Land, even had an adventure with a grizzly that came into camp one day. Moose had clients on a photo shoot and she was tending camp when the griz showed up, looking for a free hand out. Fortunately Cimarron scared it away without having to ventilate it with lead.

Another time the photographers had a grizzly charge them but this one had to be dealt with in a hurry up hurry. The bear attacked the pack string—stuff was strewn all over the tundra, hanging in birch and alder trees. Griz showed up out of nowhere spinning moss and dirt in every direction but the guide was on his toes and, in spite of the confusion and all, got the group under control. Turned out to be an overprotective mother griz and no damage.

Moose busted a griz in the hump, paralyzed it until he got a finishing shot into its skull. Seems he'd walked off into the bushes at a call from Ma Nature, carrying his rifle as always in bear country. After it roared out of the trees, straight at him like a sidewinder missile, he had the presence of mind to shoot from the hip, something he'd done since a kid growing up with his .22. Some might call it luck; others would say muscle memory.

Yore Lore

Gran told Cim about "a little neighbor girl who often came to our house after school. We thought she was locked out and waited for her mother to come home from work to let her in. I didn't know till much later that the girl was raped by her brother regularly if her mother and father were not at home. After high school the son went into the service and blew his brains out."

It's no wonder neighbor kids felt like Gran's house was a safe house. Gran's always had cookies and hot chocolate or cold milk for the kids, depending upon the season.

Dear Diary

This morning on the way to school a crop duster buzzed over us so low I thought the pilot figured we were a runway! His thundering bird, a big, 500-horse Ag Cat, all horses kicking and squealing, roared over, belching pesticide from both wings, a yellow bullet flashing like lightning. I asked Mr. Sprinkle how close it came. Everyone calls him Fuzzy but I respect him too much and call him by his mister name.

He said it wasn't that close. "Not near as close as some of the runs I had to the North Slope when I owned Fuzzy's Trucking in Anchorage."

When I asked him about the chemicals spread by the crop duster, he told me they were nasty and that he'd seen them loaded from the tanks where the operators wore masks for protection.

I knew Mr. Sprinkle lived in Alaska, probably the same time my grandparents did. And Gramps had a PA 18 A Super Cub he rebuilt. It had been used for spraying fields. He put nose art of Gran on the cowling,

Tundra Bunny.

Kids love Mr. Sprinkle—they could hardly wait to board the bus. He always remembers their birthdays, gives them cards and a special gift for the day.

I always loved Mr. Sprinkle's stories about Alaska. That's the reason that I sit behind him asking him questions. Maybe that's the reason I developed an interest in Alaska and got a job there.

Darin Parsons laid plans carefully to go dog hunting on old man Carmen's property. He figured even if the pack did not follow a circuit, he could provide enough temptation to get them coming on a regular basis. He knew it wasn't safe to ride his bike. Not even logical since he had a ton of meat scraps. So he asked his mother to help him round up the dog bait. He contacted several stores and butcher shops, actually got some bakeries to donate old baked goods. He'd have his revenge.

They drove from location to location picking up the food-scraps then home to deposit them in the chest freezer in the garage. Passing a local restaurant one day, he told his mother he remembered when his father wasn't log hauling, he was long haul trucking. Darin had seen his dad's coffee cup in the diner numbered and named among two hundred other cups on the wall.

One Friday night his mother dropped Darin and his booty near the road. He had his AR 15 gifted from his uncle, in case the K-9's had other ideas. He filled an old Army pack board with his treats and started to a tree to dump them. When he returned Saturday, the bait was gone, as he expected it would be. But he had his tree stand and set it up near the scrap area and fastened it to the tree in anticipation of another visit.

Meanwhile he continued collecting goodies for the unsuspecting dogs. And the law. Ha, ha.

More bait gathering, storing, baiting and waiting till Friday night. Darin knew it was only a matter of time before his AR 15 would bark.

The following Saturday his mother dropped Darin and another load of food which he hurriedly carried to the stand. He'd barely gotten on the seat at the top when he heard barks in the distance. It wasn't long until a German shepherd appeared and immediately zeroed in on the pile. Moments later here came the pack.

Darin picked out a large dog and looked into his 2x7 Leupold scope. At that range he really could have barrel shot but with the scope set on "2" and a chambered .223 round, he touched the trigger. *Pop!* The dog dropped in its tracks.

Instantly the pack vanished into the grass and underbrush. He had thought he'd take several of the dogs with his semi-auto but did not expect them to be so skittish. He didn't know if they'd return but at any rate, it looked like he was going to have a long wait until his mother returned for him.

On a Thursday Cimarron talked with her math teacher Mr. Brock who also taught economics, "Mr. Brock, since you teach economics and are far more aware of finances than I, is it okay if I ask a question regarding taxes?"

"Sure, Cimarron, what is it?"

"If the finances of our government are paid for with taxpayer monies, what would happen if that money dried up?"

"You mean, if the tax payers stopped or…

"No, let's say it costs a thousand dollars a year to run the country. What if the tax payers can only pay, say $500. That leaves half the amount of running the government unpaid. How will that affect our country?"

"Obviously the government needs taxpayer monies in order to operate. I don't see a situation wherein taxpayers will stop. It's the law."

"But, what if the taxpayers come to a point where their tax payments are overshadowed by government spending? We have numerous examples of people receiving government payments, such as health, housing, food. What percent of those receiving government handouts are working? What percent are able to pay back the monies? Is it true we're paying illegals…that we're paying them more than our citizens?"

"Whoa there, Cimarron. I don't know if I have time this period to answer all those questions. Let's just say if government spending exceeds taxpayer monies, we'll be in real trouble. I don't know the percentages you've asked about exactly but we are providing lots of people finances, including illegals…though I don't know the amounts."

Yore Lore

Cim asks her grandfather, "Gramps, what was it like when you taught?"

"At least one thing would probably be a major change. Instead of writing on the desks like they did in my day, kids today would probably save on ink and just text the recipient. Don't you think?"

"Probably. All my friends have smart phones."

"Little Darlin', I remember reading a Dear Abby piece several years ago, comparing-contrasting the concerns teachers had from 1940 and into 1988. It was shocking. The great concern in the 1940's was students who talked too much. Following that were chewing gum, making noise, running in hallways, getting out of line, improper clothing and failing to put paper into the wastebaskets. Fifty years later numbers one and two were alcohol and drug abuse, followed by pregnancy, suicide, rape, robbery and assault. In the schools! Where has our country gone?"

"That's interesting, Gramps. Today's probably about the same as the last list. There is a greater shift in educational policy I think. Some teachers dock students a letter grade for each minute they're tardy; some teachers make it a point of not noticing late students. Nowadays students are bribed to attend class, actually paid money to show up. How dumb is that?"

"Different times, different people."

Circular File

Who said, "It's your responsibility to be responsible?"

Did you ever consider The B.G. battleground like a wilderness battleground…and wonder how much time we spend wandering in the wilderness before we find our way? Or what about the idea that we're all lost until we're found?

Amid the chatter about saving feral dogs, Alana Marie Holland and Gramps wrote back and forth a few times on Facebook and emails. They made arrangements to meet at the Double K. Gran and Gramps wondered so many years later how the meeting would go and agreed to focus on Alana and her life since high school.

Gramps felt Alana, in some ways like Cimarron, carried the overpowering weight of the world on her shoulders. What she endured as a pregnant teen, facing parents, grandparents, aunts-uncles, friends, teachers and boy friend. Facing tough decisions and choices such as keeping the baby and its ensuing challenges.

Gramps reminded Gran that Alana was a young woman of persistence, courage and commitment who left the shadowed silence, stood tall and emerged the victor…in spite of a painful past and very uncertain future. They agreed Alana was a heroine. Big time.

Alana arrived at 7:30 PM sharp and Gramps introduced Alana to Gran. Turns out they had a great visit, until 11:30 PM when Alana left. She sent an email the next day expressing her delight in the evening they spent together and adding that she had completed a few pages on her "book."

Dear Diary

Question. How are the dogs and the kids alike? Answer: they are considered throwaways, targeted by adults.

It's probably time to talk with daddy again. My brain's bubbling with concerns. So many things, so little time. How can our community be salivating about saving dogs when our teens are going down the toilet?

It's not bad enough that kids are targeted by industries producing and distributing alcohol, drugs, music, games and multiple other harmful items. But I'm learning more about other things, maybe not even those of a physical nature, like school and college professors pedaling propaganda, media lies.

Dear Diary

I'm listing some of my concerns and compiling a list for Daddy to chew on while he's on the road. I won't list all but will touch on topics like pornography, video games, teacher BS, vaccination, fluoride, chem trails, diet pills, TV, abortion, music, emasculating men and parents bribing colleges.

Hopefully we can discuss the dangers of fantasy as opposed to reality when he returns

I'll ask him about the concept: when you're the measure, you're the measure. How do you stack up against other standards?

Liberty Heights Journal

Letter to editor

Dear Editor,

There are numerous teachers, coaches and/or staff members in our community who deserve our kindest thoughts and highest praise. They matter because they know our kids matter.

Mrs. Grace Lovington

Teacher Quotes

To read a book you've got to open the cover.

When the girl told Mr. J, "I won't be here for two weeks. I have to go to the doctor," Mr. J replied, "You mean the vet?"

When Josh Tremain told Mr. Weldon he wouldn't be able to do his homework because he'd be playing, Weldon said, "Take it with you; you can do it on the bench."

One of the troubles with America is that people mistake sex for love, money for success and Walkman's, Blue Ray or I-phones for civilization.

Gramps told Cimarron about a friend coming from Alaska to visit. "We'll probably be spending next Sunday after church worshipping at the Temple of the Holy Goalposts. You're welcome to watch with us. Bring Mr. Darcy and Trinity…and that new little pup you got named Nellie."

"Gramps, now I know you're kidding."

"Well, Little Darlin', I can try. I guess you know my references to the House of the Glorified End Zone or the Temple of the Bruised and Battered or some other 'sainted' venue is my way of having fun. No, I don't watch football on the tube."

Gramps, "Why do people proclaim you're not a man unless you drink? That you're programmed to have a beer while watching sports on TV? That there's no life without booze? What's so hot about booze, anyway?"

"That's a good question, Little Darlin'. I'm told it's an acquired taste. I quit drinking alcohol when I was 14-years-old. Couldn't see any purpose in it. I'm told a cold one is great on a hot day. I'll never know. I've had a wonderful life without drinking…it gives me no regrets about beating my wife or kids or neglecting them."

"Gramps, don't you find it interesting that when we hear about the glories of alcohol, how millions of dollars are spent portraying it as the ticket to happiness, that we never see divorced families, drunks or their victims, family abuse or hospitals admitting those injured as a result of alcohol?"

"We are surrounded by slick marketing techniques. We all love the Budweiser Clydesdales…right? But they are not drinkers."

When her father returned from his latest trip she followed up on her litany of concerns.

"Daddy, do you think we'll have a civil war?"

"Cimarron, a civil war? Are you serious?"

"Yes. Our country is so topsy turvy and so many differences of opinion I'm concerned."

"Well, I looked at your list. So I'm not surprised by your concerns. You mentioned numerous topics. I understand several like the one about parents bribing college officials regarding their kids. And the age old TV dilemma...the one eyed monster. Some think that and the smart phone will be the ruination of the nation. I guess only time will tell.

"Dad. Instead of MVP for most valuable it seems like MVP has devolved into Mommies Vanity Pays. And what actual value is television. It destroys the family. And what about the movies?”

“Okay, Cim, I’ll give you those. My work revolves around promoting numerous products and companies. Yes, some are harmful. I’m not sure where music and games come in but…”

“Dad, games? Look at the games that promote killing. It’s like all a kid has to do is kill everyone and hit the replay button and the game begins anew. Is it any wonder we have so many kids killing today?”

“You can’t blame kids’ killing on video games. What is your proof?”

“I haven’t researched it, but it seems logical.

“Dad, the lyrics of a lot of music is aimed at cop killing, romanticizing it. When Elvis Presley and the Beatles were popular, they were considered a threat but they didn’t talk about killing cops and other detrimental things…

“How many babies have been aborted in the last fifty years…and now a kid can be aborted when it’s born. What about selling baby parts? And what about child trafficking and the sexual perversion and collecting of blood for Satanic rituals, as well as child human sacrifices.”

“Okay, Cim. I get your points.”

“Dad, how many poisons can a person absorb and live? We’ve got the poison of corruption in politics, in legal circles, in school. My head’s spinning. Where will it stop? And guess what? Kids do NOT pedal this stuff… adults do. What’s going to be done about it?

“Dad, I’m not smart enough to know some of this stuff. Help me out. Some in this community want to save the dogs. Terrible, wild animals. Isn’t that what people represent? Isn’t it time to save the children from the adults? If feral dogs matter, shouldn’t kids matter?”

Circular File

I saw you in the ocean.
I saw you in the sea.
I saw you in the bath tub.
Oops! Pardon me.

One evening at dinner Gran told Cimarron, “Your photo guide friend in Alaska sent a batch of frozen high bush cranberries. They’re very small berries but worth the effort so I’m going to make you some of your favorite jelly. Remember last year when you brought home the crowberries and I made you that delicious jelly?”

"Yeh, Gran, it's a tossup as to which is better. They're scrumptious. I love 'em both."

Then Cimarron brought up the subject of family. She asked her grandparents how many families eat together, even one meal a day…or week? How many families are families? How many families have both a husband and a wife? How many have male and a female parents?

Where's our country going?

Cimarron questioned the wisdom of mothers pursuing a career instead of staying at home with their children.

They mollified her to a degree by stating the divorce rate was higher than the past and the structure of society nearly demanded a two-parent income. They couldn't pacify her regarding the number of families with a male and female parent.

Yore Lore

Since you're attending Liberty High, another story of interest, Little Darlin'. After I left Liberty, I got the dope on Coach K. The shaft he got from Mr. Wild had nothing to do with recruiting. Instead Mr. Wild's ego got in his pathway…got a little bruised, you might say.

Mr. Wild used the list of misdeeds as an excuse to fire Mr. K. I learned through others that what really happened was that Mr. Wild called Mr. K that summer, informing him that he had an ineligible wrestler living with him. Seems that Tom Benson's dad called and asked Coach K if he'd let Tom live with him his senior year. Coach told Mr. Benson to check with the state high school athletic association to insure Mr. K wouldn't be accused of recruiting. It's kind funny in a weird way because there was at least one area coach who recruited kids from other states…and one wrestling coach in a nearby town who offered Mr. Benson a job and home if he brought his kid to that town…so the rumor goes.

Anyway some time later Mr. Benson called Coach K and told him it was okay. Little did Coach K know that Mr. Benson lied to him.

Mr. Wild insisted the wrestler could not live with Coach K and wrestle. Coach knew the kid had college potential and told Mr. Wild he'd give up coaching and coach the kid on his own. It didn't come to that but in the meantime Coach K wrote each member of the state association for clarification. He chose to use the actual situation instead of a hypothetical case.

Boom! Mr. Wild received a copy of Coach K's letter from a committee member and that's what caused the excitement. Mr. Wild was humiliated that Coach went over his head, so to speak.

So instead of Mr. K's misdeeds as falsely represented by Mr. Wild, it was Coach K's interest in solving the matter for the good of the athlete. I suppose in retrospect Coach K should have sent a copy of his state association letter to Mr. Wild also.

Don't you know?

The three S system seemed to have taken effect—locals took the wild dogs to task and trapped, poisoned or shot them. Didn't bother telling the law. It was kind of "good riddance to bad rubbish." Folks saw the pack and it was diminishing in number.

At noon one day Gran and Gramps talked. He jokingly commented, "My steel trap brain seems to have taken considerable rust these past years. There's nothing like good, old-fashioned truthfulness, that's the reason I can state unequivocally and in all honesty that my arrogance is exceeded only by my humility. Like I always say, Gran, I'm the eighth wonder of the world and God is still wondering."

"Howard, you're such a hoot. Both serious and humorous. What will you come up with next?"

"Well, I'm not going to bore you with my list of ongoing nitwittery, as in government agencies or those they fund like planned parenthood. How many of these guvment agencies have done rogued out on America, gone coyote wild and sneaky and have no chance of being believed. We've got a nation overcome with an avalanche of snowflakes, weak kneed wimps—those unable to engage with reality. Like I always say, we need leaders who are men, not men who are leaders!

"We're so used to driving into McDonald Land, the City of the Golden Arches, and being spoon fed. They slap together a fat mac, fries and drink and we're on our way. Whatever happened to building our own burger? When do we get off our duffs and think for ourselves? When do we do more than what's expected of us?"

In the midst of his mini-tirade Gran interrupted him to say the phone was ringing. Gramp's hearing wasn't the best. He answered it. "Yeh, I'm home. Yes, I'm sitting down. Shoot."

"Grandpa T, you remember Lane La Blane saw the pack around his place and set some traps or snares for the feral dogs?"

"Yeh, I know. Lane came by our place. I guess you know he's an old-time Alaska trapper."

"Right. Seems he snagged that big Lobo. We're pretty sure that wolf was the last of the group. May have no more wild dog problems."

"You don't say? That's great news. I'll let folks know. You're welcome."

Teacher Concerns

Disallow "toys" in the classroom, like smart phones, etc.

Eliminate running in halls

How about some serious discipline for all in building, including teachers

Who gives counselors power to change report card grades issued by teachers?

What's with the inordinate amount of empty soda cans throughout the building?

Yore Lore

One night my friend Jim Emerson, who spent his senior year with us, and I decided to go for a drive. In our pajamas and thongs we jumped into my 1942 Chevy and headed for the strip. Nothing was happening, even at the Arctic Circle so we decided to go deer hunting.

Only problem was that neither of us had a license and most every place was closed. Jim knew Mrs. Hogan, the owner-operator of a bar that sold hunting equipment, so we drove to the bar to see if we could swing licenses. We saw Mrs. Hogan behind the counter and two lady patrons on stools.

Jim knocked on the door. These women had to stifle laughter when they saw two high school guys in pajamas knocking on the door after closing hours. Mrs. Hogan admitted us just after 10. We bought licenses then headed home to gather gear for the next day's hunt, figuring if we got a deer, we'd be back in town in time for the last day of school that week.

Since we were only thirty miles from the hunting area with six hours till daylight, it proved to be a slow drive and then a cold night sleeping in the front seat and starting the car occasionally to get warm.

As daylight pried open the eyes of the eastern sky, I cranked on the starter and my 6-banger crawled in the gray dawn, four eyes straining up the ridges on either side for deer.

In a short time I spotted a mule deer silhouetted on the skyline and hollered, "Deer!" Before I brought the coupe to a stop, Jim was out the door, rifle ready. I shouted, "Doe. Don't shoot!" Too late. Boom.

One shot. One dead deer...did I mention ILLEGAL?

Leaving the doe was no option. We dressed it and tossed it into the trunk and headed for the barn/house.

Thirty miles later I backed up the driveway to the back door where we grabbed it front and rear and carted it into the basement furnace room. We hung it up on its hocks from the ceiling.

Dear Diary

Liberty High represents the ascension into adulthood, a pathway through the minefield of adolescence...

away from childhood...

away from innocence...

do we not recognize our need to grow up?

Is it a step toward freedom and a way from bondage...or a step through possible bondage and into the freedom of life and what it has to offer? What are we running from?

The grandparents and Cimarron discussed a solution to her growing list of concerns. She stated, "We have had a succession of mythological saviors. Some cite numerous literary characters. It used to be Superman, then Batman, we had Neo of *The Matrix*. Some far out ideas. If there is solution, what is it?"

"Little Darlin', you're loading the wagon with a ton of questions. Which one do you want us to answer first? I think we've always had heroes... or, you might call them saviors. Those who keep us safe from the bad guys. And I think humanity has always had fear. In fact, today's commercials play on fear to the max. Whether it's health, male enhancement, your stolen identity. Advertisers play that big time.

"Do we need a savior? Was the world created with a savior in mind? How do we respond to our fears...how to we slay the dragon? What is the dragon? Do we each have individual dragons...or do we all face the same dragon?"

"As far as the dragon...it seems we've always had a dragon to slay, at least metaphorically. Probably our individual one and our societal one. I could go into detail about a savior but for now will say one of the ways to save ourselves is not to fall victim to those who proclaim they are the answer. We're smart enough to find the real answer."

"I know about the fears and people who faced them. There was

Noah and the flood; David and Goliath; Moses and the Hebrew children; the Crusades; racism; WWI; WWII; socialism; communism/Mc Arthy-ism; the fear of fear; illegals invading America. And now we have the disconnect between parents and children because of the smart phone—thumbs replacing action toward the one's needing attention. Too many to name. Now our community is dealing with wild dogs."

Gran offered her opinion, "Cimarron, we'll always have dragons or some other something to face or 'slay' but we have the hope of our ability to think. We have the promises of the Bible that assure us that those who believe will be protected. You're right in saying that we do not need to fear fear. Your recent comment about knowledge and Liberty High was quite apropos. We need to face reality and to be prepared to make knowledgeable decisions."

Wall Talk

Spidey: "You beat that kid like a rented mule. I think he learned his lesson."

Jake: "But what if he charges me with assault. I heard his parents were pushing that. That they wanted to know the name of the assaulter. We need to find or manufacture a witness to clear me."

Spidey: "No one else was there. You trounced him in the locker room. When he crawled out and she found him, she cleaned him up after calling 911. And she doesn't care about your innocence. I'm sure he told her who you were."

Jake: "We need to change her mind."

Spidey: "How?"

Dear Diary

And we're surrounded by instant gratification...if you need to know something yesterday, just whip out the phone and dial it up. Or get an ap so you can find out what the fridge needs tonight so you can buy it at the store. Gran asked me if I wondered whatever happened to ice boxes?

One of Cimarron's favorite teachers told the class one day he would take questions from the floor. Coach Terry taught history and coached volleyball and softball. He cared about kids and they considered him one of the good guys.

"Mr. Terry, may I ask a question relative to the wild dogs in our community?"

"Absolutely, Cimarron. Shoot."

"It appears the dog problem is representative of a predator-prey relationship between adults and teens."

"What would you say to me if I told you that your concern is insignificant? What if I told you to forget it?"

"I'd be disappointed in you. I'd go to someone who would listen."

"You make an excellent point. Let me give a true example. A history colleague of mine was given the opportunity to expand student learning. One of his students asked him what effect Jesus Christ had on the history of the world. What do you think the teacher said?"

"No clue. Maybe he suggested the student and other interested students do a little research and present their findings on a given date."

"An excellent idea…the very thing I would have suggested. But the teacher told the student his question was insignificant and changed the subject. Is education about opening or closing minds?"

"Mr. T, what if I told your question was unimportant? What would you say?"

"Touché."

"I'm playing with you, Mr. T. I get your point. We both know a teacher's job is to be objective. You have always presented both sides and let the students choose."

"Okay, Cimarron, what is your issue?"

"What's your opinion regarding hazardous substances and activities promoted by adults that affect teens negatively?"

"Where do I begin? I'm assuming you're talking things like tobacco, drugs, cosmetics, right?"

"Yes, but my original list expanded greatly."

"Let's do this. How about throwing the door wide open and getting input from the class? What do you say, class, can you think of anything harmful to students besides drowning? Actually, we could consider the metaphorical aspect since our society is drowning in so many areas."

The students inundated Mr. T like a Southwest gully washer.

"Human trafficking."

"Satanic rituals, *kuru*, drinking adrenal filled blood and human sacrifice. Can't be true, can it?"

"Human trafficking."

"Big pharma."

"FDA, GMO's, fluoride…"

"Abortion."

"Our government!"

"Hollywood and the liberal establishment."

"What about this nonsense about diapering livestock and dispensing with oil related travel? What is the sense of eradicating gasoline powered travel? Will travel be replaced by the flatulence of looney-tick politicians? Who's in charge?"

"Media that once was news, not propaganda."

"How free are we? Aren't our freedoms being eroded on a continual basis? What kinds of politically correct garbage are we being fed today? Since when do we tax the flatulence of cattle? Or taxing water? What kind of idiocy is banning the gender terminology? The word *man*?"

"What's that all about?"

"How about hatred?"

"Whoa, whoa, whoa, class. You're creating a whole new syllabus of topics…one that will take a lot more time than today. Since the beginning of mankind, we've been subjected to harm. Look at the caveman and the predators he faced. Seems like every generation we face new challenges in this arena. What say we prioritize your list of dangers, do some research and discuss later? Does that make sense? After all the bell is about to ring."

There was a united affirmative response.

After class Cimarron thanked Mr. Terry while telling him he was one of her favorite teachers. He then told her about a student who had graduated years past, that he had asked to name some of her favorite teachers. She was unable to name even one from K through 12. He found that very disturbing.

Dear Diary

Dad agrees. He's going to see what he can do to call attention to dangerous products provided by adults.

I'm going to look into starting a national organization for getting truth…to discover what's really happening to our children and our country. Maybe I'll call it GETRUTH or LEARNOW. And maybe we can have protest or boycott groups to support the concept.

Gramps said Truth is already here in the form of Jesus. That karma is coming and it's going to get real uglier…Jesus warned us by telling us what we give, we get. Gramps says the reason our country has remained strong as long as it has is because of conservative people, maybe those clinging to their Bibles and guns…as in Christian, Judea-Christian values. If people found Him, they'd know the truth and wouldn't have to be so concerned about it. Like he always said, "Life is like a game of checkers.

God makes His move and waits for us to make ours."

I think I'll also contact my legislators to get them educated, motivated and activated.

Seems like Liberty Heights returned to normal after the dog scare. Time to joke about the bump in the landscape called Startup Mountain and forget about the calf the dogs killed at Granger's Grove, the patch of woods near Grandpa and Grandma T's place. Time to return to the educational pursuits of Liberty High.

Is that a yo or a no?

Don't you know?

Faculty Lounge

"I know of one of our colleagues who ingests nostril nuggets in class."

"You don't mean loogies, do you? Eats 'em?"

"You got it."

"*Eewwww,* tell me no more."

Student Writing

What I Learned from "Daddy" Kandel

English 10 has been great! It could be because it was easy, or it could be because I had an awesome teacher. ☐

One of the many things that I learned was common sense. The quotes on the board every day made me think about life on a simple basis. I also learned from "Daddy" was to laugh at myself. His stories helped me learn the reason for doing things and about life.

I've learned a lot and have had fun doing so.

You've been an awesome teacher and friend. Someday when I'm a famous movie star, call me up and we'll do lunch—that is, if you're not still a married man! Have a great life. I'll never forget you. (smile emogi)

Mr. K—Studman

Your class is really cool, best class I ever had. You're a great teacher, your down to earth, ya know whats goin' on—what I'm tryin' to say is you're not a stuffy old English teacher! This is a great class to come to everyday. Everyone loves coming to this class. Cya next year Yo, gommer!

Melanie Morgan

Teacher Concerns

Morale is at an all time low.

Department chairpersons could schedule students in four days instead of all year.

How about teachers voting on retaining or dismissing new principal?

Can we have a tardy policy that works?

Locker Room

Don: "Why can't girls figure out that sex rules. They don't make the rules. We do."

Carey: "It just shows they're dumber than our dads. My old man is so anal that he knows exactly when I do something…like taking the car when I sneak out at night. I have learned to park it in exactly the same spot so that he doesn't catch me."

Don: "Yeh, my dad's so tight. He did a lot more than I did. He partied. But he won't let me out of his sight."

Carey: "I'm going to let my kids party. They can pay me for the booze. I might even buy it and profit from it."

Don: "Yeh. Tease me. Seize me. Squeeze me. Please me."

Dear Diary

Crap happens. We can either let it define us or use it to better ourselves. It's always easy to blame those around us. It takes a lot of inner strength to accept accountability for what we have done in certain situations, and move forward with a happy heart. Sure, another party may have been a part in some crappy situation, but it's our choice not to dwell on that. We are all human. We all make mistakes. We all have choices. It's that choice that we are going to move forward, enjoy the short life we are given, and make the most of every day. God didn't put us on this earth to be miserable. He gave each of us a passion and a reason to live, and it's up to us to strive for both.

Suggestion Box

Survival Mode
My father is a recovering acholic & my mother is a current alcoholic.

Their addiction to achole caused my sisters to move away as age 14 & 16 & my mother to move away after 17 years of marriage. This destroyed my brother & myself. In the future don't let this addiction do the same to you & your family.

We can learn from crayons in a box that all colors can live together. Those who mess with slugs get slimed.

Blacks, Hispanics, Pacific Islanders and others are just like Caucasians—they just have different parents.

Student Comments

Having a teacher who really cares about you is a real plus. If that teacher gets involved with what you are doing, then it gives you more enthusiasm and you'll get it done knowing that your teacher supports you. Whenever I have problems on my papers or personal problems, Mr. K, you are always there to lend an ear...which surpasses other teachers in this school.

You have treated me with the same respect you treat your other students regardless of my appearance. You have been a new inspiration to me. Thanks.

There is a teacher at Liberty High who inspires his students to do better, he inspires by his actions. I have learned more in this class than any other.

Mr. Kandel is the best teacher in the school because we have fun and thought provoking lectures. He actually cares about the kids and doesn't just do it for the pay check.

I wish you weren't leaving, Daddy K, cuz I had fun learning alot in your class. I even learned how to spell a lot!

Student Writing

"No Saved My Life"

Nothing comes before drugs. It has no rivals. Not even God.

This jealous lover comes in many flavors. Dope arrives in cigarettes, needles, pills, bottles. And it controls your thoughts, money, priorities and time. It takes no prisoners, does not allow family, work or pastimes in its presence.

Once in its grasp, dope enslaves you by destroying your will and your self-respect. Dope becomes your master, turning you into a dependent, liar, con artist, thief and loser. Your drug of choice will control your very being, strangling you in its talons like so many before you.

Dope has but one enemy. The word *no* will stifle the drug. But you must be man enough to utter "no" and to change your direction before the drug engulfs you totally, choking your life out and killing whatever good you possess.

If you say "no" and escape the scene, you relinquish nothing of necessity to the Evil One; you gain over the drug and create a life of worth and value. You escape the death of mindlessness and the threat of future incapacity. You become a new person. Once you say "no," you escape the merry-go-round of incapacity and begin the journey toward the freedom of life and its offerings.

Another student wrote:

I lost a lot of brain damage becase of pot. I can feel it becase I used to do it constalty, day after day. But I got some sense into my head and said to my self, "why should I haev to be stupid just to be cool." I wish I could of known this in Junior High that way I would of never got involved with drugs and today I could be as smart as I was in elementary. I used to get A's and B's until I started smoking pot, then my grades just suddenly dropped. Today there is nothing I can do to regain those missing brain cells.

Word got out that BDK was retiring. He said in the *Angels' Halo* that: "Teaching at Liberty High has been very rewarding for me. Opportunities such as teaching, coaching, civic activities have been a blessing for my family and me. I wish students learned as much from me as I did from them. If there is a pot of gold at rainbow's end, it is the rays of hope called students that lead the way to the riches."

Student Comments

"I always enjoyed being in your class. You're one hell of a teacher. Sorry to see you retire but I can't wait until your book about teenagers comes out."

"Big K

"You're the best teacher my mom (Big Al) ever had. You're the best teacher I ever. I want my kids to have you. Thank you for seeing my mother before she passed. It was one of her wishes.

"It's been awesome having you as a teacher. You have taught me a lot, not just school work, but attitude, and how I should stand up for what I believe in! You have encouraged me to be a teacher, you're a perfect example of someone to look up to! (and I do) Stay cool and I'll come see you sometime!"

Leon Dwiggins, AKA Twiggy

Student Writing

Someone said, "If you don't know the King, you ain't getting into the kingdom. I'm not talking knowing ABOUT the king...but knowing Him. A friend has written a lot of songs about Jesus but he doesn't know Him—he just knows about Him.

Before we knew it, the twenty-five to thirty year Angel grads scheduled their reunion. Tons of planning had gone into the event. The reunion was kind of an eye opener…as most reunions are. Some of those kids have achieved beyond imagination while others may not have been so successful but were definitely pleased with the outcome of their lives. All in attendance were twenty-five years to thirty years older…and wiser.

Some of the students shared their thoughts during the intervening years. Bob Droege thought Mr. K was a little strict and maybe too idealistic as his teacher but "now I know he was right."

Victoria talked about her happy, married life with four children, none of whom bleed blood because of their overwhelming athleticism which they ooze. With no pressure from her she has allowed them to participate in sports, music, drama, student government and community affairs. They have thrived on this stratagem.

Joe Ayers and Bill Bivins showed up at the reunion. Both are happily married. Joe is an Arizona designer of swimming pools and Bill is a railroad man, an engineer for Alaska Railroad.

Bad Mas had gotten into fiber-optics and done extremely well, quite the contrast from the days when Mr. K teased him in English 10. Kandel always asked Marty the reason he carried a *Wall Street Journal* under his arm when he entered class, "You're a football player. You probably can't read. Ha, Ha."

Dawn is also married and volunteers several days a month at a suicide prevention clinic.

Matt Janisiciewich hoped to see BDK, the only man who ever made him think, to tell him "I love you."

Unable to attend the reunion, Mr. Kandel sent a telegram to the class congratulating them on their two-plus decades of life after school.

He said, "My happiness is yours. My goal was always to help you reach yours. My joy and reward was seeing students achieve happiness in their activities."

Although some predicted Lu Lu would make the big stage, he didn't. He made a larger splash than the stage. He married Angie Webb, had a family of kids who adored him and raised the community and state awareness of alcohol consumption.

After the head on collision which resulted in the death of his classmates Marshall and Mazzie, Lu Lu never drank another drop of alcohol. He initiated the MarZie Bend name change and the statue of the high school sweethearts holding hands next to the road, helped raise most of the money, was completely remorseful, even wrote the inscription on the pedestal and has always wondered what would have become of Marshall and Mazzie.

Lu Lu's tribute to them reads: "Marshall Allen Perry and Mazzie Wenatchee Mc Kenzie, high school sweethearts, lost their lives on this corner, struck head on by a drug impaired teenage driver. Formerly called Dead Man's Curve, it was renamed MarZie Bend in their honor. This statue is a testament to them. They symbolized the very best that comes to high schools everywhere when students like they attend. May they rest in peace."

Who knows how many lives Lu Lu saved. Unfortunately he didn't make it. He died in a freak motorcycle accident a year ago. However he left an amazing legacy.

Clancy Fitzsimmons and Tuffy Bidar showed up, discussing the old days. Clancy is a high school English teacher whose life was turned around by a caring, thoughtful BDK. He has chosen to make a difference in this world because a person was there when Clancy needed him. Fitz was named teacher of the year and Tuffy tells him, "If BDK were here, he'd approve. I heard he thought about becoming a principal in order to remove lousy teachers and to further protect our children….but that was before he remembered tenure."

Along with Lu Lu, Tuffy and Clancy were instrumental in getting Dead Man's curve changed in name and they helped with the fund raiser for the Marshall and Mazzie statue.

Clancy has two sons: Tuffy and Marshall.

Tuffy Bidar is a global airline pilot and has a boy named Clancy and a girl named Mc Kenzie.

Alana Marie Holland attended. Although she did not graduate with our class, she did graduate…and kept her baby. Her son is now 25-years -old. She's the head of her mega-company's accounting department and can work from anywhere in the world, thanks to her boss to whom she's his right hand.

Myrna Garfield is married with three kids, Ashley, Chelsea and Mindy. She had her breast implants removed. She stated, "I realized the outside is only one facet of a person and what matters is on the inside. Since I had my implants removed, I've heard horror stories about other women. Like exploding implants, burned skin, life threatening events. I'm a very happy lady."

At the class picnic Clancy and Tuffy reminisced, "I can't tell you how many times I've thought about the parallel between The Beeg and life. Many a time you and I ran head to head on the runway, practiced on the wrestling mat, enjoyed triumphs, the great people we grew up with. Many, many happy memories."

"Yes, Tuffy. We raced many a time at The Beeg, our personal battleground on the concrete but we also shared the battleground called high school. What percent of our peers cruised through school like we did on the strip? How many of them suffered travail and tribulation. How many of them did we know…but really did NOT know? How many of them never made it through school…or through life? It's heartbreaking to think of it all."

They agreed that if they had learned nothing else from high school, it was to accentuate the good and eliminate the bad.

"But we do have good memories—those many times."

The former racing rivals agreed there are things far more important than racing a Chevy and a Ford. Much greater things.

"So, Fitz, we used to say 'the sky's the limit,' but it isn't."

"Not a chance, Tuffy. God is."

"We've learned a bunch in our years on the planet and have a bunch to learn before we cross the great divide."

"Yeh. A ton. Hopefully we'll measure up in our eyes, our family's, our community's and His."

"Well, you've certainly made the grade."

"Thanks, Tuffy. The sky's as high and as bright as we choose to make them. Emphasis upon choose."

We're the Liberty High Angels. Some fantasize about being America's team but we're not. We're like any high school—the good, the bad, the aborted. Change the era, change the locale, change the culture. We pretty much share the template of high schools everywhere,

whether we're talkin' racin' the bay, the chariot, the Porsche…

whether the cliques include stoners, Geeks, Dagos, preppies, parking lot crowd...

whether you name those good and those lousy staff members...

whether our parents are together or not and love us or not. We share the teenage affliction called high school...and...

That's a Magoo!

Epilogue:

Every student attending an American public high school encounters events that affect him. I chose to substitute intitails B.G. for the words "battleground" thus representing the battleground of high school.

Appendix 1

a bee in your bonnet
a bone to pick
a whipping boy
according to Hoyle
as old as the hills (and twice as dusty)
a shot in the arm
ace up your sleeve
ax to grind
baker's dozen
bats in the belfry
beat around the bush
beat(s) the living daylights out of me
behind the eight ball
best foot forward
between the Devil and deep blue sea
bit off more than you can chew
bite the dust
break the ice
burning bridges
burning a candle at both ends
burning the midnight oil
bury the hatchet
by the skin of your teeth
can't see the woods for the trees
can't never did anything
carry the ball
cash on the barrel head
casting pearls before swine
cat got your tongue
cat out of the bag
cat's meow
caught flat footed
come off your perch

cut and dried
cut off your nose to site your face
cut you down to size
crack the whip
crazy as a jaybird
cry wolf Davey Jones' locker
dead as a herring
die is cast
don't care a fiddlestick
don't get your dander up
easy as rolling off a log
every dog has his day
eyes too big for the stomach
fat is in the fire
fatten or sweeten the kitty
fish or cut bait
fish out of water
fit as a fiddle
flog a dead horse
fly by night
full of prunes (or beans)
get a kick (charge) out of it
get cold feet
getting your feet wet
get your nose out of joint
gird one's loin
give him the third degree
give it a lick and a promise
go against the grain
go hog wild
go off the deep end
got his comeuppance
hang by a thread
hanging on by my eyelids
happy as a lark
have other fish to fry

hell bent for breakfast
hide your light under a bushel
  (basket)
hit below the belt
hit the nail on the head
hoe your own row
hold your horses
holding the bag
hunky dory, peachy keen
in a pretty pickle
in an ivory tower
in hot water
in the dog house
Jack or all trades (master of none)
Johnny-come-lately
keep a stiff upper lip
keep your eye on the ball
keep your eyes peeled
keep your shirt on
keep up with the Joneses
lay an egg
leave no stone unturned
led by the nose
let sleeping dogs lie
like a lump on a log
like greased lightning
Lord willing & the creek don't rise
mad as a wet hen
mad as hops
make no bones about it
met his Waterloo
neck of the woods
nip and tuck
no dice
no skin of my nose
not the size of the dog in the fight
  but the size of the fight in the dog
not worth a hill of beans
nothing to write home about

off the top of my head
on the cuff
on the Fritz
on the level
over a barrel
paint the town red
pass the buck
plain as the nose on your face
play cat and mouse
play fast and loose
play possum
playing with loaded dice
pull a boner
pull one's leg
pull the wool over one's eyes
pull yourself up by your
  bootstraps
put that in your pipe and smoke
  it
real McCoy
red headed step child
resting on your laurels
ride the gravy train
root hog or die
rule of thumb
rule the roost
sawing logs
shake a leg
skating on thin ice
skeleton in the closet
skinny as a rail
slower than molasses
snowball in hell
something/nothing to write
  home about
something's rotten in Denmark
sparse as hen's teeth
step up to the plate
stick to your guns
stick your neck out

straight from the horse's mouth
strain at a gnat and swallow a
   camel
strike while the iron is hot
swallow hook, line and sinker
take a leaf out of one's book
take a powder
take one down a peg
take under one's wing
talk a blue streak
that rings a bell
the bigger they are, the harder
   they fall
throw a monkey wrench in the
   machinery
throw cold water on it
throw in the sponge (or towel)
tilt at windmills
toe the line or mark
tongue in cheek
too big for his britches/breeches
too many irons in the fire
to the bitter end
turn over a new leaf
turn the heat on
turn the tables
up the creek without a paddle
up to my neck
walk the plank
water under the bridge
well heeled
what do you have up your sleeve?
whole kit and caboodle
whole nine yards
wild goose chase
win one for the Gipper
win one's spurs
without rhyme or reason
wringing my hands

you stepped in it, put your
   foot in it

Other terms:
ace in the hole
blowing one's top
cotton picker
chowder head
chum
dark horse
Don Juan
duck soup
dunce
elbow grease
even Steven
gorilla
hell on wheels
high jinks
lame duck
lead pipe cinch
loaded for bear
no ifs, ands or buts
old hat
pork barrel
punch in the nose
split hairs
tin horn gambler
tooth and nail

Appendix 2

Alana Marie consented to summarize some of her anguish about pregnancy as a prelude to a book for teens. Following is that introduction. I hope she completes it in order to benefit the readers.

I walked into the nurse's office as I often did the past couple of weeks. Mrs. T had to be the coolest nurse anyone could ask for. "Mrs. T, I just don't feel good, can I just lie down for a bit."

"Alana you've come in every day this week. You can talk to me. Is there something you would like to talk about?"

My mind was whirling. Even being 14 and a girl (young woman) I knew…my brain wouldn't accept it. It was incomprehensible. In my mind it was not real yet, but I knew…I knew…but I had no idea where that would lead my life for the next 12 years.

The thoughts…"I'm sorry Mrs. T, I think I just have the flu." Mrs. T sat on the edge of the cot I was lying on. I wanted to open-up, share my life and fears with her, and my impending news. Hoping someone would make me feel like I exist. All she had to do was look at me, in that motherly way (the only one I've always wanted from my own mother) and I spewed out words and tears for the next 30 minutes. She sat and listened to everything I felt safe sharing. For the first time someone actually looked at me with kindness and understanding. For the first time in my life I felt alive and understood.

There were many weeks I would visit the nurse's office. Actually, almost every day. At this point, at 14, I still didn't know what was happening to my body and energy. I was a young teenager a few months ago with endless energy, now all I want to want to do was sleep.

Mrs. T, and the nurse's office, was a safe place for me. Easy to get to if you rotate your teachers… being a girl and saying you don't feel good is the easiest way to the nurse's office, especially with male teachers.

I went to school on a typical day, as far as I was concerned. Second hour was all I could take. I was exhausted, my stomach was in overdrive and there was no reason for it. I had purchased a pregnancy test at the store. I don't' know why, but I just did. During this moment of "what the hell is happening, I took that damned test" to my horror, it was positive. I honestly can't tell you what I felt when I say that. Numb, indifferent, ignorance… in my head it was not happening!!

As I was waiting for Valerie to pick me up, I stared at that test strip for an hour. There was a little tiny being growing inside my stomach. But how could this be. I'm 14. Just 2 years ago I was playing with dolls… damn I'm only a freshman in high school.

My thoughts… my life is over. How Alana…how…I never even thought about birth control. That was a conversation my mother and I never had. I was too fearful and shy to discuss those topics with her. So, here I was pregnant at 14.

1984

After I went to the doctor who confirmed my pregnancy, he said because of how far along I was I only had one week to decide whether I was keeping my baby or aborting it. My father was pushing me for an abortion. He said this would ruin my life and that I would never be able to do any of those things that normal teenagers do. My boyfriend was also pushing for an abortion, that was not surprising to me. However, when I went home and told my mother what the doctor said, she said "No, Alana you don't have a week, you one day." I looked at her in disbelief.

I knew she was furious with me for getting myself in this position, but why was she being so heartless. Not only did I only have one day, if I decided to get an abortion, I would immediately be made to leave the house and my mother would never speak to me again. I was being pulled in so many directions. Everyone had an opinion. But none of them were me.

I knew that no matter my decision, I was literally on my own. No one was showing me any love or compassion. All I saw when people looked at me was pity or anger. I can tell you, that was one long night. I shed many tears, yet I had no one to share those with. No one wanted me, yet I was desperate for love and understanding. I also knew deep down that they were hurting too. We just did not know how to talk to each other. We never had and never would.

1985

Here I sit on an airplane holding my 6-month-old baby boy. I'm headed to Shreveport, LA, to stay with my grandparents for a while. Not only am I holding my 6-month-old, I have just found out that I am pregnant again. I don't even have time to process that because my little boy is very active, and I try not to think of the real reason I am on this airplane…I was cooking dinner for my family, Steve, my boyfriend and child's father, was over. I asked my parents if they wanted to eat dinner at the dinner table. That infuriated Steve, and he dragged me into the laundry room and started grabbing me around the throat, smacking the side of my face. I tried to break free, but he grabbed the front of my hair and pushed me down at the same time. He literally ripped out a chunk of my hair and somewhere in the struggle ripped off my shirt and shredded my bra.

This was the first time my parents realized how badly I was being abused. I had been being abused since right after my son was born. It was just getting worse, so my mother sent me away. They immediately kicked Steve out.

A few days later my stepdad tells me that my mother had felt guilty for kicking Steve out and let him move back into my bedroom at their house. She didn't even ask if that was something I wanted. I cried. I had thought I would finally escape him and the abuse. So there again, people are making decisions for me and making me feel that my voice meant nothing. My whole life I lived with people who said sit down and shut up because whatever you say is worthless.

At the same time, I am getting to know my grandparents. I had never met them. My grandmother was very controlling and was not impressed by having a young girl and a baby in her space. She made her discomfort very well known to me. I tried to stay in my room and keep out of her way, but I really believe she enjoyed being so hateful to me. The night before I left, she thought I had gone to bed and started yelling at my grandfather about what an ungrateful little bitch I was and that she was going to stay in a hotel until "that little whore gets out of my house."

I left the next morning and walked right back into the arms of Steve. I felt hopeless and alone. I felt like my life was spinning out of control (that's because it was). I did not want Steve, but it was very difficult when my mother seemed to be more on his side than mine. Again, I cried.

1986

My son was born today, he's beautiful. I am now the mother of 2 at 16. I have a lot of hopes and dreams for this family I've created. I dream that we can make our little family work and that Steve gets the help he needs to overcome his anger issues. I want the boys to grow up to be strong independent gentlemen. I have faith that this will happen. I am going to be the best mom I can be to these 2 small souls. Life will definitely bring trial and tribulations, but I have faith in myself that I will overcome and come out the other side with more life experiences and stronger because of it.

SOURCE NOTES

Elliott, Charles, "Feral Dogs: Threat to Man Too? ," *Outdoor Life*, March 1977, pp. 88,180,182 and 186.

"The Little Girl Who Refused to Die," *Good Housekeeping*, August 1991, pp. 90, 132-134

"Not all adults are insensitive to problems…" Oct. 6, 1992, *Anchorage Daily News*

Wetherell, Barbara, *"Taking On the Booze Merchants," Listen*, pp. 11-15, June 1984

Young, Andrew (Atlanta Mayor), "What my Family Taught Me," *Listen*, pg. 18, December 1984

Personal-archived files going back to 1966—student papers (notes, journals, compositions, poems) and school related communiqués.

Michael Mewshaw, *Life for Death*, Avon, NY, NY, 1983

About the Characters:

Many of the characters are exactly as portrayed except for the fictitious name.

Some of the characters are composites of more than one person. For instance:

Clancy Fitzsimmons is based on at least four of my former students—a teacher actually wrote in his evaluation that Jay was "absolutely worthless." Another student had all "F" grades except one "D" from grades 7 through 10. One guy was tossed under the bus in the second grade. And the fourth came to our home asking for help in stopping his case of beer a day drinking habit. (Matt told me, "You're the only man who ever made me think. I love you.")

Tuffy Bidar is a former student-wrestler who moved to Oregon, got involved in housing and donates a lot of money to his church and charities

Alana Marie Holland was a genuine, real student who was a heroine in that she chose to keep her child…and raise it by herself. How many other students have suffered her anguish and surmounted the travail?

Some of the <u>teachers</u> are real or composites—some good, some not so.

Some of the <u>writing</u> was very well done and quoted verbatim or nearly so. Students willingly gave me copies of their work. (Jodee Garrells, Michelle Frigillana, Deborah Wood, Denise Rusk)

Suggestion box, Corner of the Shadow, circular file, student writing, teacher-student-janitor-secretary concerns, teacher's lounge, class discussion, Angels' Halo, wall talk, locker room are genuine or close to it.

In the third grade I had a witch for a teacher and an angel the next year—one Wanda Whitman at Cherry Valley School in Duvall, Washington, gave me a new perspective on life. Kids would love school if all teachers were like Wanda.

About the Author:

Born in Deer Park and growing up in Washington before obtaining his English and master's degrees from Linfield College, Larry had no plan to write. His efforts to acquire a classroom anthology of Alaskan adventures for his literature of the North students resulted in more than one book. He and his wife Pam drove the graveled Alcan Highway in 1966, planning to spend that honeymoon year in Anchorage. They have honeymooned fifty-four years in the Great Land where they reared three children and explored the outdoors via boat, plane and highway vehicle.

Larry Kaniut's thirteen books to date include both non-fiction and fiction—bears, adventure, survival and romance. His contact information:

web site is www.kaniut.com
personal email is kaniut@alaska.net

BEAR-MAN ENCOUNTERS

Alaska Bear Tales   - Comprehensive research from false charges to fatalities.
"Anyone looking to read real life drama this is the book to start with."
Amazon reader, Daniel Bird

More Alaska Bear Tales - more stories, greater emphasis upon humor than original
"…open minded look at attacks…a lot of effort in research…hope there is a book three in the works." Reviewer jdmiles

Some Bears Kill - 38 stories re: man vs. bear
"Larry Kaniut is destined to join Beach, London and Service as one of the best of Alaskan writers." Attorney Wayne Ross, Alaska gubernatorial candidate

Bear Tales for the Ages - classic American stories (rescued from out of print)
"Plan to stay up all night to finish this book…you are not going to sleep."
MyShelf.com

SAFE with Bears (Stay Alive From Encounters) - how to stay out of a bear's mouth

"Alaskans are lucky to have someone in their midst who helps to make time in the bush more enjoyable and safe and is willing to withstand the continuous assault from those who want to overprotect bears."

James Gary Shelton, king of the bear book writers (Bear Encounter Survival Guide, Bear Attacks the Deadly Truth and Bear Attacks II Myth and Reality)

<u>ADVENTURE-SURVIVAL</u>

Cheating Death - highlighting Alaskan outdoor mishaps
"All your stories are good reading."   Lowell Thomas Jr., former
                                                                    Alaska Lieutenant Governor

Danger Stalks the Land - from saltwater to mountaintop adventures
"I urgently recommend…Danger Stalks the Land…Don't leave home without it."   Paul Harvey, legendary radio commentator
"Everyone interested in survival should read this book."
                    Lars Monsen, ultimate Norwegian adventurer and explorer

Alaska Air Tales - personal pilot experiences aloft; includes center foldout page of WWII Anchorage aviation bone yard
"This book is an excellent addition to anyone's Alaskan aviation library that might already include such books as Wager with the Wind and Glacier Pilot."   Amazon reader Alaska Guy, 5 stars

<u>NOVELS</u>

Trapped - New York photojournalist finds more than she bargained for in Alaska, including romance
"I really enjoyed the story. I loved the sassy by-play."   Katie Sturgell

Brachan - Brachan departs Rome for Judea on a secret mission
"I absolutely love Brachan. You have something very special here…you nailed it…this is big time."   Randy Mc Kenzie, Bookmasters

The B.G.
"We share the teenage affliction called high school."

<u>ALASKANA</u>

Instant Sourdough - humorous booklet of old Alaskan terminology, like Spenard divorce and bear insurance

COLORING BOOK

Alaska's Fun Bears - one of a kind. 94 fun-packed pages bears performing human activities, word find, maze, alphabet, etc. Designed for adult-child interaction

www.ingramcontent.com/pod-product-compliance
Lightning Source LLC
Chambersburg PA
CBHW050009070726
47598CB00015B/2611

Books by Larry Kaniut

Alaska Bear Tales

More Alaska Bear Tales

Cheating Death: Amazing Survival Stories from Alaska

Danger Stalks the Land: Alaskan Tales of Death and Survival

Some Bears Kill

Safe with Bears: Bear Conflict Survival

Bear Tales for the Ages: From Alaska and Beyond

Alaska Air Tales

Brachan: A Soldier's Secret Mission

Trapped: An Alaskan Romance

The B.G. High School Flashbacks

Heavenly Rose, Angel in Disguise

Instant Sourdough

Alaska's Fun Bears